THE TEMPTATIONS OF PATIENCE

"Miss Cheswick, may I inquire what you are doing?"

The duke stood close enough that she could see the small swirls of blue and gold in the pattern of his brocade dressing gown. "I was just looking for something to read."

One brow arched as he glanced at the shelves behind her. "I could not have supposed a historical account of the rise of the House of Norwick to be to your taste."

She blushed but held her ground, her chin lifting in defiance. "No, Your Grace, I was merely seeking to . . . to familiarize myself with the arrangement—assuming, of course, that the books *are* arranged in some order?"

He nearly grinned. She was the one caught in his library at two in the morning, clad only in a thin wrapper, yet she had the audacity to criticize the placement of his books. It irked him to admit the library was not in any kind of order, but it also gave him an idea.

"I have meant for some time to engage someone to set them straight. Would you be willing, Miss Cheswick?"

Surprised, she looked up at him. As her gaze met his, she was suddenly conscious of his nearness.

Gregory forgot what he was saying. He was suddenly aware of the way Patience's thin wrapper draped her slender figure.

Suddenly aware of the impropriety of their being alone together at this hour.

Suddenly aware of the tug of desire that make him wonder how it would feel to hold her in his arms . . .

from THE VIRTUES OF PATIENCE, by Carol Quinto

WATCH FOR THESE ZEBRA REGENCIES

LADY STEPHANIE   (0-8217-5341-X, $4.50)
by Jeanne Savery
Lady Stephanie Morris has only one true love: the family estate she
has managed ever since her mother died. But then Lord Anthony Rider
arrives on her estate, claiming he has plans for both the land and the
woman. Stephanie soon realizes she's fallen in love with a man whose
sensual caresses will plunge her into a world of peril and intrigue . . . a
man as dangerous as he is irresistible.

BRIGHTON BEAUTY   (0-8217-5340-1, $4.50)
by Marilyn Clay
Chelsea Grant, pretty and poor, naively takes school friend Alayna
Marchmont's place and spends a month in the country. The devastating
man had sailed from Honduras to claim his promised bride, Miss
Marchmont. An affair of the heart may lead to disaster . . . unless a
resourceful Brighton beauty finds a way to stop a masquerade and
keep a lord's love.

LORD DIABLO'S DEMISE   (0-8217-5338-X, $4.50)
by Meg-Lynn Roberts
The sinfully handsome Lord Harry Glendower was a gambler and the
black sheep of his family. About to be forced into a marriage of con-
venience, the devilish fellow engineered his own demise, never having
dreamed that faking his death would lead him to the heavenly refuge
of spirited heiress Gwyn Morgan, the daughter of a physician.

A PERILOUS ATTRACTION   (0-8217-5339-8, $4.50)
by Dawn Aldridge Poore
Alissa Morgan is stunned when a frantic passenger thrusts her baby
into Alissa's arms and flees, having heard rumors that a notorious
highwayman posed a threat to their coach. Handsome stranger Hugh
Sebastian secretly possesses the treasured necklace the highwayman
seeks and volunteers to pose as Alissa's husband to save her reputation.
With a lost baby and missing necklace in their care, the couple embarks
on a journey into peril—and passion.

*Available wherever paperbacks are sold, or order direct from the
Publisher. Send cover price plus 50¢ per copy for mailing and
handling to Kensington Publishing Corp., Consumer Orders,
or call (toll free) 888-345-BOOK, to place your order using
Mastercard or Visa. Residents of New York and Tennessee
must include sales tax. DO NOT SEND CASH.*

For Mother, With Love

Dorothea Donley
Martha Kirkland
Carol Quinto

Zebra Books
Kensington Publishing Corp.
http://www.zebrabooks.com

ZEBRA BOOKS are published by

Kensington Publishing Corp.
850 Third Avenue
New York, NY 10022

First Printing: April 1998
10 9 8 7 6 5 4 3 2 1

Printed in the United States of America

Contents

Makeshift Mama

Dorothea Donley

One

"What a wretched day," said pretty Susan, spoiling her face with a moue as she watched the rain pattering on the window at which she waited. She was by nature a bright creature with bouncing, golden locks and smiling lips.

"Do you mean the weather or the event for which we are waiting?" asked her elder sister, Audrey, with a wry look at Mr. Howerfield.

"Well, both," Susan admitted.

"Now, my dear young ladies," said Mr. Howerfield soothingly, "you have known for years that Rampton would have a new rector when your papa had gone to his place in heaven. I daresay he has an eye on you now—and St. Peter does, too."

"Yes, but so *soon*. He was so young," objected Susan.

Mr. Howerfield nodded. "Not yet fifty. It surprised us all. Now the living has been awarded to Mr. Nunley, who is said to be an estimable young man. It is only natural that he would want to bring his wife to see the rectory, so they can plan arrangements for their own family."

"We understand, Mr. Howerfield," Audrey interposed calmly. Though she resembled her sister, her hair, also being golden, was sleekly drawn back with only a few curls escaping a ribbon at the nape of her neck. Elder by nine years, she was clearly in charge of the rectory, now that her papa was gone. "It is very kind of you to come all the way from Salisbury to be with us at this time. I expect the rain and gloom have made the day seem more difficult."

Susan said, "A carriage is coming up the street. Yes, it is stopping here."

"Do come away from the window," begged her sister, and Susan obeyed. The three of them waited without further talk until the knocker had sounded and their little maid, Polly, had come up the hall to answer it. There were subdued murmurs, followed by Polly's leading the guests into the small drawing room.

The new rector was unsmiling, yet his face was pleasant enough as he unerringly addressed Audrey: "Miss Malton? How do you do? You are kind to let us come."

She greeted him civilly and exchanged curtsies with his wife, who eyed her frostily. "May I present my sister, Susan, and Mr. Howerfield, who has been my father's financial advisor and friend?"

Several bows and nods having been made, the men ventured into conversation while Mrs. Nunley ignored Susan and cast her eyes about the drawing room as though condemning it for being outmoded.

"It is a pleasant house," Audrey said. "May I show you upstairs?"

"Let me see this floor first," commanded Mrs. Nunley.

She declared the stairs looked "steep." The dining salon was "crowded" by the width of the table. Fortunately, all was spotless, even the stone floor of the pantries and kitchen, so no adverse comment could be made about them.

"You will find the bedchambers airy," Audrey said in a colorless voice.

But Mrs. Nunley condemned all of them as "very small."

"We have been comfortable," Audrey replied.

"Well, Mr. Nunley has accepted this call, so we must make the best of it. Suppose you point out which pieces of furniture belong to you, so that I will know what must be replaced," said the visitor in a businesslike manner which so exacerbated Audrey's feelings that she immediately decided she would carry off every item which they could claim, down to the last bar of soap and a newly purchased bucket.

When they returned to the drawing room, Mr. Howerfield was

assuring the rector that the ladies would be prepared to move within a month or two. They did not intend to remain in Rampton, he said.

Actually, Audrey and Susan had thought of doing so, but they now knew it would be painful for them. Rampton was not a large town. One met one's neighbors regularly. To be condescended to by Mrs. Nunley would be unbearable. Evidently Mr. Howerfield understood this, for when the visitors had departed, he bade them sit down and listen to what was in his mind.

"I think, my dears, you will have to make a life for yourselves in another place. What are you now, Miss Audrey? Twenty-five or so?"

"Yes, sir. Almost twenty-five," she admitted.

He made humphing sounds. "I thought so. Should have been settled in a home of your own before now."

"Papa needed me—with Mama gone."

"Yes, yes. Very true. Now, however, you must find a husband, and if you will stop giving Miss Saucy"—here a wink at Susan—"all the bright-colored frocks, you will take very nicely."

"But where?" interrupted Susan.

"One of the watering places, I daresay. You decide. Your Papa left enough funds to keep you respectably smart. All it will take is for you to be penny-wise. Think who can come as chaperon, and look into spas, my dears. You are due for a bit of pleasure, I am sure. No extravagances, mind; buy a few pretty things, rent rooms in some other town."

"Oh, dare we?" whispered Audrey.

"Well, now, not London of course; you would be gobbled up there. And not Brighton, for the prince's cohorts have taken that over. You must choose a place which you think will be congenial. Tell me. Then I will obtain rooms for you."

Evidently forgetting he was in a rector's home, he added, "I'll send a carriage to take you on your journey, and damn me if I won't send m'nevvy, David, to escort you!"

The next morning rain had ceased, though pavements and streets were awash with brown water in low places. The girls set out, not taking Polly, for they did not want her to know exactly what was in their minds.

"Before we buy any fabrics," Audrey said, "let us see what may be in the attics."

"But we will need a fashion journal," urged the younger and giddier of the two.

"Yes. We shall want to look smart. But first we must find where we can store our furniture until we have a permanent home. Then the real problem will be to find a chaperon. I can think only of Mama's great-aunt, but she lives north of York, and must be too old to come to us or endure the simplest season."

"Mr. Howerfield may find us a suitable place very soon," Susan pointed out.

"But, dearest, we have a great deal to do before we go any-where. Papa's books must be packed—breakables packed—fur-niture moved—and all that is to be left behind must be spanking clean, for I would not want to give Mrs. Nunley a chance to complain of us."

"No, of course not. But, Audrey, can you not almost *swoon* when you think of balls and beaux?"

At the draper's shop, Mrs. Smith, the draper's clerk, asked if it was true that they would be leaving Rampton. "No one can like to see you go," she said quite earnestly. "The town and the church won't seem the same."

Oh, thank you, Mrs. Smith," replied Audrey in gracious tones. "Mr. Nunley will be coming with his family, and I am sure you will like him very much."

"Where will you go?"

"We are not yet certain," Audrey said. "First we must find a way to store the furniture that was Papa's until we know where it is to be sent."

Another customer, who had been listening unabashedly and was a devoted member of St. Leonard's, interrupted to say that the whole loft of her stable was vacant. "Nice and dry it is, miss, and I am sure my husband can get men together to move whatever you need to store away."

"Why, thank you, Mrs. Cranny," said Audrey fervently. "This

would be a perfect solution and will relieve my mind immensely. Of course we *expect* to pay a fee as long as the furniture must stay there—we do not know where we will definitely settle or how long it will be before we have a new permanent residence. Please tell Mr. Cranny that we will be grateful for this help."

"Well, miss," said the woman, "haven't we all been blessed by Mr. Malton in years past? I am sure St. Leonard's will never be the same again."

Audrey hastened to say that Mr. Nunley seemed a very real gentleman who was bound to be a blessing to Rampton. She could say nothing agreeable about Mr. Nunley's wife, but did offer the information that the Nunleys had several children to brighten the parsonage.

When the rector's daughters had purchased needles, pins and thread, ribbons, and a pattern book, they went away leaving goodwill behind them and taking away wishes for their own comfort and happiness.

"Do you think we will meet folk as kind as the ones here?" asked Susan wistfully. She could not remember anything before the rectory of St. Leonard's church and the quaint houses of Rampton.

"Of course we will," promised Audrey. "Some maybe not so nice, even *wicked,* but there are kind and pleasant people everywhere, especially in a church—so wherever we go, we must look for a church."

After they had eaten a nuncheon, Susan retired to her chamber to lay out frocks and try assorted new ribbons with them. Taking her mama's ring of keys, Audrey climbed to the attic and set about opening trunks, some of which, she could see from the top layer, were infant things. Another contained old clothes of her father, and these drew tears to her eyes, though she did not give way to weeping; these she would have to send to the needy of the parish.

The treasure trove was her mama's trunk, evidently packed privately by her papa to spare his young daughters' feelings. Such pretty things—though not youthful. Evidently her mama had had a good sense of values, for the simple gowns were fine lawn, and the evening ones, though in muted colors of plum and gray and forest green, were heavy silk in excellent condition.

Holding the plum gown pressed to her bosom, Audrey was assailed by a sudden idea. Could she dare to deceive people, dare to pass herself off as Susan's mother? *That* would solve the problem of a chaperon! Oh, not in Rampton, of course. But in Bath, where they knew no one. After all, she was as old as many a governess, and Susan, at sixteen, *could* be thought her daughter—or her stepdaughter. Who was to question it?

Struggling to her feet, and clasping the plum gown, she sped down to her chamber and scrambled into her mama's dress. It was a near fit and could easily be altered. She could actually remember her mother wearing it to a village assembly long ago. Of course she had not been present to see her mother dance—if her mother did so—but no one had doubted that Mrs. Malton was a married lady with a daughter almost old enough to be Out. Audrey knew she was not as beautiful as her mama, yet if she put her hair into a knot and used rice powder to subdue her youthful complexion, was it not possible to pass as older than she truly was?

Susan scratched at the door, and Audrey said "Come in" breathlessly, turning from the mirror to face her sister.

"Audrey!" cried Susan. "How—how very elegant you are! So . . . so sophisticated—"

"Enough so to be your mama?" asked the lady in question, kicking aside her demitrain to stroll across the room.

What did she mean? The words tumbled out, explaining Audrey's sudden plan, which was just daring enough to delight a maiden on the threshold of Society.

"But what will Mr. Howerfield say?" Susan asked, awestruck.

Audrey lifted her chin slightly. "Of course he must not know. It is a risk for us to take, yet I think there is a chance of making it work. Mr. Howerfield will probably not come near Bath while we are there. After all, he will think that his nephew has settled us respectably."

"But his nephew—David Howerfield—will have been told he is to escort two *sisters!*"

"Oh, no," corrected Audrey firmly. "I expect you to charm him into thinking he misunderstood."

"But he will never believe such a thing!"

"He will decide to do so if you dazzle him with languishing glances."

Susan began to giggle. "I never thought of you as so—so outrageous. Wicked! Leading the young astray!"

With another glance at her reflection in the mirror, Audrey said more soberly, "It is not the best sort of behavior, but in Bath we will behave like the perfect ladies Mama and Papa expected us to be, and if you do attach a suitable gentleman, we will, of course, tell him the truth, but he will be so besotted as to think you the most intriguing young lady in the world."

Susan, who had had in Rampton nothing that faintly resembled a suitor, was enchanted, though not so self-centered as to forget her sister's plight. She said slowly, "But, dearest, why should you sink yourself into a widow? That is not fair to you."

"Well," Audrey returned, "it is only for long enough to settle you happily. Then you can invite me to visit at the great house to which you go live with your husband, and I daresay there will be neighbors or friends or kin to furnish me with a suitable mate. I am nearly an ape-leader now, you know, and must not be particular."

"Ape-leader!" howled Susan. "How can you say such a scandalous thing?"

"Easily," said Audrey, laughing. "Perhaps I shall go on the stage. If I succeed in fooling Bath, I will know I have sufficient talent to be an actress."

As Susan was sure this was all nonsense, she fell upon the bed in a fit of giggles. "The duke who marries me will undoubtedly take me to Drury Lane to see you dazzle London!"

But Audrey was sobering. "We are only funning now," she said, "but it is a serious matter. I owe it to Papa and Mama to see you settled respectably. It can be done—you are so pretty . . . and sweet, which is even better. I am hoping to win the approval of some lady of title who will take us under her wing in Bath. Bath is your choice, isn't it?"

Susan rose from the bed to embrace her sister fondly. "Whatever you decide will be my choice," she said. "I do not care a bit about Grand Matches, but I understand a respectable match is what Papa would want for each of us. Now, what will you tell Polly?"

"Oh, Polly! I had not thought of her. She will know the truth, of course. Perhaps I shall tell her a kind lady in Bath is to sponsor us. Indeed, that is what I hope to find—a kind older lady to lend us respectability."

"Audrey! You know Papa's children are respectable!"

"Yes, dearest, but Bath Society does not know it, and someone must be persuaded to believe it."

Two

Did Audrey feel guilt at their planned subterfuge? As her father's daughter, she should be quaking with shame. How shocked the rector would be if he knew! But situations, she told herself, required action. So she purchased two new lengths of fabric for Susan, laid out appropriate pieces, and while the younger girl was cutting and basting, she climbed to the attic to plunge into trunks.

Actually, the attic was very neat, with no furniture relics except a baby bed and a rocking chair that needed mending, though it had not been wanted for a long, long time. The trunk of infant clothes she decided to save for sentimental reasons; might not the dainty things be needed some day?

She set aside some of her mother's garments for her own use—several gowns, a heavy pelisse for next winter, and three bonnets which, if retrimmed, would be as good as new. There was also a beautiful embroidered shawl, which she could remember her mother wearing for special occasions. She thought Mama had said Papa bought it for her, which was perhaps the reason Papa had packed it carefully away in tissue.

The door knocker sounded just as Audrey was carrying her mother's garments to her bedchamber.

It was Mrs. Cranny and two other ladies from the church.

She ran down the steps to welcome them.

"Miss Malton, we thought you might use a bit of help," said Mrs. Cranny, reinforced by several nods from the two other women.

"Indeed, I can!" she assured them warmly. "There are some

good things that may be useful in the parish—some almost new. I beg you to decide. Do you mind a climb to the attic?"

The three women, with no frills about them but plenty of practical sense, declared their whole aim was to help dear Miss Audrey. They shed plain bonnets and cloaks, handing them to Polly, whom they called "dear child."

"Susan and I could not manage without our Polly," Audrey said, which made the little maidservant blush with pleasure. She was the eldest child of a widow with several others to feed. This enterprising woman managed a vegetable shop; she was glad for Polly to have proper employment with the Malton ladies who treated her well and taught her useful things, like how to press *ruches* and pass teacakes without spilling them.

"Well, Polly," said Mrs. Cranny kindly, "I hear you are to travel from home." To this Polly glowingly replied, "Oh, yes, mum."

"Indeed! I trust you will take good care of our young ladies."

Polly curtsied the best she was able with armfuls of cloaks and bonnets.

"May I lead you ladies to the attic?" Audrey reminded gently.

They went up after her, leaving Polly to hang their wraps on hooks behind the staircase.

"Are we to see dear little Miss Susan?" asked one of the women, as they neared the top of the second flight.

"Of course you will," Audrey assured her. "She is busy with some sewing now, but will want to greet you before you leave. Oh, we are going to miss our friends of Rampton!"

After looking carefully through the trunk containing her papa's clothing to see that nothing should be held back, she sighed and moved away so the women could see what was there. While they were busy, she examined the things of her mother that she had left in another trunk, but found nothing more that would be useful for her own camouflage.

The baby bed, not being an heirloom, and the rocker which needed mending, and a few other things, would go along with the clothes to needy persons. She kept back an empty trunk and two portmanteaux which she and Susan would need for their travels.

Susan, quick to laugh and easy to cry, might have shed tears, had she been with them. Audrey managed to restrain her own tears and offer tea, and Susan came down to the drawing room to partake. The impromptu tea party passed off very well, with the visitors thanking them again and again and saying they would send men to fetch the things in the attic.

There was nothing to hold the girls in Rampton. When Susan's new dresses were made and their mother's altered for Audrey, the elder girl wrote to tell Mr. Howerfield that they were ready for "new places."

They waited only two more days for the arrival of David Howerfield with a traveling coach to whisk them to Bath and adventure.

Susan, somewhat nervous about the part she was to play, received young Mr. Howerfield first. So struck was she by this vision of a young dandy with dancing eyes and tall, slim form elegantly garbed from head to toe in the latest of Fashion, that she lost all thought of herself and smiled at him delightfully. For his part, he began to think his uncle had sent him to a romantic encounter.

"Miss Malton?" he inquired.

"Miss Susan Malton," she replied breathlessly. "M-Mama will be down in a moment."

He was momentarily at a loss. "I thought—two young ladies, my uncle said."

"Well, yes," Susan managed to reply. "M-Mama and me. Mama is very youthful, you see."

Mr. Howerfield did not exactly see, but Audrey was coming down the stairs now, swathed in a gray cloak with a veil from her black bonnet partially hiding a pale (powdered) face. She held out a hand encased in a gray glove.

"Mr. Howerfield, so good of you . . ."

"Madam," he replied, bowing over the hand.

"You see. Our luggage is ready." She motioned to the bags which were watched over by Polly, also garbed for travel.

"Then there is nothing to wait for," he said briskly, going onto the stoop to beckon a footman from his uncle's coach to fetch the bags and small trunk.

In no time at all they were seated in the coach, the Malton ladies facing forward, and Mr. Howerfield facing them, with Polly beside him. As the vehicle wheeled out of town, Audrey lowered her head and pressed a handkerchief to her mouth, which was not so much playacting, as restraint of tears. She could not bear a last look at her home and dear St. Leonard's, close by. Susan, however, was too interested in the dashing gentleman facing her to spare a glance for Rampton.

He did not seem bored. Indeed he was not. His uncle, besides confusing him about *two young ladies,* had not prepared him for the delightful spectacle of Miss Susan Malton. He began to think this trip would not be so onerous after all.

Out of consideration for the ladies' comfort, they did not travel at a breakneck pace, yet made good time, with smooth and rapid changes. Although the carriage had no crest upon its doors, it was a handsome vehicle, well kept, and obviously belonged to someone of importance. It received excellent attention at all posts.

By not much past midday they had reached Hungerford where Mr. Howerfield suggested they stop for luncheon. An assorted number of vehicles were crowding the yard.

"I am afraid," he said, "we may have trouble finding a table free. Let me go inside and ask."

They did not wait long, for Mr. Howerfield's charming manner—or the pourboire he slipped to the innkeeper—was successful. "Two gentleman at a small table have agreed to share their private parlor. A table is being added for us," he told them.

Audrey was somewhat dismayed by the glare given her party by one of the two other occupants of the parlor. He was an elderly man whose face was somewhat disfigured by scowls. Hanging over the arm of his chair were two canes. In one quick glance at him, Audrey, a pastor's daughter, diagnosed pain rather than bad nature.

"Why can we have no privacy?" he mumbled to his companion

who somewhat resembled him, though many years younger. "Must we share our room?"

This gentleman replied softly, "The inn is crowded, Father. I believe the lady is a widow. Surely we can allow them the comfort of a quiet table . . . Do you wish more to eat?"

At this point a servant set a dish of fruit before the gentleman with the canes.

"Yes. This fruit." He shifted slightly in his chair so as not to be facing the interlopers.

Meanwhile, the "widow" and her party were giving quiet orders to a waiter. Audrey had lifted her veil, and when she had made her choice of a meal, she raised her eyes to find the younger man staring across the room at her. He quickly averted his gaze, which she took to mean that he had no interest in a widow. If he had any interest in pretty Susan, it was wasted, for her sister was chatting happily with David Howerfield. Much out of place, Polly sat like a stone, though that did not interfere with her youthful appetite.

Presently, a servant in livery came in to address the disabled man's son: "Your carriage is ready, Mr. Aintree."

The two of them hoisted the invalid to his feet, handed him his canes, and the small procession withdrew from the parlor, Mr. Aintree saying, "We have your house waiting in readiness for us at Bath and will be there in time for you to rest before dinner."

Susan whispered to her sister, "Audrey, do you suppose they are a sample of Bath beaux? We might as well have gone to Tunbridge Wells!"

"Shhh!" cautioned her sister. "You *must* remember to call me 'Mama'!"

Fortunately, Mr. Howerfield was conferring with their waiter about desserts and did not hear. Polly was looking round-eyed, but would have cut her throat rather than expose her dear Miss Audrey to criticism by anyone.

With forty-odd miles to cover, and a later start than Mr. Aintree and his father, Audrey and Susan were slower in reaching Bath. It was close to six-thirty when they were decanted at Trim Street.

"I will be only two hops away on Wood Street," David Howerfield explained, "so you can send for me if you encounter any difficulties." He escorted them into the house, where his uncle had reserved a ground-floor suite for them, and they were received by a middle-aged woman to whom David said blithely, "Good day, Mrs. Dawes. I have brought you Mrs. Malton and Miss Malton as promised by my uncle, Mr. Howerfield."

The tall, plain-faced woman greeted them with sufficient warmth to make them feel welcome, but not enough to demean herself. After all, did she not have Sir John Sallinger and his wife occupying her first story?

Meanwhile, Mr. Howerfield's footman was bringing in their luggage, and was directed to their suite on the left of the hall.

"Our dinner is not quite ready," said Mrs. Dawes. "I hope you will feel like joining Sir John and Lady Sallinger in our dining parlor behind the sitting room across the hall."

Audrey replied they would do so.

David Howerfield bowed and said he would call upon them in a day or two. He and Mrs. Dawes went out; and Polly, with pride in her office, gently closed the door.

"We are here," exulted Susan, spinning around. "Did not this town look beautiful as we came down the hill? I had glimpses of the river! And wondrous buildings! I am sure even London could not be so delightful."

Audrey was removing her bonnet and detested black veil. "It looks expensive," she said. "I wonder how long we can stay."

"Oh," begged Susan, "say for weeks and weeks!"

Her sister admitted that Mr. Howerfield had not set a limit to time, but they must be cautious about expenditures.

Their sitting room was small and cozy, with a vase of violets on one table. Already Susan had gone into the bedchamber to investigate it.

Audrey went toward the flowers and, sure enough, there was a brief note beside them from their father's friend, Mr. Howerfield, wishing them a pleasant visit. She felt a slight twinge of guilt at her false identity and hoped Mr. Howerfield would never know. With luck, pretty Susan would meet a suitable husband

and be comfortably settled for the rest of her life. If David Howerfield's admiration was a sample, surely other young gentlemen would be attracted to Susan. She could not think David was ready to be serious about settling into matrimony, but other men might be. At all levels of society, Audrey knew, mothers manipulated marriages for their daughters, and now she was going to be trying the same thing. It would not do to talk to Susan much about such a subject; she would simply encourage her to become acquainted with as many Bath visitors as possible—all ages and sexes of persons who seemed respectable. Even an elderly gentleman might have a grandson he doted on—or a maiden aunt might have an unattached nephew. No one, meeting Susan for the first time, could know—as Audrey did—the sweetness of her nature, her generous ways, her lack of self-interest. As Susan's mama, she would have to make sure these assets were recognized.

Fortunately for Audrey's plans, Sir John and his wife proved to have the one thing the girls needed: friendly connections with everyone in Bath that *mattered*.

"There is to be dancing in the Upper Rooms tomorrow night," Lady Sallinger told them that night at dinner. "You will have to go."

"I need to enter our names on the subscription books, do I not?" Audrey asked. She had heard about those.

"Yes, but you must do it promptly in the morning," advised Lady Sallinger. "We will be going to the ball in the evening, which means taking our carriage, for it is all uphill from here, so we will be happy to take you and your daughter with us. There is nothing so dismal as going into a crowd of strange faces."

"Yus, yus," amended Sir John fervently.

Susan clasped her hands in delight, as her "mama" offered grateful thanks. It seemed a miracle that they had encountered such affable people within an hour of reaching Bath.

Yet the rector had many times told his daughters that they were more apt to *find* good in people if they *looked* for good.

After the meal, alone in their small suite, the girls spoke of how fortunate they were to encounter the Sallingers.

"I had thought," Susan said, "that Mr. Howerfield might have offered to escort us."

But Audrey answered seriously, "He has already given up a long day to our affairs. It is better this way. To be under the aegis of an older lady—Lady Sallinger—is more appropriate for unknowns. She will be sure to introduce us to persons Papa would want us to know. Indeed, I begin to feel we have found guardian angels right here in Bath!"

The next morning, while Polly tenderly pressed all their dresses, Audrey and Susan walked out to explore the town, admire Georgian architecture, and enroll at both Upper and Lower Assembly Rooms. Though they were out early in the day for most visitors to Bath, they did climb Milsom Street and did reach the Assembly Rooms, where on the register, a short space above where they inscribed their own names, were written "Viscount Chalbert and Mr. Charles Aintree." Would those gentlemen be coming to the ball that night? Even one with two canes?

What mattered more to Susan was the registration of Mr. David Howerfield, who did not have a handle to his name, but who was handsome enough and jolly enough to appeal to *her.*

The Malton girls did not want to make themselves conspicuous by poring over the register too long, so even though few people were there to notice, they read but a portion, only to find no other names they recognized, except Sallinger, of course.

Three

"I have had the most frightful thought. How could I have over-looked it?" said Audrey as they explored George Street, intending to reach Gay, which Lady Sallinger had said would take them down to Trim Street again.

"What can be that bad, when all is so delightful here?" Susan asked, not the least dismayed.

Audrey was not soothed by beautiful scenery. "Just think!" she said, keeping her voice low, so as not to be overheard by passers-by. "What will you do if Lady Sallinger should present some young gentleman and he asks you to dance? You have never *learned*."

"Oh, but I have!" laughed her sister. "The Ethan girls have taught me. We practiced in their drawing room several times when their mother was at tea somewhere else."

Audrey shook her head in disbelief. "You never told me! I do not think their mama keeps a proper eye on those two. She is very good *ton* and will launch them socially in a year or two, but our mama never expected to do the same for us."

"Well, I hope David Howerfield—if he is present tonight—will ask me to dance. Surely he is not a stranger."

Audrey said reluctantly, "I suppose that would be all right. We *did* come here to make new friends, to present you socially in a small way; and I know Bath is considered less formal than London. I shall not dance myself, of course."

"Do you not know how?"

"I know a bit—learned much as you have done." She smiled

ruefully. "However, I am a widow, you must remember, and in half-mourning."

"A clanger!" declared Susan.

"You did not learn words like that in Papa's house. If you speak like that in the Upper Assembly Rooms, you must soon be an outcast."

"Well, then," Miss Susan said mildly, "I will not. Perhaps if we sit dutifully watching with Lady Sallinger, we may learn new steps."

That evening, as they waited for Sir John and Lady Sallinger to come downstairs, Audrey was almost regal in her mama's plum silk dress, a dainty lace cap upon her carefully knotted hair. Susan, by contrast, was youthfully captivating in pale pink gauze, her hair flowing beautifully.

Audrey, who thought her merry sister would attract many partners, reminded her that there might be men of less than refined antecedents mingling with the gentle folk. "You must take your cues from Lady Sallinger," she insisted. "If she pretends not to see someone, you must not see him either; and if she is hesitant, that is your signal to be very sorry but your program is full. Or you can always fall back on a plea of needing rest."

"How can I need rest, if I am to refuse partners right and left?" demanded her sister. "And why," she said, changing subjects swiftly, "are you wearing that wretched lace cap?"

Audrey was not obliged to answer, for they heard Sir John and Lady Sallinger descending, so they went into the hall carrying cloaks and small reticules.

"How pretty you look!" exclaimed her Ladyship. "Do they not, John? Do they not?"

"Aye," said her spouse, but stiffly, as though he was laced into a corset of some sort.

The girls wondered if his wife would expect him to whirl young women about the ballroom.

In no time, all had entered the Sallinger carriage to make a very slow trip up the hill to the Assembly Rooms. As they progressed, the pace became even slower, for other carriages and chairs were converging on the same space.

At Bennett Street there was a brief wait for them to be set down. Then they had entered the building, and Lady Sallinger was sweeping them up to the Assembly Room, whispering how glad she was they could commandeer chairs on a front row, which would make them accessible to dancing gentlemen. She cast a hard look at Audrey's lace cap, but was tactful enough to say nothing at that time.

"I will take a girl on each side of me, John, and you can sit next to Mrs. Malton, for I am sure you two will have things to talk about. I shall be introducing Miss Malton to partners. Do you not see? There are several looking at her already."

Susan blushed rosily. She had already spied David Howerfield diagonally down the room, though he gave no sign of noticing her. Other young women were standing about the dance floor with partners, waiting for the music to begin. Surely he could not ignore her!

Either he *could* . . . or he had not seen her—or perhaps he did not recognize Audrey in her dark plum dress, her lovely hair drawn back tightly to a severe knot, a frothy lace cap on her crown to proclaim her widowhood.

Susan bit her lip. She had counted upon David to launch her on the dance floor, yet he was busy talking and had not even glanced her way. She watched the dancers, nodding her head in time to the music.

On the long side of the room, opposite the entrance, was an elevated bay for the musicians, which made them more readily visible and had the effect of amplifying their music, so Susan concentrated on them. The chair next to her was empty, a lady there having gone onto the floor to dance. From time to time Lady Sallinger called her attention to some lady or gentleman swirling before them. She could not see her sister.

Audrey, at the other side of Lady Sallinger, was concentrating on looking like a proper matron, though to do this involved making conversation with the taciturn Sir John.

"Do you come often to the balls?" she asked him.

"Aye. M'wife enjoys lively scenes," he responded. "Don't dance much, myself."

No gentlemen had approached them, so Audrey and Susan had met no one. Perhaps, Audrey thought, it was better to watch quietly for a while. There was not a great deal of conversation while the musicians played and many feet pattered on the floor. Then, as a line moved past her, she saw Mr. Aintree partnering a handsome woman, and he must have glimpsed her, for he nodded slightly. She wondered if Susan had noticed him. Evidently she had, for Audrey caught a whisper to Lady Sallinger: "My lady, do you know that gentleman?"

And her Ladyship replied sufficiently loudly for Audrey to hear, "Oh, yes. Charles Aintree, Chalbert's heir. First time on the social scene since his wife died a year or so ago."

He must be surprised to see us in the company of a knight, Audrey thought. Like Susan, she had seen David Howerfield, and wondered why he had ignored Susan and herself. She hoped Susan was not hurt.

Then all was explained during an intermission between dances, when a stranger approached with David and addressed Lady Sallinger.

"Good evening, my lady. May I present my friend from Cambridge days, Mr. David Howerfield?"

"Henry, dear boy!" she responded, delighted. "Happy to see you. John, you remember Miriam's son. How do you do, Mr. Howerfield? Mrs. Malton, Miss Malton, this is Mr. Wells . . . Mr. Howerfield."

David immediately asked Susan for the next dance and led her away to meet other young people, and Henry Wells sat down in Susan's chair to chat with her Ladyship about his mama and various events in Dorset. When the tuning of violins was heard, he went away as suddenly as he had come, and Lady Sallinger and Mrs. Malton soon had the pleasure of glimpsing a flushed Susan dancing tolerably well and happily.

Susan did not return to her seat at the end of the set, for she stood conversing with the young people that David had introduced to her. When the music resumed, she had another partner.

"A good beginning," said Lady Sallinger with satisfaction.

"Yes," agreed Audrey, pleased that her sister's informal "dancing lessons" with the Ethan girls in Rampton had been useful.

"I do like to see well-bred young people enjoying themselves. Matchmaking is my hobby—or so John says. I would like to see all sweet young ladies settled in a marriage as happy as mine has been with dear John," her Ladyship said. "Your daughter is charming, Mrs. Malton, but I see no reason for you not to enjoy the evening also. A widow, are you not? Ah, there is Aintree who lost his wife a year or so ago. He will want to meet Miss Susan, I daresay. Yes, here he comes."

"Good evening, Lady Sallinger."

"Good evening to you, Mr. Aintree. Mrs. Malton, this is Mr. Charles Aintree, whose mama was a dear friend of my second cousin, Cecilia Calne. Not a relation of mine, but one of my favorite young men. You have not met?"

"Not exactly," Mr. Aintree responded before Audrey could decide how to reply. "Our paths . . . er . . . crossed at Hungerford." He looked into her eyes with a faint twinkle in his own. "Do you care to dance, Mrs. Malton?"

"I-I had not thought—"

"Certainly, she will dance," interrupted Lady Sallinger. "Go along with you!"

Audrey wondered uncomfortably if her Ladyship was trying to make a match for *her.* But Mr. Aintree had a hold on her elbow and was propelling her down the room toward a group of his friends. She faltered in the dance steps only once. The whole set was nerve-wracking, but pleasurable.

"There, you see!" said Lady Sallinger when Mr. Aintree had returned Audrey to her side and gone away. "I predict you will be a belle, if you will just cast away that cap!"

"It belonged to my mother," Audrey protested faintly.

"Very nice for your mother, I daresay," said her Ladyship tartly, "but you are too young to wither away. I shall introduce several eligible men to you. Bachelors and attractive widowers, you know."

"Susan—" began Audrey.

"Yes, yes, you feel you must first settle your daughter. But what will become of you then? You must be a good deal younger than I, and I am not ready to abandon pleasant society. I cannot see you wasting away in a Bath-chair or retiring to Good Deeds in a village!"

Laughing, then, to hear Lady Sallinger so nearly describe her existence in Rampton, she said pluckily, "Do your worst!"

"Ah," said her Ladyship triumphantly. "John. *John,* fetch Sir Roland to meet Mrs. Malton. I see him down at the end of the room with Lord Combe. Bring Combe, too."

Soon, with Susan returning in the company of several beaux, they were crowding over the edge of the dance floor, so that the Master of Ceremonies had to come and ask them to disperse or withdraw to the anteroom. No offense was taken, the group broke up, and Susan and Audrey settled in their proper places beside the Sallingers.

"I shall send notes tomorrow," Lady Sallinger informed her husband, "inviting these interested gentlemen to a sherry party the next day." To Mrs. Malton she said, "We have a very nice drawing room on Mrs. Dawes' first floor. She does not mind if we entertain from time to time."

Audrey protested, "You must not go to so much trouble on our account." Where all this was leading she did not know.

"No trouble at all. Indeed, you must realize by now that I enjoy people. John and I have very pleasant friends, and we are always delighted to acquire more. What you can do for me is *remove that cap.*"

By this time Audrey was wondering if Mr. Howerfield, her papa's banker who had placed them here, was acquainted with Lady Sallinger's propensity for acquiring friends and shaping their lives.

Twenty minutes before the ball closed, Lady Sallinger was collecting her small party. "It is always best, I think, to leave any public ball ahead of time, for that way one will be *missed,* and to linger means making bland conversation with persons who are interested only in finding their transportation."

Much struck by the practical sense of this, Miss Susan and her supposed mama went readily. Neither had ever danced at a ball or even seen one before this night. They trusted Lady Sallinger's advice implicitly.

In the lower hall at Trim Street, the girls thanked their companions again, and Audrey asked if she could be of help in addressing invitations.

"Mama writes beautifully," Susan said, not offering her own scrawl.

But kind Lady Sallinger refused, saying they were to be honored guests.

When her Ladyship and Sir John had started up the stairs, and the rector's shamefully deceitful daughters had closed themselves into their own small suite, Susan said ruefully, "I feel a bit guilty about misleading Lady Sallinger."

"So do I," Audrey admitted.

"Is it very bad of us?" persisted Susan.

"Papa would think so. I keep wondering if it could be possible that Mr. Howerfield purposely placed us here, under Lady Sallinger's influence. Can he even have *told* her our circumstances?"

The younger girl breathed out an "Oh!" and pressed three fingers to her mouth.

Then Audrey said, "N-no. No. Our lady genuinely likes people. You and I are fortunate to have met a lady both kind and well placed, but I am beginning to feel ashamed."

Without talking further, they went through their bedchamber to rouse Polly from her cot in their dressing room.

Polly was wide awake in no time, asking if they had danced all these hours, and whether they were tired.

In garbled talk, sometimes both at once, they let her know that all was divine and they were quite exhausted and wanted to sleep till noon, so Polly might do the same.

Four

Next day Lord Chalbert, wearing a robe in preparation for a morning at the baths, was having breakfast with his son in his house at Number 4 of the Royal Crescent, when a footman laid before him a note that had just been hand delivered.

"What's this?" he muttered. "Looks like an invitation. Folk ought to know I never accept them."

"Well, open it and see," said Mr. Aintree reasonably.

His Lordship tore open the seal. "It's for you, too, Charles. Lady Sallinger is inviting us to what she calls 'a small sherry party' tomorrow afternoon. I like that female, but of course I shall not go. What about you? Will you do so?"

"Why not?" returned Charles, having a suspicion that Lady Sallinger was conducting a campaign to promote Miss Malton—and indirectly her mama. "Do you remember the two ladies who shared our parlor at Hungerford? I have an idea this affair is to draw some attention to them."

Lord Chalbert said he remembered two females who invaded his private parlor. "Didn't pay them much attention. Why should Lady Sallinger care about provincials?" He tossed the note to his son, who immediately saw mentioned the names of Mrs. and Miss Malton. "If they are pretty, I suppose you will go."

"I shall go," said Mr. Aintree, "whether they are pretty or not. First new faces this season."

Lord Chalbert scowled at his son. "Three days here. Are you bored already? I suppose I am a burden to you."

Charles ignored the word "burden" and said, "You always used to notice handsome women before I did."

"Yes, but these invaded our parlor!" objected the viscount.

"They were hungry, too."

"And had a maidservant—obviously a *maidservant*—eating with them."

"Where could they have left her in that crowded inn? There was also a young gentleman with them, Father. David Howerfield, kin to the Howerfield I think you know."

Lord Chalbert looked up from his meal. "Howerfield, the banker of Salisbury?"

"Yes. Nephew, I think. Pleasant chap."

"I suppose you met all these people at the assembly last night?"

"Yes." Seeing that his father no longer ate, he added, "Time for the baths now." He motioned a footman to come forward to assist Lord Chalbert to his feet.

"I think they are beginning to do you good," he added, noticing that his father had eaten a better breakfast than usual.

Lord Chalbert growled something indistinguishable.

The carriage was already waiting. With some difficulty his Lordship was hoisted into it, and they set out. Twice a day they went down to Stall Street, for Lord Chalbert to have a long soak in the soothing hot water. Charles Aintree hoped today would continue to increase the old man's comfort. He rather looked forward to Lady Sallinger's sherry party and hoped his father would decide to go to it.

For his part, Chalbert was pleased about the sherry party, if it meant his son had not only ended his period of mourning, but also was ready for the company of other people, even strangers.

At the baths, Charles turned his father over to a bath attendant and went up to the Pump Room. It was too early to find many persons present, but he did encounter several acquaintances with whom to talk. They greeted him enthusiastically, glad he had come out of retirement, but not wanting to mention the loss of his wife. All save one were bachelors of assorted ages, that one being a hearty squire whose wife was across the room swilling mineral water as if she depended upon it to maintain her youth. The others had come to see and be seen, to hear the latest gossip.

"See the new Beauty last night, Aintree?" a young dandy asked.

Charles Aintree raised a brow quizzically.

"Miss Susan Malton." The dandy rolled his eyes with a roguish grin. No mention was made of Miss Malton's mother, as others joined in to describe Susan's sparkling eyes and friendly ways. Not top-lofty at all, though clearly a lady.

"Yes," said Aintree. "I had a dance with her mama."

Several jeers greeted this.

"A youngish lady. Quite pretty," he added temperately.

At this moment, looking down the length of the room, he saw the Malton ladies enter with Lady Sallinger. They came nearer, and he heard her Ladyship say, "Now, I am going to see that you both taste the mineral water. Very healthful. If you do not like it, you can at least claim to have tried it, and no one will bother you further."

The Malton ladies accepted glasses and were just sipping from them, when Mr. Aintree approached them.

"Enjoyment of the drink depends upon a strong desire for improved health," he said, smiling.

"Ugh!" said Susan, lowering her glass hastily.

"Very true," he replied. "Good day, Lady Sallinger, Mrs. Malton. My father drinks the water sometimes, as well as bathing in it, to restore his health."

"Well, I visit Bath for pleasure, not punishment," said Lady Sallinger firmly, "though my husband sips Bath Tea now and then. Here comes my husband now for his glass. I suppose," she added to Mr. Aintree, "you must sip some from time to time, too, to encourage your father."

He said mildly that his father preferred the hot baths. "None of you ladies require medication or hot pools, as is plain to see."

"You are being gallant, as usual, Aintree. I hope you are coming to my small sherry party?"

"Indeed I am. Thank you. As for Father, he does not feel equal to convivial groups. The sherry party will be his loss. Mrs. Malton, is Bath as pleasant as you expected?"

She replied, "Very much so." To which Susan added, "The

town is beautiful, and everyone we have met is most cordial."
She looked both young and happy, which was an endearing combination.

"I saw many young men being 'cordial' last night," he said,
offering an arm. "May I escort you on a circuit of the Pump
Room?"

Glad of an excuse to set aside the noxious beverage, Susan
gave her glass to her sister and went off happily with Mr. Aintree
to meet his friends.

Lady Sallinger immediately said to Audrey, "I do not think
you need to worry about settling *that* one. Such a happy nature!"

"Yes, she is always in good spirits," responded the false
mother truthfully. "She is very young, however, and I hope to
keep her under my eye until she is somewhat older and can make
a sensible choice."

"She will have choices enough," Sir John chimed in.

"Besides," said her Ladyship, who loved to arrange—or re-
arrange—lives, and had no qualms about doing so, "Susan is
very young. It would be wise to catch a beau yourself, before
she does . . . and do not claim to be an old, settled widow! You
would find a husband very helpful in negotiating a match for
that saucy creature."

Blushing furiously, and not knowing what to say, Audrey stammered, "Oh, no! I mean, I am a widow and do not intend—"

"I know you think only of the girl. Am I not right, John? You
do think Mrs. Malton must not be *wasted?*"

"Yus, yus," he mumbled, then cleared his throat and added in
a rush, "Don't press the girl, m'dear."

His "dear" laughed heartily. "John knows I am really not
pressing you to do anything hastily. You have not been a widow
very long, have you? Miss Susan is a gay creature, who must
spread her wings for a while, but you are not so old either, are
you? Quite amazing you could have a daughter sixteen—if that
is what she is. Must have been a child-bride yourself."

Feeling backed into a corner, where to affirm or deny would
be equally embarrassing, Audrey took a deep breath and said,
"Mr. Malton has not been . . . gone . . . long. We are feeling our

way. I hope you understand that I cannot say what we intend, for we do not know. M-Mr. Malton and I lived quietly. Susan has not been spoiled. I pray you will not—rush us."

"There!" said Sir John. "The girl has a head on her shoulders."

Lady Sallinger was willing to surrender most of the way. "Just do one little thing for me, Mrs. Malton. Leave off your cap tomorrow afternoon."

"I will," she said, "if you will call me 'Audrey.' "

Sir John Sallinger was happy that all had been settled so amiably. Susan was free to subjugate as many gentlemen as she pleased, which would delight both her "mama" and Lady Sallinger. And Audrey would be rid of her sedate cap.

On the following afternoon, when the girls were dressing for the sherry party, the elder admitted to the younger that she was obliged to abandon her widow's cap to please Lady Sallinger.

"Well, that's good!" declared Susan forcefully. "I do not like you to be *drab.*"

"Oh, was I that?" asked Audrey chagrined.

Susan said, "Our mama was pretty, wasn't she? My makeshift mama should look her best, too, so I can be proud of her."

"You are a scamp," declared Audrey. "You are trying to manipulate me as you do the beaux!"

Susan looked astonished. "I am? I do? No, no. I want everyone to be happy."

"But what makes you happy may not serve for others," her sister said seriously. "Two gentlemen cannot be happy if they both want the same girl."

"Well, I do not intend to settle on anyone for years, so no one will be unhappy today!" Susan declared triumphantly.

This being moderately reassuring, Audrey said no more.

They climbed a flight to Lady Sallinger's drawing room, Susan delectable in a white muslin dotted with marine blue, blue ribbons looping gracefully beneath her bosom. Audrey was wearing a discreet gray muslin to which she had added a blush silk rose at the center of a modest neckline. She hoped she looked old enough to have a daughter who was sixteen, though actually she did not. Fortunately, people they met seemed to have accepted the supposed relationship. She did not realize there was a maturity in her manner that came from her having assumed her mother's duties a number of years ago.

"Dear me!" said Lady Sallinger, receiving them. "You look alluring. It alarms me a little, for it is the men who may be swooning on my carpet."

"Well, my dear," said her spouse, surprising them greatly, "we will just step over them."

The first guests entered then, to find the four laughing heartily. The unexpected appearance of Viscount Chalbert, accompanying his son, sobered them, although he seemed to have left his grumps behind.

"I *was* invited, wasn't I?" he asked.

"Glad to have you," said Sir John sincerely. He did not know that most people, including his wife, found the viscount something of an old bear.

This afternoon Lady Sallinger settled him on a comfortable sofa and went to welcome David Howerfield and several other youthful blades who had been invited for Susan's benefit.

Mr. Aintree had found his way to Susan's side, and Audrey watched them covertly, thinking how gracious he was, seeming to listen courteously to Susan's youthful prattle. Of course, he was a gentleman—a handsome one with wonderful broad shoulders—poised in any situation, and seemingly dependable, which was a characteristic she admired most. Was there any hope that his attention to Susan could be more than courtesy?

Other people had arrived until the Sallingers' temporary drawing room was convivially crowded. Then Audrey noticed that most people were standing with their glasses of sherry, and no one paid any attention to the viscount, who was beginning to look as if he wondered why he had come. Having learned long ago in ecclesiastical circles that *everyone* must be included in a group activity, Audrey dutifully went across to him and sat upon the same sofa.

"It is good to see you out in Society, my lord," she said. "I hope this means the baths are helping you."

"Well, they are. I should have tried them sooner," he admitted, changing the subject because he knew his infirmities would not be of interest to a pretty young woman: "Kin of the Sallingers, eh?"

"No, my lord. We met only a few days ago, when we took rooms here. They have been kind. Two women alone do not have an easy time."

"That's right," he agreed. "Recent widow, Charles said."

"A matter of some months," she corrected gently. "Mr. Malton's post as rector of St. Leonard's in Rampton has been taken over by Mr. Nunley."

"After Bath, what?"

"We may settle here. We are beginning to like Bath very much."

"Not a great deal happens in winter," he pointed out.

"Susan and I would not mind," she said with a slight smile. "We are accustomed to a small town, you see." Changing the subject from herself and her supposed daughter, she asked him to tell her about the baths. "Are they very hot?"

"Not enough to scald," he replied, smiling for the first time. "Very warm. Much like a good, deep bath at one's home, with minerals added."

"Did the Romans really build these pools?"

"Yes, found the wells boiling up and put them to use. Had baths in Rome before Christ, you know."

"But not from springs like ours?"

Pleased to find a female who knew a thing or two, he said, "Obliged to heat them. Rather erratic. Oh, we are living in better times, I think."

"Would you like to wear a toga every day?" she asked teasingly. Across the room Mr. Aintree was surprised to see his father smile.

Lord Chalbert was finding it pleasant to be teased, so he said with a genuine grin, "I wear a bathrobe most hours. Do you think a toga might be more dignified?"

In their carriage, going back up to Number 4, Royal Crescent, his Lordship did not mention young widows, nubile girls, or lonely widowers. "It is pleasant here. Great deal going on. You might fetch my grandson to brighten my days." It was one way to assure Aintree's staying longer.

Charles knew he would do just that, since his father's suggestions had the force of commands. "Do you miss Jamie, sir? So do I. How can we amuse him here?"

"Oh, the ladies will think of things—carriage rides, boating on the river, picnics, and so on."

Lord Chalbert was being unusually casual.

"Can you manage without me?" Charles asked. "It will take me two days—maybe three—to get home and back."

"Yes. I am feeling stronger, less hobbled, and I have my valet, you know."

"Then I will leave in the morning," Charles promised.

Five

Mr. Aintree was not seen the next day by the ladies of Trim Street.

Lady Sallinger, who had begun to spin a few fantasies about him, thought merely that he was busy with his father. When another day passed, she began to wonder first if he had gone to a mill or some such masculine pursuit, then second if he was ill, finally if he had lost interest in the young ladies under her fond supervision. She did not mention these doubts to Mrs. Malton and her daughter.

"Shall you wish to attend Sunday Service at the abbey?" she asked them.

It was a superfluous question to the family of a rector. Of course they did, and were happy to accompany her Ladyship. Sir John escorted them in his courteous way, telling them things his wife did not know, or in any case had forgotten. It was in a previous abbey church on the same site that Edgar was belatedly crowned in the tenth century, he said. In the eleventh century a son of William the Conqueror built a cathedral which later burned and fell into decay. In the late fifteenth century, Sir John said, Bishop King built the present structure according to a dream that had come to him in his sleep.

Miss Susan Malton was enthralled by the story, while her mama declared herself amazed.

Mr. Aintree was not seen here, though no one spoke of that.

He was traveling fast, staying at home only long enough for Nursie to pack the child's clothes and admonish him to be a good boy. Jamie was blissful, leaving his faithful Nursie behind and having his papa all to himself. They reached Bath in time for a late Sunday dinner with Grandfather, whose aches and pains, already abating, were forgotten for several hours.

On Monday the three Aintree gentlemen went to the baths so that Jamie could see his grandfather soaking in the hot pool. He was allowed, firmly held by his papa, to reach out to feel the warmth of the water. Then he was taken upstairs to be presented to various of Mr. Aintree's friends who happened to be gathered in the Pump Room.

It was somewhat early for a Monday morning. Lady Sallinger and her protégées were not present, yet before a small boy could become tired or bored, they had entered, and Mr. Aintree led his child across the room to be presented to them.

All immediately declared him to be a "fine boy." Audrey, however, stooped down so as to be on Jamie's level, and said she was pleased to know Master Aintree who was a perfect miniature of his papa. Truly, the child did closely resemble his father, although he had big brown eyes which Audrey could not know were inherited from his mother.

The child, responding to the warmth of her smile, and glad she did not tower over him like all the others, said that Papa changed horses often, so that they came very fast. At the last posting stop, they got Papa's own horses, and they were fastest of all.

"Would you like to taste the well water?" Audrey asked.

"It smells bad," Jamie objected.

"Yes," inserted Mr. Aintree, "Jamie has been to watch his grandfather in the bath. The odor there is strong, of course."

She turned her face up from about the level of his knees, and he thought how incredibly young she looked to be the parent of a grown daughter. "I daresay Jamie will want to tell his nanny and others at home that he has *tasted* the famous Bath mineral waters. I tried them myself," she added to the boy. "Just a sip, so as to know what they are like. Your grandpapa drinks them sometimes—doesn't he, Mr. Aintree?"

"Yes," admitted the gentleman, smiling. "I have been known to do so, myself. Would you like a wee taste, Jamie?"

If his papa and grandpapa could drink the stuff that smelled strongly at the bathing pool, Jamie thought he might do so, too. "I will tell Nursie when I go home."

Effortlessly, Audrey stood up before Mr. Aintree could reach down to help her. She led the boy to where glasses were being filled and asked for "a wee, wee bit."

So little in a glass would be less odorous than down below at the baths. Jamie took a small sip, handed back the glass, and said, "Nasty!"

His father and Audrey laughed, and Susan came to see what was so amusing.

"Time for honest tea!" said his father.

While he went to procure tea for all of them, the girls took Jamie to a vacant table. Mr. Aintree, followed by an attendant with a tray, was obliged to say "Excuse me" several times, in order to make his way through the group of beaux which had gathered around them.

Susan chatted happily with the gentlemen who had been presented to her, as Audrey helped Jamie with his tea, and Lady Sallinger extracted from Mr. Aintree the details of his fast trip home. Secure in her position as a wife of a knight, her Ladyship could ask what she pleased of a gentleman who had not yet ascended to a title.

His manner was everything gracious, yet she thought Susan might be less interested in a widower than in some dashing fellow nearer her age. Of the gentlemen clustered around, David Howerfield was just the handsome chap to appeal to a young girl.

Unfortunately, Mr. Howerfield was heard to say: "I am off for Salisbury today. My uncle has ordered me home. Says 'All play is demoralizing.' "

There was a groan of sympathy, which led one scamp to promise: *"We* will watch over Miss Malton for you, old chap."

Susan colored becomingly and said she and her mama would never have been so comfortably settled without him.

"What time do you leave, Mr. Howerfield?" asked Lady Sallinger, sorry to lose such a personable fellow. She doubted he was a real prospect for matrimony, yet his attention to Susan sparked a general interest in the girl.

Mr. Howerfield said he should already be gone, but had hoped to catch Mrs. Malton and her daughter here, to explain he was not deserting them. "I will be sure to see you another time, Mrs. Malton. Are you quite settled in Bath? Is it all you hoped?"

"We may never leave Bath," Audrey replied with some exaggeration.

Mr. Howerfield promptly said she was gracious to give him hope that he might see her and Miss Malton when next he came to town.

"Will you be returning?" asked Lady Sallinger, alerted to the possibility.

"My uncle sends me hither and thither," he said lightly, trying unsuccessfully to catch Susan's eye.

But Susan, very interested, pretended not to seem so.

David Howerfield was obliged to leave, and looking back, he saw that the ranks closed about Susan as if he had not ever been among them.

"Who can tell me," said Mr. Aintree, "what other young people are in town? We may want to gather a group at my father's house."

"William Talbott," someone suggested. "Henry Wells."

"Thomas Medbury," said another.

"Miss Crowell." This brought out a burst of laughter and one young gentleman blushed hotly.

"We will certainly include Miss Crowell," Aintree said, jotting the names and adding one or two others. "Come along, Jamie. We will see if your grandpapa is ready to go home."

Tiring of the big people towering over him, the boy slipped a hand into his father's, and they went away.

Lord Chalbert had had enough hot mineral water. He was ready to leave, and not disapproving of his son's intended party. "Why not a luncheon, if the weather is good? Then your friends will like a stroll on the sloping parkland below. Ladies, you will find, like to twirl their parasols."

"Yes, I know," his son replied, smiling faintly.

Aintree's departure had been a signal for the group in the Pump Room to disperse.

"Lord Chalbert," Lady Sallinger said privately to Audrey and Susan, "must be feeling a good deal better, if he is willing to have guests in the house. It will give you an opportunity to see the interior of a Royal Crescent mansion."

To young ladies reared in the rectory of Rampton, the whole of Bath seemed quite splendid. They were gently born, yet unacquainted with much that was truly elegant. Their papa's firmly implanted values prevented awe or ambition to influence them. Audrey wished only to find a mate for her sister, one who was kind, gentlemanly, and able to support her in comfort, if not splendor. Susan, on the other hand, dreamed only of romance, not sure what it might mean, but convinced it was essential for happiness. She liked the young men she had met but had not yet measured them against her papa.

The Malton girls were grateful to Lady Sallinger for guiding them through the somewhat rural society and relaxed manners of Bath. They were pleased to be invited to Number 4 of the Royal Crescent, but not overawed. Mostly, they were surprised that the crotchety lord would open his home to the invasion of youth.

"I wonder," said Audrey later in their suite, "if there are any children in Bath with whom Jamie can play. I suspect he has been fairly well isolated on Lord Chalbert's manor."

"Perhaps there are some not yet mentioned," Susan suggested.

With Susan fairly launched and flirting with first one young man and then another, happy, and not thinking about possible exposure of their ruse, Audrey devoted her motherly instincts to young Jamie. She rather thought he would turn out to be much the sort of man his father was, which could only be good. Such steadiness of character, such quiet good humor! How wonderful it would be if Aintree were to take a serious interest in Susan. She thought he would be a kind and caring husband; someone who would be amused by Susan's romantic flights and general good nature.

Perhaps it was too soon to think of such things . . . but the whole reason for this experiment in Bath was to settle Susan's future within a compatible marriage. From the time of her mother's death, Audrey's attention had been on consoling her father, keeping the household serene so he was free to deal with matters of his church, and filling Susan's days with love and understanding. Now she was focusing on Susan's future.

Loving Susan had never been difficult, for her sister's nature was a happy one. Already Audrey could see that the young men whom they met were warming to her sister's sunny disposition. Susan spoiled? Certainly not! Her amiability was quite obvious.

David Howerfield was the first bonny fellow that Susan had encountered, and it was not surprising that she should admire him, but Audrey hoped her heart was not engaged, for a match there would not be what Audrey had in mind for her—something better than a banker's nephew who had not much to offer beyond an engaging personality. Though Susan must regret David's leaving, and hope he would return sometime, she seemed to be responding sweetly to others at hand—Henry Wells, William Talbott, Thomas Medbury, for example. And Aintree, too, yet she made no special favorite of him.

Since Bath was still rather thin of company, those invited by Charles Aintree to a luncheon were pleased to accept, the ladies bringing parasols, of which Audrey and Susan had only one between them.

The whole meal was put into the hands of Lord Chalbert's housekeeper, which meant they sat down, sixteen of them, to a lavish repast in Lord Chalbert's beautiful dining room, with its soft gray-green dado and scenic mural depicting the same view that was to be seen through Lord Chalbert's front windows. The setting would almost have made the food superfluous, had not an excellent housekeeper planned a tempting assortment of salads and whole salmon in aspic. There was a superb white wine, of which Audrey and Susan were each cautious to drink only one glass.

Lady Sallinger was, of course, at his Lordship's right, and she seemed to entertain him well. There were, in fact, few that could remain dour in her company. Besides, she drew him out skillfully about his adventures in hot baths, saying she could almost feel the soothing warmth.

Charles Aintree anchored the foot of the table, with Miss Crowell at his right, and Audrey separated from him by Jamie, on a cushion, at his left. Awed by the elegance of both meal and company, the child was a model of good behavior. His papa and his grandpapa had every right to be proud of him.

After the meal, Lord Chalbert retired for a nap, and the rest flowed out the door of Number 4, across the Crescent and down sloping lawns of parkland with scattered trees and distant views of the Avon valley. As Susan veered off with Mr. Wells and Mr. Medbury, she flirtatiously twirled the Malton parasol, for which Audrey had no use at all, for Jamie had her hand and was urging her toward a particular tree.

"Look, Mrs. Malton," he said, "I can reach the branches. Please . . . may I climb?"

She thought it rather remarkable for a small boy to speak so politely when contemplating daring exploits.

"Oh, dear me, no! I would like to try it myself, but I must not give permission for what your father might think dangerous."

"But Nursie lets me at home!"

"Does she, indeed?" said Mr. Aintree, coming up quietly on the soft turf. "On what trees does Nursie permit you to climb?"

"The apple trees in the orchard, Papa. She says boys must be *tough* as well as polite!"

"I could not take respon—" Audrey explained.

But Mr. Aintree did not let her finish, "Of course not. It appears that I must do so, since the courage of a future viscount is at stake. Go ahead, son."

Jamie grinned and hauled himself onto a low branch, with some disarray to his clothes. Then, by grabbing another branch, he was able to stand upon the first, an exploit he then repeated.

Audrey was torn between amusement and anxiety.

When the child had climbed about five feet successfully, which put his head above his father's, Mr. Aintree said calmly, "Very good, but high enough. You must come down now. I will have to commend Nursie for her nerves of iron."

He astonished Audrey by casting a wink at her, which disconcerted her. She was not able to breathe freely until the boy was safely on the ground again.

"Boys are so daring," she murmured.

"What?" said Mr. Aintree. "Did you never try to climb to the sky when you were a child, Mrs. Malton?"

"No apple trees in our garden!" She gasped, and began to giggle, which Jamie did not exactly understand, but he laughed too, and leaned confidently against his father's leg. It was clear that they had a warm relationship.

As they turned back toward the Crescent, Susan, with Wells and Medbury, joined them. She seemed pleased with the small triumph of *two* escorts. Others followed them. Ahead, they could see Mrs. Crowell chatting with Sir John and Lady Sallinger beside waiting carriages. It was time to say good-bye.

"I am glad we came to Bath, Mama," Susan said to her sister when Sir John had stowed his ladies in their vehicle. Jamie and his father were waving as they turned into Brock Street.

Shocked, Audrey heard Lady Sallinger say, "Lord Chalbert has taken a fancy to you, Audrey. I gather that is why we were invited here today. With a bit of effort on your part, I believe you could be a viscountess."

"Marry that old man! I would not do that!" she protested. Susan was looking at her with an odd sort of expression. "I am sure he is very nice and all that, but no old man is going to lure me into being his keeper!"

"Hoity-toity," said Lady Sallinger, though her tone was not critical. "Widows have less chance for exciting marriages. They must consider practicalities."

"Susan will tell you," Audrey replied firmly, "that I am *very* practical. Too much so to consider marriage as an unpaid nurse. The thing I hope for is to see Susan wed to one who will make her happy. She would not wish to be *bought!*"

"Oh, no!" said Susan fervently.

"My dear wife," Sir John interposed, "the girls have not known you long enough to realize you turn everything into a joke. Miss Susan, she only means that she wishes to invent partis who are noble, as well as everything you would like."

"I see," Audrey said. "You mean a noble of any age, who is presentable, civil, and able to afford a poor, self-effacing, not-so-young widow."

To her surprise, Lady Sallinger was laughing. "You are not describing yourself, Audrey!"

Six

For the next ball in the Upper Rooms, Susan wore her only other evening gown, which was white with flounces edged in green embroidery. Any sort of flowers would have done well with it, except for the fact that Misters Talbott, Wells, and Medbury had all sent dainty bouquets. At first Susan was unable to solve the dilemma of which she should wear. Would Audrey like to wear one?

"No, no," said Audrey firmly. "Any of your beaux would be offended to see his gift on anyone but you. Wear Talbott's mixed corsage at the center of your décolletage, but be sure to tell Mr. Wells that you have put his sweet-smelling roses beside your bed, where you can smell them day and night."

"They could not expect me to wear all three," Susan agreed. "What about Mr. Medbury?"

"Well, tell him that you have placed his in water in our sitting room where every visitor will see and admire them."

"And that I hope he will see them there himself?"

"Yes. Perfect!"

"How," asked Susan, "do you know all these things?"

But Audrey only felt such strategies would work; she had no idea how they had jumped into her head.

"Born wise," Susan declared, and Audrey shook her head but began unwrapping the stems of the roses.

There was no choice for Audrey. Her mama's green gown was handsome, yet too severe for a ball. It would have to be the plum silk again, though without a lace cap. She would wear her mama's pearls for the first time; they were too heavy for a debutante, but quite suitable for a widow.

Although David Howerfield had left, available rooms at Bath were filling now, and the crowd at the Upper Rooms might have overwhelmed the young ladies from Rampton, had not Sir John Sallinger proved his worth admirably by opening a path for his three ladies to the ballroom, where they did find seats at one end. Lady Sallinger was not so pleased about this position, for she complained that her protégées might be overlooked. What she feared did not happen, however, since Susan was solicited for several dances, even without David Howerfield to start her off.

Mr. Aintree arrived earlier this evening than the previous time. When he reached Susan, she was about to walk out on the floor for the first set, and hastily promised him a later one. He spoke graciously to Lady Sallinger, then stretched out his hand to Audrey, saying, "Will you honor me, Mrs. Malton?"

She thought it was gentlemanly of him to suggest that it was an "honor" to dance with *her* when it was Susan that he wanted. However, she was happy to be among the dancers in a way she had missed when blossoming into a young lady seven or eight years ago. Probably, she told herself, his interest in Susan was enough to make him want to curry favor with herself.

"I wonder if you will save the first waltz for me," he said as they danced, presuming an "older" lady had long ago been approved by the superior dames of Almack's. "Can I assume that Miss Malton has not yet appeared in London?"

"Susan has lived quietly in Rampton," she replied evasively, letting him also assume that she, herself, would waltz with him, although she wondered anxiously if her knowledge of that daring dance would be sufficient. She had learned it years ago from a friend. Would dear Papa be scandalized to see her now?

When the music ended, Mr. Aintree escorted her to Lady Sallinger's side, where Sir Roland was waiting, apparently expecting to win her for the next dance. It was heady attention for a widow, especially a false widow.

They did not see much of Susan, who was happily handed from one partner to another.

"I declare!" said her Ladyship. "I do not know when I have enjoyed a ball so much—my young ladies being so sought after by the beaux. John, *John,* do you see what a belle Susan has become? And here is Lord Robert Combe, too. Good evening, Lord Combe. Have you come for Mrs. Malton?"

Lord Combe said heavily that was his plan. "Mrs. Malton?"

Blushing like a young girl, Audrey went onto the floor a third time with this middle-aged gentleman. Her dancing was not very experienced, and his was not adept, yet they were able to hold up their part of an energetic set.

Later, when a waltz sounded, Mr. Aintree was on the spot to guide Mrs. Malton around the room. "I think," he said, "you can cease to be concerned about your daughter."

"Oh, yes," agreed Audrey. *"Your* attention to her has been an encouragement to other young men, and I thank you. I could not bear for her to be disappointed at her first venture into Society."

"A true, motherly sentiment," he observed, steering her gently in a circle of the dance floor.

Sometimes she could see Susan, and sometimes she could not. "I suppose you think me overanxious, but Susan is such a dear girl that I cannot bear her to be disappointed . . . or misled."

"Would it help," he asked looking down at her seriously, "if I keep an eye on her and hint away any unsuitable young men?"

As this confirmed his interest in her sister, Audrey said, "Oh, thank you! I am not the most knowledgeable guide."

Mr. Aintree smiled his small smile, and she diverted her eyes to the white of his waistcoat.

"Lady Sallinger has been kind and helpful," she ventured.

"Yes," said Mr. Aintree, "you can rely upon her advice."

Audrey wondered what he would think of her Ladyship's proposing a match for her with his papa. That might alter Aintree's opinion of the lady!

They advanced halfway around the room. Waltzing was not difficult, at least not with Mr. Aintree guiding her deftly, one hand holding hers and the other at her waist.

"What do you think of my son?" he asked.

This was safe ground.

"Adorable," she said, "though he might not like to hear me say that."

"He is not quite five yet. 'Adorable' is what Nursie is sometimes heard to say. Also, 'naughty' and not infrequently 'dirty face.' She is dealing well with him . . . though of course it is not the same as a mother or a grandmother."

Audrey's step faltered. *Oh, dear, was he implying she would be welcome as a wife for his father?* She could say nothing.

He glanced down, but she was scrutinizing his waistcoat again, so he had no clue to her feelings. Was it strange for a matron— even a young matron—to be so uncertain of conversation at a mere Bath ball? Her daughter, though infallibly ladylike, seemed more at ease with teasing beaux.

"Father and I hope to make some plans," Mr. Aintree said. "When he asked me to fetch Jamie, I wondered how we should entertain a small boy during the Bath season, but Father thought he would enjoy the simpler things—like picnics in the countryside or boating on the Avon. Do you think Miss Susan would care about such things?"

"I am sure she would," Audrey said. "Bath is a far cry from Rampton. She will not want to miss any new experience."

Mr. Aintree said, "Good. Then I will see if I can hire a boat or two. There are no waterways large enough to carry boats where we have our home—oh, yes, shallow-draft ones that are propelled with a pole, but nothing with oars or sails. Jamie will think the Avon as mighty as an ocean."

"I almost do myself," she admitted.

"But you have seen the Thames."

Which she had, though not as a debutante in London. She was silenced. They ended the waltz at the far end of the room from Lady Sallinger, so they had to make their way slowly through the throng upon the dance floor in order to reach her.

"I will let you know when I have located a boatman," Mr. Aintree said, a guiding hand on her elbow.

Audrey answered that Susan would be pleased.

She did not see Mr. Aintree again that evening. Evidently he had gone home, having done his duty by dancing with Susan's mama.

Mr. Aintree, satisfied by the welcome of his idea for a boat ride, was in town the next morning, inquiring for boats, and as he found two clean ones, propelled by an honest-seeming fellow and his gawky son, he went at once to pay a morning call upon Lady Sallinger and lay his plan before her.

"La, Mr. Aintree," she said, "you will never get me into a rowboat! But I daresay the young people will take to the idea like old salts. Two boats, did you say?"

"Yes. Do you think Sir John would like to go?"

"He does not talk much, but he is usually game for anything."

Charles Aintree smiled. "That makes a boatload—the Malton ladies, Sir John, and myself. We can tuck Jamie between two of us. I will invite Medbury and Wells and Talbott. There is room for one more in the second boat. We need another lady. Miss Crowell, I suppose, if you won't come."

"Well, thank you, but I will not," Lady Sallinger said. "Mrs. Crowell may not permit her daughter to go; though, now that I think about it, she will not want the girl to miss anything."

"Then all that remains to be settled is where we will meet the boats. I will let Sir John know."

He descended to the ground floor and knocked at the Maltons' parlor, but they were not at home. It would have been nice to see the pleasure with which they greeted his arrangements. Mrs. Malton, looking anxious, as she often did, would acquiesce to the boat ride, because of the enthusiasm with which Susan would greet the plan. Susan was young and enjoying a new sort of existence, but Mrs. Malton would be wondering if his plan was reasonable, respectable, and promised enjoyment. He thought it was natural for such a young matron to be serious about her daughter's safety and happiness, and he promised himself to make them see the simple pleasure of a ride upon the Avon. Jamie, who would love it, might have to be restrained from falling overboard or rejoicing in being splashed by backswing from the oars.

It was only fourteen months since his wife had died. He had

almost forgotten what simple things can alarm women—although he did not imagine that Mrs. Malton would spoil the small cruise by tittering nervously about tipping over. If Mrs. Malton worried about shipwrecks, she would see how tame the Avon could be on a balmy day of summer.

He tapped at the Maltons' door and told Polly that the excursion was set for the next morning and he would call for her ladies at half after ten.

Polly, who saw Mr. Aintree as positively godlike, curtsied and nodded vigorously to assure him that she would faithfully convey his plans for the next day.

As he had supposed, Susan was overjoyed by an excursion so novel. Audrey realized she could not say no without being a perfect ogre; besides, if Jamie was to be present, it must be safe.

Accordingly, Mr. Aintree and Jamie called at Trim Street to pick up Susan, Audrey, and Sir John. Others of the party, coming in two curricles, met them where they were to board the boats just above North Parade, from which point they had a hurried and interesting view of Pulteney Bridge. From there, with a gentle current that required little work on the part of the boatmen, they would circle the lower end of Bath and disembark where the river turned slightly northwest, ultimately to reach Bristol and the wide mouth of the Severn River. Most of the work of the boatmen was to steer them around other watercraft and maintain an even keel to keep the ladies from being alarmed.

Mr. Aintree, traveling backward, had little chance to see scenery or admire the pulchritude of the Malton ladies, for he was obliged to keep secure hold of Jamie, who had colossal curiosity and no fear at all. Enchanted by the child's enthusiasm, Susan and Audrey begged to take Jamie between them.

"Certainly not!" Aintree said, "I could not rescue the three of you if you toppled overboard."

Secretly, Audrey agreed with him, for she knew two females who did not swim could not be trusted to rescue anybody.

After a leisurely journey they landed safely at the bottom of Southgate Street, where carriages met them. No one had been soaked, no one lost overboard. Thanks were exuberant.

But in the hubbub of parting, while Mr. Talbott was flicking his reins to drive off with Miss Crowell, Audrey discovered her sister was being assisted into Mr. Wells' curricle, leaving Mr. Medbury to Aintree's carriage.

"Oh!" exclaimed Audrey, "but—"

"It is all right," Charles Aintree said calmly. "He will enjoy driving her home, and we will be right behind them."

Sir John, who was anticipating his nuncheon and a nap, seemed to think nothing was untoward. She smiled uncertainly at him and Mr. Medbury, as Aintree drew his son between Audrey and himself, and signaled his father's coachman to proceed.

If Audrey knew little about conventions of Society, Susan knew less. She hoped her young sister would not disgrace them.

Needless worry! Susan was too well brought up, and too genuinely a lady to disgrace the late rector of Saint Leonard's at Rampton. She thanked Mr. Wells prettily, and allowed his tiger to help her down at Trim Street, so as not to keep Mr. Wells' horses waiting.

Aintree's carriage pulled up just behind them, and he sprang down to escort Audrey to her door.

"It was everything delightful," she said. "Good-bye, Master Jamie . . . He is a precious child, Mr. Aintree. One's children make life worth living, do they not?"

"Yes," he replied soberly. "Children and other things."

It was useless to berate Susan for driving off with Mr. Wells. However, when Mr. Wells began to haunt Trim Street and capture Susan's attention here and there, Audrey wondered if she should be anxious about *him* as she had been about David Howerfield. The young men whom they had met were well bred and accepted everywhere in Bath, but she doubted any were old enough, financially sound enough, and mature enough for matrimony. Of course Susan was very young herself—perhaps not ready for anything as serious as married life—unless it were with someone as sound as Mr. Aintree. Would Susan deal easily with housekeeping and children? Yes, certainly in time. But now? Audrey had begun to have doubts.

She had brought her sister to Bath in hopes of settling her in a suitable union. Was she rushing things? This was not something about which she could consult Mr. Aintree, for he was obviously the best candidate, so far. Yet, Mr. Aintree seemed to sense her problem, for he had promised to keep an eye upon her sister, had he not?

Would her own folly ruin everything?

Lady Sallinger, for one, seemed to notice nothing out of the ordinary about the swarm of bees about Malton honey. She did not interfere, except periodically to point out the attributes of this gentleman or that. After insisting Audrey do away with the pretty but offending lace cap, she seemed to find everything pleasing about the sisters, to whom she continued to lend her support and encouragement. In serious moments, the Malton girls agreed they were as fortunate as orphans could be, although the future was unknown and worrisome.

A fortnight later, David Howerfield appeared in Bath, sent by his uncle, he said, to see if the Malton ladies had settled comfortably. Evidently David had not dropped any remarks in Salisbury that one of them was apparently a widow, and was wise enough to give no inkling to his uncle of an attachment to the other, for Mr. Howerfield would never encourage his nephew in a union with any damsel as impecunious as a rector's daughter.

David was obviously a favorite with Susan, ready to help with a slipping shawl or to fetch a cup of tea. Audrey, watching closely, could not see that her sister made a difference between him and Mr. Wells, and Mr. Medbury and the others. Susan was gracious to all . . . but all were not as handsome and charming as David Howerfield, who might disappear in a day or two, as suddenly as he had come. As a matter of fact, in three days he was gone.

Mr. Aintree had told Audrey not to worry about Susan's beaux. *He* was certainly calm, content to watch them skirmish for Susan's notice. Very likely Charles Aintree had survived similar warfare when he captured his wife; he was not competing now, as near as Audrey could see. Nevertheless, his presence kept the young men on their toes.

They did not see Mr. Aintree every day, Obviously, he was busy attending to both father and son. Often, when they did see him, he had Jamie in tow, as Nursie had been left behind at Lord Chalbert's manor. Not many gentleman of their acquaintance burdened themselves with small children, so this spoke in Aintree's favor to the Malton girls, though they did not talk about it. Audrey felt sure that Susan must admire Charles Aintree's attitude.

A small squall, passing through, dampened activities for a day or two. Then Mr. Aintree and his son paid a morning call on Lady Sallinger to propose, if she approved, a visit to the Sydney Gardens.

The number of Miss Susan's admirers had grown. One ran into them at the Pump Room, Milsom Street, and the dwelling on Trim. Aintree felt it would be best to consult her Ladyship in the privacy of her own suite.

"Aintree! Dear fellow!" she welcomed him, bestowing a sweetmeat on Jamie, who was with him, before giving Charles her full attention. "What is on your mind?"

"Another outing, my lady. I have a suggestion."

"Well, your suggestions have been fine so far. What is this one? Do you need Sir John's opinion?"

"It will be the same as yours, I daresay," he said with a naughty grin. "I have been thinking of Jamie, you see."

"Oh, Jamie. Of course. Must we all be lively?"

"And run?" inserted Jamie.

"Perhaps. Small boys always run, if ladies do not. I was thinking of a visit to Sydney Gardens—a larger group than our boating experience. The Gardens should be beautiful this time of year, with ample sunshine and shade to suit varied tastes. Perhaps even races, Jamie. And I believe Father keeps a set of balls for lawn bowling, though they have not been out of the closet for ages, and what their condition may be, I do not know."

"You will not expect me to play games, will you?" Lady Sallinger demanded.

"No, indeed. What I want from you, dear lady, is advice about the guest list and the food to be brought in hampers."

"Lemonade," she said decisively. "No wine in the heat of the sun, please!"

"You are right," he agreed. "After all, it is a youthful group."

They consulted on a guest list, and Jamie was rewarded for good behavior with another sweetmeat of crystallized fruit. Then they chose a day.

"Father's coachman considers himself a notable weather prophet. He says it will be sunny all this week."

They settled upon Friday, and Jamie was promised a labyrinth, whatever that might be.

Seven

The return of David Howerfield yet another time surprised everyone, for he was supposed to be in the employ of his uncle, the banker of Salisbury. Perhaps, it was only out of family feeling that he obliged his uncle in useful ways. The Malton ladies could not think he had come to check on their progress, as he was known to be three days in Bath before he called upon them. Even then, they did not meet for another day because of having driven with Sir John and Lady Sallinger to visit cousins of her Ladyship in Bristol.

Upon their return, Audrey and Susan found his card and lamented missing him, though Lady Sallinger said, "Depend upon it. You will see that young fellow before twenty-four hours have passed."

And, sure enough, he was at the Pump Room when they went there the next morning.

"My uncle wants me to be of use to you," he said after greeting them. "What can I do? Are you having edible meals? Are your rooms comfortable? Are the beaux of Bath wearing a path to your door?"

That last was not an easy question to answer, so Audrey ignored it and said that Mr. Howerfield had arranged for them perfectly. Lady Sallinger was watching from across the room, so she added, "Sir John and his wife have been the best of acquaintances—well, more than that, splendid mentors. You must tell your uncle what dear friends and advisors they are." *That* should mislead the elder Mr. Howerfield nicely!

Young Howerfield bowed in her Ladyship's direction and received a pleasant nod in return.

Glowing with pleasure, Susan said, "She will want to talk with you." She led the way across to her Ladyship with David and several beaux trailing behind.

From a window, where he stood with friends, Mr. Aintree sent Audrey a slight nod to indicate she need not worry as long as Susan was surrounded by half a dozen beaux. It was as if he said, "Safety in numbers." There was no sign of jealousy on his part.

Audrey was truly puzzled. Charles Aintree paid Susan every courtesy, danced with her, even had once taken her driving in a curricle, yet she saw no sign of jealousy in his manner when other gentlemen were claiming Susan's attention.

But he was watching now, and presently drifted across to Audrey to say, "You must stop worrying. With so many admirers, Miss Susan is perfectly safe. Though all are gentlemen, they are too young to be seriously attached."

"Then my hopes in bringing her here will be for nothing," Audrey murmured. "I do so want her settled in life."

"Yes," he returned, "but she is very young. In two or three years most of these chaps will be turning to matrimony."

"So long? Oh, dear. Well, better she remain single than wed the wrong sort. The only thing is, we cannot stay . . ." Chagrined, she wondered if she had revealed too much. If Mr. Aintree was seriously interested in Susan, he would have to be told the truth of their circumstances.

"Perhaps you will take her to London in the spring," the gentleman suggested.

If he thought that, he could have no understanding of their precarious situation. Here in Bath, with the sponsorship of kind Lady Sallinger, who might be enraged if she discovered the deception played on her, they were accepted socially. Exposure was hanging over Audrey's head like the sword of Damocles, which made it difficult to do more than smile weakly and ask where Jamie was this morning.

"Watching his grandfather in the bath," Mr. Aintree said with a smile. "He is under military orders to get no closer than three feet to the rim of the pool."

"Oh," she exclaimed, "but will he obey when you are out of sight?"

"Yes, because Father's valet is close beside him today. Todd has very heavy, black brows and can look sterner than Father or I."

This made Audrey gurgle with delight, and Charles Aintree went on to explain that there was also the promise of a visit to Sydney Gardens and a picnic luncheon.

"Jamie will like that," she said.

"Will you?"

"Oh, are adults included?" Audrey asked.

"Included and wanted," he assured her.

"What of Lady Sallinger?"

"She has helped me to plan the event. Shall you mind if I do not call for you and Miss Susan? It has been a long time since I organized a social event of any size." From this, she understood that more guests would be invited than the sixteen who had lunched at the Royal Crescent recently.

"Sir John's carriage will transport you and Miss Susan," he added. "Perhaps the two of you will explore the labyrinth with Jamie and me."

Audrey clapped her hands. "Oh, is there a minotaur?"

"You know there is not! But something will be there to surprise Jamie."

"Perfect!" she declared, and he could see, from the sparkle of her eyes, that she meant it.

But she forgot to look like a proper widowed mama.

It was fortunate that Lady Sallinger beckoned her then; she went across the room to be presented to a new dowager, just arrived in Bath.

"Your Grace," said her ladyship, positively cooing, "this is Mrs. Malton, mother of the young lady you admired in the midst of all the beaux."

This was somewhat of an exaggeration, as Susan was surrounded by only four, three Audrey knew, and one stranger.

Her Grace said "Ah?" and raised a quizzing glass, though Audrey had a good idea that the lady could see perfectly well without it. "Too young," she announced.

"No lady can ever be too young," Lady Sallinger said firmly. "Audrey, my dear, this is Her Grace, Catherine Du Cros, Duchess of Wembly."

Before she had finished speaking, Audrey was already making a graceful curtsy.

"Who or what or where is Malton?" demanded the duchess.

"Mrs. Malton," said Lady Sallinger superbly, "is my dear friend."

The duchess said grudgingly, "Curtsies nicely enough, but would not do for Albert."

Amused, but wisely hiding it, Audrey stole a glance at the young man in question, a duke or heir to one. She saw at once that he was dazzled by Susan's radiant face, and she thought how sad that he should be so undistinguished . . . but perhaps a dukedom could offset thin, sandy red hair and a weak chin. Standing by Susan, who was small, he was half a head taller, which was enough to lend him some distinction; beside his ample mother he would look negligible.

"Bring Susan to meet Her Grace," Lady Sallinger commanded.

Audrey at once made a slight bow and went across the room to summon her sister. Lady Sallinger presented His Grace, the duke of Wembly, which told Audrey that the young man had indeed come into his title. From his mother's attitude she realized that daughters of a country rector would never do for this gentleman, but he looked slightly ill at ease and unhappy, so she forgave his having the mother that he did and gave him a kind smile before leading Susan away.

The duchess's sense of decorum obliged her to greet another nobody tolerably well, Fortunately Sir John came along to lend his welcome to his wife's friend, so the Malton sisters were able to withdraw without attracting criticism from the ogress.

"Poor young fellow," whispered Susan to Audrey. "He needs befriending."

"Ah, well," returned her sister, "his title will provide a place for him in Bath society." She was not surprised, some time later, when the duke was again graciously received into a group about Susan. Audrey was pleased to notice that Susan was neither awed by so noble a young man, nor unduly attentive to him.

Whatever there was about Susan's manner, she was not intimidated by Wembly. He could not know that all persons were received equally well by the late rector and his family. That he was attracted to this particular young lady soon became evident, and Audrey hoped Her Grace would not notice.

It was no surprise when Mr. Aintree was seen talking with Duke Albert, for apparently Charles Aintree was acquainted with everyone. Audrey imagined that the duke would be included in the picnic at Sydney Gardens. Would Her Grace come too, to spoil her son's ease? Poor fellow! He must long for friends and independence.

There was one advantage, Audrey thought, in being a widow: her every word, smile, and gown were not scrutinized and subjected to criticism. She noticed that Susan's manner to the young duke was a wee bit gentler than her teasing ways with the other gentlemen. Could this mean anything special? She decided it did not, for Susan was sensitive to the unspoken needs of everyone. That she, herself, had set Susan an example in this did not occur to her. At Rampton or Bath or St. James's Palace, Maltons would always be responsive to the feelings of others . . . but she could not think jolly David Howerfield would do as a husband for her sister. In fact, each young man they had met was pleasing in some ways, though not what she wanted for Susan.

Presently, she saw Mr. Medbury lead Susan to a table with another couple to take tea. She thought the young duke's eyes followed them, even though he did not.

There was no doubt that Susan was enjoying her popularity, yet at home—on Trim Street—or in company, as now, there was no sign that popularity was going to her head. She simply radiated happiness, which only added to her charm. If only there were a suitable match for her . . . Mr. Aintree had implied that

Audrey was expecting too much too soon for a girl too young. Was Mr. Aintree interested enough to wait for Susan to mature?

Anyone watching now would think Susan was enchanted by Mr. Medbury, yet moments ago she had been smiling on Mr. Talbott. Oh, dear, it would be a disaster if Susan was believed to be a flirt! How could one steer her safely through the shoals of Society?

"Is Susan too *forthcoming?*" Audrey whispered to Lady Sallinger.

"No, no," returned the lady promptly. "She is charming. A perfect credit to you. If you fancy a duke for her, you might get him."

Audrey gasped. "I would not dare to think such a thing!"

"Well, Wembly cannot take his eyes off her."

"Neither can Cerberus," Audrey pointed out with a nod in the direction of the duchess.

Lady Sallinger laughed heartily and said she must guard her tongue, for gentlemen liked to reserve wit to themselves and a display of it might hinder her own chances.

Audrey looked shocked and opened her mouth to protest, but Lady Sallinger tapped her with her fan and turned away.

It had not been long since Audrey had formed the plan to display her sister at Bath, and already its success was greater than she had hoped, for at least four likable men were fawning over Susan, not to the point of quarreling with each other, but noticeably dancing after her attentively; and now here was a young duke added to the group! It was very exciting.

Yet Charles Aintree had doused her hopes with warnings about them all being too young. Surely he did not consider himself *that*. Was he not a suitor of Susan after all? If not, how disappointing that would be, for he was the best of the lot . . . though a little older than might appeal to Susan, until she was thinking of more than social enjoyment.

Audrey concluded that she must not trouble Trouble. The summer stretched before them. Surely someone suitable would come to Bath and fall in love with her flirtatious sister.

Susan gave no sign of preferring one particular beau; she

treated all the same. Even the shy duke received no special attention, though he danced with her when allowed to do so, and otherwise watched her from the sidelines. Mr. Aintree was awarded smiles, but no more nor less than anyone else.

"You are wise to make no favorites," Audrey told her sister.

"But I like them all!" Susan declared.

In some surprise, Audrey realized that she, herself, had acquired a small court—older men, of course, yet noticeably faithful, if not exciting. Though the Malton sisters failed in making convenient connections, she and Susan were happy to spread their wings. She could look back on Rampton as times of quiet contentment; this life—here—now—was a little period of interest and stimulation. Would her papa think them wickedly frivolous? No. He was no killjoy. He would say that as long as they held to Principles, it was all right to be happy.

Afternoons, if not devoted to excursions, became times when tea was served in the Maltons' small, ground-floor parlor on Trim Street. Young gentlemen found their way there, sometimes one or another escorting a young lady, who was made just as welcome as the beaux. From time to time friends of Lady Sallinger brought daughters. If chairs were insufficient, no one seemed to mind; ladies got available seats, and gentlemen stood about in casual poses to exhibit their fine legs and broad shoulders.

The duchess of Wembly never came, having no interest in anything less than the Royal Crescent and the first pew in the abbey. Her son, however, found his way to the parlor of the Malton ladies, and received as warm a welcome as anyone else. He did not talk much, though the expression on his plain face was intelligent.

He is shy! Audrey thought, surprised that even a duke could feel his own shortcomings. She was kind to him, and pleased to notice that her sister tossed pleasantries to him as often as to others. It was the rector's training and influence on his daughters that made them consider the feelings of everyone.

When the day of Mr. Aintree's garden party came with cloudless skies, the Sallingers' carriage took Sir John, his wife, and the Malton girls across Pulteney Bridge, around two sides of

Laura Place and into Great Pulteney Road, which led them to the gardens. There they found Viscount Chalbert's servants had set blankets on the ground, along with a few chairs, and tables with humping cloths that concealed what must be platters of food.

Some blankets were in shaded areas, some in pleasant sunshine. Lady Sallinger chose a chair near the Duchess of Wembly and seemed not unwilling to exchange verbal arrows with her; she enjoyed a good squabble.

Charles Aintree had greeted them with Jamie by his side, the child displaying perfect manners in speaking politely to each newcomer, as taught by the absent Nursie.

When it seemed that all thirty-odd guests had come, Susan found that her particular beaux were there and eager to surround her, vying for attention, and carrying her from sun to shade and back to sun again, as they disputed where she would be most comfortable. Audrey noticed that her sister was laughing, willing to walk this way and that in such good-spirited company, and not affecting the blasé manner of some rich and spoiled beauties.

There was contemplation of this tree or that, and no matter how much farmers might feel the need of rain, no one would admit to such a thing.

Whether the Duke of Wembly was being cautious in the presence of his mother, Audrey did not know. He did not hang upon Susan's sleeve, though he did manage to exchange a few words with her supposed mother, saying how much he admired Miss Malton "as all the gentlemen seem to do." Audrey, liking his modest manner, replied that her daughter had a singularly good disposition, which she could not claim, as it came from Susan's father, the rector. Since neither Audrey nor the duke wished to attract the attention of the duchess, they soon separated.

When luncheon was announced, Audrey was seated with a flourish by Lord Combe in a chair he had commandeered, while Sir Roland fetched a plate for her with more heaped upon it than she could possibly eat. Neither gentleman sat upon the ground, Sir Roland dreading dirt on his new fawn-colored breeches and

Lord Combe fearing his corset would not permit him to bend sufficiently to get up again.

While the meal was still in progress, though nearing its end, Mr. Aintree and little Jamie came to fetch Audrey for their special visit to the maze. They collected Susan, whose escorts protested but must yield to their host, and walked some distance off to a labyrinth of clipped ilex aquifolium.

Jamie was allowed to choose their route, which meant they reached numerous dead ends or came back to where they had started. The girls wondered at Aintree's serene manner, especially when Jamie's choices brought them to where they had been. His papa merely whispered that they need not worry; he knew the key to the route. Eventually, they were deep in the maze, and sounds of the picnic only faintly reached them.

"We will never get out!" Susan declared, though not worried.

"Then perhaps we will get to see the minotaur," Audrey said. Susan shuddered delightfully, and Jamie demanded to know what a minotaur was.

Mr. Aintree said solemnly that it was a large creature that ate bad boys.

"But I am good, Papa!" his son declared, having been told that often enough to believe that he was very good.

His father laughed and promised to protect him and the ladies—for he was sure the ladies were very, very good.

Susan and Audrey, feeling extremely guilty, said nothing, when their host suggested, "Let us try *this* aisle."

He had led them to the small center clearing where waited *a wonderful wooden sailboat* with a royal ensign atop its mast. Forgetting all about man-eating monsters, Jamie was awed; then he was clapping the boat to his chest.

"See," said his father, bending over. "Here is a cord that we can fasten to the bow, so as to set your boat sailing on—"

"The river, Papa? The river?"

"Well, a good captain must consider shoals and dangerous currents. A pond would be best. Or the brook at home."

The Malton ladies watched benignly, not minding that they were forgotten.

Eight

As Audrey thought back over that pleasant afternoon, carefully considering the young men who vied for Susan's smiles, she could not settle on one who would suit her ideas of a husband for her sister. They were likable enough, but—as Charles Aintree had warned—none actually looking for a wife. There were too many mills and balls and hunts to be enjoyed. It was the style to dangle after the latest belle; besides, the excitement of competition added spice. As for matrimony? Not yet. Someday . . . after races and house parties ceased to hold their interest.

The older men—like her supporters, Lord Robert and Sir Roland—were past the age of wanting to chase after girls as young as Susan. Finding a suitable husband for her sister was not going to be as easy as she had imagined. Not that Susan wasn't a daughter of whom to be proud. The fault was her own, for thinking a marriage could be achieved in so few weeks.

She suspected that David Howerfield, who was neither too young nor too old, did appeal to Susan most of all, yet she could not be easy about a match *there,* and she imagined his uncle would like it even less.

There was Charles Aintree, though neither he nor Susan gave any indication of being romantically attracted. That would be a wonderful match . . . if they had *cared*.

And there was the young duke, Albert, whom she suspected to have a serious regard for Susan. Her sister did not lead him a merry dance, as she did the others, which made her wonder if Susan sensed his basic goodness. But to have the duchess for a mother-in-law would be horrid. In fact, it would be impossible, for his mama would never allow it, and the duchess would not care how many hearts she broke.

Albert now outranked his mother and might surprise everyone by defying her, but then she, in the pose of Susan's mother, would have to put her foot down, rather than let her sister live unwelcomed by Albert's family and in a perpetual state of war.

The day following the picnic in Sydney Gardens, Mr. Aintree arrived in a curricle to invite Susan for a drive, which was a lesson of sorts to the young beaux, for none appeared until after luncheon when she had already gone. They were shocked. Two left notes, asking Susan's company the next day. Another was turned away deflated. The youthful duke was one who left a note.

In a way, Audrey was amused. She wondered if Charles Aintree was becoming more interested in Susan, or if he was bent on teaching the young chaps a lesson.

When Susan and Aintree returned, he left his curricle in the care of his groom, then accompanied her inside to tell Audrey he had located a gentle brook where Jamie could sail his vessel.

"He particularly asks if Mrs. Malton can come sailing too," Aintree said with an impish smile.

"Oh, yes," laughed Audrey, "I cannot develop *mal de mer* on a brook, can I?"

His eyes were twinkling, but he said solemnly, "I do not think there will be waves. We must hope there is enough breeze to make the ship's flag ripple. Will you join us, Miss Malton?"

"It sounds delightful," Susan said, "but I have here a note from Albert who expects to find me home tomorrow."

"Albert?" echoed Audrey.

"I mean," stammered Susan, "His Grace of Wembly. He—he had said yesterday in the Gardens that he would call, and I am afraid I . . . forgot."

"You must not disappoint him again," Mr. Aintree said quickly. "We may get wet and muddy. You would not like that. Mrs. Malton, are you still willing to go?"

Audrey laughed. "Yes, indeed. I shall wear boots old enough to disgrace you."

"They will not bother me," he said.

"Oh," objected Susan, "you make it sound so merry!"

Mr. Aintree advised her to ask the duke to escort her to the shops on Pulteney Bridge. "If you have not visited them, you will find them more interesting than a brook."

"Should she take our maid?" Audrey asked.

Mr. Aintree replied, "Oh, no. Not in the busiest streets of Bath. You will see other couples, and very likely some of your mama's friends, Miss Malton. Ask Lady Sallinger, if you doubt my advice."

Susan and Audrey both murmured something indistinguishable.

"Strolling Bath is all the crack," he added, which reassured them.

Nothing more was said of propriety until dinner that night, when Audrey mentioned that Susan had agreed to walk about the town with the Duke of Wembly. "That is perfectly permissible, is it not, Lady Sallinger?" she asked.

"Why, of course," her Ladyship answered promptly. "Even in London, ladies walk about Hyde Park and respectable streets with gentlemen. You can take Polly, Susan, but I do not think it necessary. No one will tell Her Grace. She is not popular, and public sentiment supports that nice young man."

"Mama is going sailing with Mr. Aintree," Susan said quickly to deflect the conversation from herself.

Lady Sallinger exclaimed, "Sailing!"

"On a brook," laughed Audrey. "With a toy boat, you know."

"Oh, I see," said her Ladyship. "The treasure from the labyrinth. Well, my advice is to wear something old, for you will be sure to get a soaking."

Sir John said he remembered a toy boat of his childhood and wished he could go along.

Audrey exclaimed, "Do!"

But his wife forbade the idea. "I do not want you to come home drenched and taking to your bed with coughs and sneezes, not when there are several fine invitations on the calendar."

The girls sent each other questioning looks. They did not want to miss any important social events. But then Lady Sallinger reassured them that The Young Never Catch Things. Unless Susan pitched out a window of Pulteney Bridge or Mrs. Malton tumbled headfirst into the brook, neither would suffer any danger of losing their dancing feet.

At eleven the next morning, His Grace and Mr. Aintree met on the doorstep of Mrs. Dawes' House in Trim Street. They looked at each other somewhat askance, but soon discovered they had separate appointments, and went inside amicably. Susan was looking edible in a pink muslin frock and pink bonnet tied saucily at her left ear. Audrey was less presentable in shabby boots and the protection of Polly's old brown hooded cloak. They were perfectly arrayed for their diverse appointments.

"Come along," said Mr. Aintree, who was also sensibly garbed. "Jamie is bouncing with impatience."

Outside the house, the duke and Susan, after speaking kindly to small Jamie, turned left along the pavement, while Mr. Aintree and Audrey entered Aintree's curricle, squeezing Jamie between them; the groom sprang up behind and they set off westward out of town, the sailboat resting beneath Jamie's feet.

"What have you named your ship?" Audrey asked the child.

"The Dandy Lion," Jamie answered promptly. "Papa said he should be a she but that did not seem right for a royal frigate, and you will see there is a yellow beast on the flag."

"Oh," said Mrs. Malton superbly, "of *course* a beast must be male!"

There was a muffled sound from the groom behind them, though the three in the seat politely ignored it.

After a pause, Mr. Aintree said, "The brook I found has a small weir near our road. If you don't mind, Mrs. Malton, we will walk up the vale of the stream to where the water is more shallow and a nice pebble beach will make a good launching place."

The area of pebbles proved to be only about two feet wide and maybe six long, but it was a perfect place for the child to stoop down to ease his boat into the water. When Mr. Aintree had attached the cord, he called, "Launch!" and Jamie slid his boat into the water.

For a moment, it still touched bottom, then, as a gentle current caught it, it began to bob about and the little ensign wavered realistically.

"Be sure to hold the rope," Aintree said, showing his son how to play out the cord, so that the boat moved out along the brook. "See. By pulling or easing the rope, you can make your ship change course."

Enchanted, the boy began to experiment, and his papa sat down beside Audrey on the gravel. The gentle wending of the stream and overhanging bushes separated them from Mr. Aintree's groom who was waiting with the curricle lower down, near the weir.

"Wish I had known about this spot when I was a boy," the gentleman said. "We do have a brook at home, but it is swifter and muddier. I was not allowed to splatter in it. In fact, I was forbidden to go near it."

"Did you never slip away and test it?" Audrey asked.

He laughed. "I see you know that even good boys can disobey! More than once I scouted that stream, but it is not as enchanting as this. I never fell in" He smiled at her and asked, "Did you never misbehave?"

"Not really. We had no tantalizing spots such as this." She did not explain who "we" were, realizing only in the nick of time that she might have spoken of a sister. Rather overcome by her own deceitfulness, she fell silent.

It was then that she realized how isolated they were and that their only chaperon was a child. How horrified she would be for Susan to be caught in such a situation . . . though perhaps Mr. Aintree was looking upon her as a sort of nursemaid.

At that moment Jamie squealed. He had dropped the cord and his boat was dancing downstream.

His father sprang up and raced after the boat, plunging boots and all into the water.

At the same time, the boy slipped on the pebbles and tumbled half in and half out of the stream.

Audrey struggled to her feet in time to catch Jamie who had run to her with sobs and a grazed knee.

"Good God!" yelped Mr. Aintree, looking back just in time

to see his child hurl himself upon Audrey. He sloshed back to their camping place and found the boy unhurt except for his knee.

"Boat got away-y-y," sniffled Jamie snuggling into the protection of Audrey's embrace.

"Damn the boat," said his papa, relieved to find no serious damage done. "My groom will catch it at the weir. Let me look at your knee, son."

But Jamie was unwilling to leave the security of Audrey's arms. She plopped down upon the gravel, cuddling him while Mr. Aintree examined the horrid scrape.

By this time, Aintree's groom, hearing howls, had tethered the horses and was pelting up the winding ravine.

"Good God!" he exclaimed, amending it at once to "Lord help us!" when he was reminded of a lady's presence.

"No serious harm done," Aintree said, having assessed the damage. "Flemming, if you will assist Mrs. Malton down to the carriage, I will carry my boy. Look for the boat as you go."

"Yes, sir. I didn't think to watch for the boat as I came. It'll be at the weir, sir."

Sure enough, the boat was bobbing there without enough flow of water to carry it over.

"A poor adventure," said Mr. Aintree, settling them into the curricle. "My apologies, Mrs. Malton."

Catching a mournful expression on the child's face, she replied bracingly, "At least we know the ship is seaworthy. Another time it will not get away from Jamie so easily."

"I daresay," Aintree agreed.

And the groom surprised them by saying, " 'It's one hand for yoursel' and one for the ship,' young master."

"Good God, Flemming! Were you ever a sailor?"

"Not for long, your worship. My stomach couldn't take it," Flemming replied sheepishly.

Back at a smart pace to Trim Street they went. Audrey was handed down by the sailor-groom, with Mr. Aintree apologizing for staying seated to hold Jamie snuggled against his side.

The next day Mrs. Malton had a note from Mr. Aintree, saying

Jamie was quite well, though the viscount had read his son a stiff lesson about the responsibilities of a parent.

The next day after that, Susan Malton received a note from the same gentleman, asking if she would like to view some of the buildings being erected on the bluff above the town.

It began to look, Audrey thought, as though Mr. Aintree had decided to find a mother for his boy. Would Susan be his choice? It was not certain Susan would accept Aintree, for Susan had only the day before shown her sister a wee china angel which His Grace, the Duke of Wembly, had bought for her when they visited a shop on Pulteney Bridge during their walk together.

"I . . . do not know, Susan," Audrey had said when her sister revealed the trinket to her. "I am afraid it looks expensive. Perhaps you should not accept—"

But Susan had insisted it was the merest trifle and buried it in a drawer with her gloves.

Evidently Lady Sallinger did not know about the gift, for she made no mention of it, and Audrey hesitated to raise the subject. She felt a little better this morning when a vase of roses came from young Mr. Howerfield, and Susan set them on display in the sitting room.

In the afternoon Mr. Aintree called for Susan. He was looking particularly splendid in a blue coat that sat upon his body without a wrinkle, and his face was framed by an intricately tied neck cloth. Obviously his valet had been at work upon him. The hints of gray at his temples were becoming, Audrey thought.

When the couple had gone, sunshine had left the room with them. Audrey sat listlessly, wondering what would happen next. She did not feel very brave about revealing to Mr. Aintree the trick they had played on him and, indeed, on all Bath Society. Before being confronted with actual suitors for her sister's hand she had assumed that *their* infatuation would carry her through an awkward explanation. Now she was realizing she would be ashamed to tell Charles Aintree the truth. And—oh dear!—how could she have thought she could keep the young duke's respect when he learned of her frightful duplicity. Kind Mr. Howerfield, who had helped them so much, because of being a friend of the rector—and *trusting* them—would be alienated forever. And his nephew, David, who seemed to have a soft spot for Susan, would wash his hands of them, if he learned of their deceit! What, then, might become of them? Susan would be ostracized along with the sister who had devised their scheme.

And Susan would be returning at any moment! In fact, she was returning *now.*

Seeing no escape from disaster, Audrey was standing when a radiant Susan swept into the room and engulfed her with a hug. Charles, behind her, was beaming. Neither seemed to notice her agitation.

"We had a wonderful drive, the day is glorious, and the view from above Bath is a marvel of splendid buildings and curling river and trees. Charles will take you soon to see it as I have done. If you do not mind, I will fly up and tell Lady Sallinger that I appreciate Bath more than ever."

Like a benevolent cyclone, Susan had gone, closing the door behind her.

Charles Aintree chuckled lightly. "Susan is making it possible for me to see you alone, so that I may make—"

"—a formal offer for her?"

He smiled and said softly, "No. For her mother."

"But she doesn't have a mo—" Audrey interrupted, breaking off as she realized what he meant. She sat down abruptly and twisted a fold of her skirt.

"Susan has a very special sister who has spent years in tending and guiding and mothering her in a perfectly selfless way. That, my dear Audrey, is the wife I want."

She found herself seized and pulled up from the sofa into the circle of his arms. "But I have lived a lie—told a millions lies—"

"Fibs," he corrected fondly.

"Schemed!"

"I'm scheming now," he said, "but you will not hear about it, until I have—"

Until he had kissed her. Several times.

The languorous look in her eyes and the flush of her cheeks were answer enough. Charles then drew her down to sit closely beside him. "Father will be pleased," he said. "He asked me why I was so slow to capture you."

"You mean he doesn't *mind?*"

"Did I not just say 'pleased,' dearest? Jamie will be pleased. He already says he 'wuvs' you. My valet will be pleased that I will stop being a grouch. My groom will be pleased, Nursie will be—"

"But they all—everyone in Bath—will know Susan and I have been living a sham."

"Who is to tell? I have thought it all out. You and Susan will visit Father quietly at the manor. In a month or two we will be privately wed. Then, in the spring we will present Susan at London and see if she does not do even better than she has here."

"Oh," gasped Audrey, "Lady Sallinger! So good to us—and so dreadfully misled."

"But you can depend upon me to thank her wholeheartedly for befriending you. She will love sharing a romantic secret. We will take her into our confidence. Carry her and Sir John off to the manor, too. What do you say?"

But she could not say anything, because he was kissing her again in the sweetest, tenderest, most exciting and compelling way that fluttered her heart.

Then the door opened a crack, and Susan's voice whispered, "Is it settled?"

"Yes, settled," muttered Mr. Aintree, "but you aren't my sister yet. Go away!"

Susan giggled happily, and the door closed.

*The Notorious
Mrs. Carlton*

Martha Kirkland

One

Dear Madam Whore...

The opening of Roger Carlton's letter—one could hardly call it a salutation—echoed inside Anne's head. So constant was the mental repetition of the phrase that it became one with the rhythm of the coach wheels upon the endless road. *Dear Madam Whore... Dear Madam Whore... Dear Madam Whore.*

It was those three words, the last her father would ever write, along with the partially burned letter in the dish on his bed table that had prompted Anne to begin this journey. Though whether it was a journey of discovery or one of revenge, she could not say; no more than she could predict what or who waited at the end of her stagecoach ride.

Roger Carlton had succumbed to a heart attack while writing those words, but what of the author of the letter he had tried to destroy? Was she truly alive? Would the woman her father despised enough to label a whore prove to be Lenore Carlton, Anne's mother?

Anne had been informed that the journey from Dover to the market town of Lamberford—a distance of little more than thirty miles—was an easy three and a half to four hours; unfortunately, nothing could have been farther from the truth. Six hours after setting out, the stagecoach was only just pulling into the inn yard at the White Dove in Lamberford.

"If I arrive in Tunbridge Wells with all my senses," said the nervous, middle-aged lady who sat opposite Anne, clutching a blue vial of sal volatile to her meager bosom, "it will be a miracle.

First there was that heart-stopping three mile stretch when the driver turned over the reins to that young coxcomb who all but ran us off the road; then there was the broken axle. And now poor Mr. Baxter."

Anne nodded politely, though she had not really been listening for the last several miles. The woman had talked nonstop the entire trip, and it was a mystery how she had managed to learn the name of their traveling companion, a dyspeptic little man who had sipped periodically from a bottle of Dr. Culpepper's Elixir.

"I mean to complain to the stagecoach line," the woman continued. "Any one of us might have been injured. A fine thing when a trunk is so poorly secured in the boot of the coach that it falls out and knocks one of the passengers unconscious."

She removed the cap from the blue vial and sniffed twice of the contents before continuing her monologue. "A broken limb. The poor, poor man. One can only hope the innkeeper was truthful about the skill of the doctor in that little village. Tilsham, was it? And other than the pain to Mr. Baxter, what an inconvenience to be forced to delay his journey when he had important business in Lamberford."

Anne had been gathering her possessions in preparation to alight once the coach stopped, but at the mention of the village she paused, suddenly alert. "Was he bound for Lamberford, ma'am?"

"Oh, yes. A place called Herndon Hall. Something to do with his lordship's library, I believe he said."

Anne licked her suddenly dry lips. His lordship? Herndon Hall was her destination, but she had not expected the owner to be of the peerage. The letter writer had simply penned the name *Lenore*. Was this Lord Herndon some relative Anne had never been told about? It was a distinct possibility; especially when one considered the monumental lie her father had told her seventeen years ago, that her mother was dead.

The coachman reined in the four horses, and as they halted, the carriage jerked forward then back, nearly tossing the passengers from their seats.

The woman screamed. "Merciful Heaven! I shall not live to see Tunbridge Wells."

Delighted to be quitting the company of her fellow passenger, Anne was not slow in exiting the coach. Only waiting for the guard to open the door and put down the steps, she took the hand he offered and let him assist her. She hesitated a moment in the busy inn yard before entering the rustic lodging house with its scrubbed pine floor, for suddenly she could no longer ignore the questions that had been niggling at her brain for the last hour or so. How was she to get to Herndon Hall? And once there, what if the owner of the establishment would not let her see the woman named Lenore?

"I will make him do so," she muttered.

"Beg pardon, miss?" said the young ostler who carried her portmanteau.

"I was merely thinking aloud," she replied, not unkindly. "Do you know a place called Herndon Hall?"

"Yes, miss. It be three miles west of here."

Anne looked at the portmanteau, wondering if she could carry it for three miles. As an instructress at a mediocre academy for young ladies, her salary was small, and her savings did not stretch to cover stagecoach fares *and* rented equipages. For that reason, she had hoped the Hall was in easy walking distance.

"You the only passenger?" asked a voice from just inside the door. The unsmiling innkeeper, a tall burly fellow, had obviously just come from the public room, for his once-white apron was spattered with ale, and he held a wiping cloth in one hand. He paused beside a row of pegs on the wall, from which hung a dozen metal door keys. Affording Anne only a cursory glance, he said, "We don't cater to unescorted females."

"Miss be bound for t'Hall," the ostler informed his employer.

Without another word to her, the burly fellow walked over to the door that gave access to the public room and yelled inside to someone named Tibbs. "The person you come for be here."

Since the innkeeper chose to continue past the public room, disappearing somewhere down a flight of rough steps at the back of the corridor, Anne was unable to correct his assumption that she was being met. For his part, the ostler set her portmanteau on the floor just inside the doorway and hurried back to the inn yard to help with the horses. Not knowing what else to do, Anne disposed herself on one of the wooden benches that lined the walls of the common room.

She had waited only a minute or two when a wizened, toothless old man in a workman's smock approached her, a leather cap in his hands and the pungent smell of ale upon his breath. Though his nose was that shade of red peculiar to the habitual tippler, he was not inebriated; still, he stared at her as though not certain if he had made a mistake. "Your pardon, miss. Thought I was to meet a man."

She was about to inform him that she was not expected when he added, "I'd'uv sworn old Pickle Puss said I was to bring back a person called Julian Baxter."

Baxter! That was the name of the passenger who had broken his leg. The last Anne had seen of that little man, he was being carried up to a room at the coaching inn at Tilsham.

"Lest my eyes be afailing me, you ain't Mr. Baxter."

Anne was about to reply that she was not, when it suddenly occurred to her that here was a way to get to Herndon Hall. Ever inventive, she said, "I fear you have been misinformed, my good man. I am *Miss* Baxter. Miss Julianne Baxter. And I believe Lord Herndon is expecting me."

It was Anne's fate that day to be paired with loquacious traveling companions.

While Ben Tibbs rattled on incessantly, working his mouth at a mile-a-minute speed, he kept the placid roan that pulled the dog cart to a pace that told Anne he was in no hurry to return to his duties as undergardener at Herndon Hall. Not that she objected to the pace of the roan. After six hours inside that stuffy, lumbering coach, she found a leisurely ride in the warm August sunshine to her liking.

Furthermore, the sky was a clear blue, and the hedgerows were filled with tendrils of greenish-white bryony and fragrant pink and yellow honeysuckle. Breathing deeply, Anne savored the soft, sweet aroma. Adding to her enjoyment were dozens of centuries-old beech trees growing just behind the hedges. The long thick branches of the trees arched over the road, and their foliage was so thick it rendered the silvery-gray bark barely visible.

Town bred, and unaccustomed to so many trees, Anne was in no hurry to quit such beautiful country. Also, the longer they took to reach their destination, the more time she had to devise a story that would get her inside the house and allow her to remain there until she had an opportunity to meet the person who called herself Lenore Herndon.

The woman in the stagecoach had said Mr. Baxter's purpose in visiting the Hall had something to do with his lordship's library. In all likelihood, Mr. Baxter was a librarian or a book seller. Anne felt confident that she could play either of those parts for a day or so, after all, she was an avid reader and she knew all about books. If not quizzed too closely, she had only to nod and say, "Yes, m'lord, and no, m'lord," and the owner would be none the wiser.

The decision made, she was free to enjoy the remainder of the ride. "Who is old Pickle Puss?" she asked once Tibbs paused for a breath.

The old man spat as if the very thought put a bad taste in his mouth. "Mr. Pilgreen," he said. "Him as be the butler. Old Pickle Puss likes to give me orders like I was a newcomer here. I was here even before his Lordship's father was the baron."

He spat again. "Why, there be things I could tell Pilgreen if I was of a mind to. He came *after* the scandal. The old butler was let go twenty years ago, just after his Lordship's father and Madam said their vows."

Madam? The old man must have drunk more than Anne thought, for he should have referred to his mistress as Lady Herndon or her Ladyship. As for a scandal, surely that had nothing to do with Anne's reasons for coming to Kent.

"It was on account of his insolence to Madam that the old butler was sacked, and—"

He stopped abruptly, as if only just realizing that he was telling something he might regret later. Giving Anne a sidelong glance, he said, "Seems like the ale at the White Dove done loosened my tongue a mite. 'Preciate it, miss, if you was to forget the foolish ramblings of an old man."

Because she did not want to be the source of any trouble for the old fellow, Anne said, "Did you say something? Your pardon, Mr. Tibbs, but I fear I was woolgathering. I did not hear a word."

The old man nodded his approval.

Almost immediately he stopped beside a break in the hedgerow, pulled a rope that opened a wooden gate, then directed the roan through the gate and onto a path barely wide enough to accommodate the cart. Since it was little more than a bridle path, Anne assumed the route they were using was some shortcut. Trusting the old man to know the way to the Hall, she took a few moments to notice the hop fields on either side of her.

Hops were a guaranteed cash crop for the farmers of Kent, but even a town girl knew the vines required a complicated system of poling which, in its turn, demanded a great expenditure of labor. Many hands were needed to tend a hop field, for even after the soil was dug and the vines trained upon the poles, the vines had to be guarded against fungus and bugs to insure the success of the crop.

"Someone has been busy," she said. "The vines look good this year."

"Yes, miss. No finer hops in the land." He smiled, then smacked his lips as if in remembered pleasure. " 'Tis our good hops that put the zest in our ale. Umm, umm, umm," he crooned.

Anne was still laughing at the old man when a horse and rider came around a turn in the lane, galloping toward them at full speed.

"Merciful Jesus!" Tibbs yelled.

Swallowing a scream, Anne stared as at least twelve-hundred pounds of speeding horseflesh bore down upon her. Thinking only one thing—how quickly she could get out of the way—she lifted the hem of her skirts and prepared to jump free of the cart. Fortunately, that measure proved unnecessary, for just in time the rider managed to yank the golden chestnut to the right. That they avoided a disastrous encounter was attributable solely to the man's strength and skill.

As for the animal, it submitted to the rider's authority, but even though the frightened gelding came to a halt, it took instant exception to the dog cart, the placid roan, and their occupancy of the path. Pinning its ears back, the chestnut made as if to rear up on its hind legs.

"Down," the rider ordered, and to Anne's relief, the horse obeyed the command. Though it pawed the ground as if not completely happy with the situation, at least it offered no more resistance.

"There's a good fellow," the gentleman said a bit breathlessly, patting the horse's neck and speaking soothing nonsense into its ear.

While Tibbs gave vent to further blasphemous remarks, Anne gulped several deep breaths, hoping to steady her racing heart. For as long as she could remember, she had been uncomfortable around spirited horses, and having an animal at least sixteen hands high coming at her full speed had revived all her old fears.

"Everyone all right?" asked the rider, a tall, slender gentleman of perhaps thirty.

"Right as a trivet," Tibbs replied none too steadily. "As your Lordship can plainly see, it'ud need more than that chestnut to put old Tibbs in a quake."

"And the lady?" his Lordship asked, keeping the horse at some distance. "From where I sit, she does not appear to be a grizzled old ale guzzler like you, Tibbs. I dare say she may have been frightened."

"I . . . I am fine, sir."

"You are quite sure?"

"Yes, my lord. No harm done." Trying for a light tone, she said, "Like Mr. Tibbs, it would require more than that chestnut to put me in a quake."

The rider made her as elegant a bow as could be accomplished while astride a nervous horse. "Good for you," he said.

Without further comment, he touched his riding crop to the

brim of his hat in salute and turned the horse around, allowing the animal to gallop off in the direction from which they had come.

As Anne watched them disappear around the turn in the path, the pace of her heart slowly returned to normal. To her dismay, both her fright and the dull thud of the gelding's hooves pounding the hard-packed earth had faded long before she was able to rid her mind of the image of the handsome rider. Using as her criteria the half-dozen members of the peerage she had met previously, she had expected Lord Herndon to be at least middle-aged, and gouty into the bargain. Not for a moment had she imagined a vigorous young man.

And never had she expected such blue eyes. Dark blue, they were, like the waters of the channel on a clear day.

A person could get lost in such eyes.

"Since you showed such pluck just now," Tibbs said, bringing her attention back to the present, "and didn't treat us to a fit of the vapors, I'll offer you a mite of advice, miss."

"Please do, for I should deem it a kindness."

The old man nodded his approval of her reply. "His Lordship be a fair master, and any as give him an honest day's work for a day's wages won't never want for food nor shelter. In that, he be just such a one as was his father and his grandfather before him."

Anne had little time to digest this information, for the roan, sensing home, had sped up her pace and was hurrying toward a rather grand stable. Since they had gained access to the estate by a back route, only now was Anne given a glimpse of the gravel carriageway that ended at the red brick building.

The little roan's metal shoes clanked upon the cobbled floor as she trotted through the arched entrance doors, and Anne was hard-pressed not to stare in wonder at the opulence of the stable. Grander than many a house she had visited, it boasted broad oak transverse arches at the front and rear of the building, with lesser arches at the back of each of the stalls—niches from which the horses ate their hay in unparalleled style.

Busy counting the neat stalls, Anne was surprised into a gasp when Lord Herndon stepped out of number ten at the far end of the building. "Be wary," he advised a young groom regarding the chestnut. "I did not give him sufficient exercise, so he is still rather fresh."

"Yes, m'lord," replied the lad.

Leaving the gelding in the groom's care, Lord Herndon walked decisively toward Anne. He moved with the confident grace of the athlete, and while she observed his progress, the suspicion that he had returned to the stables early for the purpose of meeting her caused little flutters within the confines of her ribs.

He stopped at the dog cart and made her a bow. "I wanted to assure myself that you were unharmed, ma'am."

She held her hand out in front of her to demonstrate its steadiness and her lack of nerves. "I thank you for your concern, my lord, but as you can see, there is not the first tremor."

His smile was just the tiniest bit crooked and more than a little sardonic. "What I see, ma'am, is that you are a lady with a commendable degree of pluck." He offered his hand to help her alight. "Are you expected at the house? If so, allow me to escort you there."

"Miss b'ain't exactly expected," Tibbs offered, rubbing a grubby finger across the bridge of his red nose in an attempt to keep his grin in check. "This here be *Mr.* Baxter."

Anne had already put her hand in Lord Herndon's, so he waited until she was safely down before he turned those compelling blue eyes upon her.

Rendered a bit breathless by that unswerving stare, she hurried to repeat the falsehood she had adopted at the inn. "I am Julianne Baxter," she said in answer to his unspoken question, "and though I realize you were expecting a man, I believe the very least I am owed before you set your mind against me, is the courtesy of a cup of tea and an interview. Especially since my journey here necessitated my spending the better part of the day traveling in an ill-sprung, stuffy coach with a companion whose unceasing chatter has probably ruined my hearing for life."

Because she saw his lips twitch, as though he tried to suppress a smile, Anne was not nearly as undone as she might have been when he asked what she hoped to accomplish, adding, "What if, after you have had your tea, and I have asked all the pertinent questions regarding your qualifications, I cannot find it within me to trust you with so valuable an object?"

Trust? Valuable object? Anne blinked. What on earth had Mr. Baxter come to do? Obviously not to sell the latest releases from the Minerva Press.

Vowing not to turn fainthearted at the first obstacle, she said, "If you find you cannot trust me, sir, you have only to make your opinion known. Once I have been allowed a night or two to rest up from my journey, you may have someone convey me back to the village where I can catch the return stage to Dover."

Michael James Herndon, the fifth Baron Herndon, studied the young woman before him. At first glance anyone might be forgiven for labeling her average. She was of medium height and build, she possessed unremarkable brown hair and hazel eyes, and her complexion, though clear and smooth, was otherwise unexceptional.

It was when she spoke that she was lifted from the realm of the ordinary, for her voice was pitched rather low for a lady, and it had a faintly husky quality.

And she had spirit. When he and the gelding had nearly collided with the dog cart, she had been frightened; in fact, her face had gone so white he thought she might faint. She had not done so, however. Not her. And when he asked if she was all right, she had made a joke that it would take more than the chestnut to put her in a quake.

"Did your mother never tell you," she said, calling him back to the moment, "that it was rude to stare?"

There was that spirit again. She was nobody's pawn.

"If my mother so advised me, ma'am, I fear I do not remember. She died when I was a lad of ten."

The young lady blushed rather prettily. "Forgive me, my lord. My tongue sometimes runs away with me."

"No apologies necessary. Actually, I have a stepmother, an exemplary woman, who tried her best to teach me manners. Though, as you can see, her valiant efforts were for nought."

"The poor lady. I am a teacher, so I know the frustration of trying to drill lessons into children who will not bother to learn. My sympathies are with Lady Herndon."

Here it came. The explanation Michael had never quite learned to give without feeling a traitor to the woman who had provided the love and security to his childhood. "There is no Lady Herndon. Mama Lenore is generally referred to as Madam."

Anne was so busy reproaching herself for admitting to being a teacher, she very nearly failed to hear Lord Herndon's explanation. *Mama Lenore?* His stepmother was Lenore? The woman Anne suspected might be her own, resurrected mother?

Before Anne could ask him how a woman married to the previous Lord Herndon, a baron, could not be Lady Herndon, or at the very least the Dowager Lady Herndon, he took her by the elbow and propelled her toward the imposing red brick edifice that sat at the top of the gravel carriageway. As they walked, he said nothing more. The atmosphere had changed somehow, altered at the mention of his stepmother.

Still several yards from the house, he let go of her arm and bid her continue to the front entrance. "I have something that wants doing before I join you, Miss Baxter. Pilgreen will see that you get your tea."

Remembering that Tibbs had called the butler old Pickle Puss, Anne could not suppress a smile.

Lord Herndon had been about to walk away, but at her smile he stopped. "Do I know you?" he asked, studying her face. "Have we met before?"

"I do not believe so, sir."

"Are you quite certain?"

She nodded. "I think I would have remembered."

"Odd," he said. "When you smiled just then, there was something in your expression that put me in mind of someone."

Two

Anne watched Lord Herndon follow a flagstone path around to the east wing of the house and disappear behind a row of well-pruned hawthorns fully seven feet tall. At the sound of a door closing, a reddish brown nightingale, not yet migrated south, fled the top of the shrubbery, its flight smooth and swift.

"You might be wise to do likewise," Anne muttered, "for who knows what may come of this rash journey."

Having spent the majority of her twenty-two years at the Misses Thwaite's Academy for Young Ladies, as a student and later as a teacher, Anne had learned to moderate her exuberance and behave in a circumspect manner, at least before her employers. However, it had been an uphill struggle. It went against her nature to stand aside and wait obediently while others told her what was best to do, and in coming to see Lenore Herndon, Anne had merely followed a natural impulse toward action.

Still, there was no point in deluding herself, the action had been rash.

"But," she said aloud, "you have made it this far by acting bold as brass. No point in turning coward now."

Taking a fortifying breath, she continued around to the front of the house which had, for the most part, been built some time in the sixteen hundreds. It was constructed around an ancient hall—possibly of Norman origin—whose entrance was enhanced by a projecting two-story porch adorned by stone pilasters. The masonry appeared fourteenth century, while the timbered, overhanging second story must surely be fifteenth century; and adding to the general hodgepodge, the windows were definitely Tudor.

It was certainly a house representative of its many generations of owners, yet the whole was not unpleasant. The various parts seemed to have blended together with the years to form a solid, seemingly unshakable structure.

The wide oak door swung open before Anne could sound the knocker, and a tall, rather formidable butler made her the briefest of bows. "His Lordship bid me make you welcome, Miss Baxter. Please to come in."

Anne entered the marble-tiled vestibule, but as far as being made welcome, she doubted old Pickle Puss knew the meaning of the word. From his carefully combed salt and pepper hair to the tips of his well-polished shoes, Pilgreen was every inch the proper butler. *Starched-up,* some of her students would have said.

"Please to follow me into the hall, Miss Baxter. His Lordship will join you directly."

Anne entered the half-timbered hall, from which the house got its name, expecting an apartment as formal as the servant who directed her there. To her surprise, the room was delightful. Though still dominated by massive tie-beams in the center and in the end walls—features not greatly changed from medieval times—the trestle table upon which my lord's knights once ate their meals was gone from the center of the room, replaced by a handsome round mahogany table and four chairs. Upon the dais where the lord and his honored guests dined, there now sat a pair of wooden settles bedecked with pillows.

Behind the dais stood the original smoke screen, but there was no sign of the companion screen at the far end of the hall. As well, the original beaten earth floor had been cobbled some two or three centuries earlier, and was now warmed by carpets of inestimable value.

Choosing one of the wing chairs that flanked the fireplace, Anne composed herself comfortably and waited for the present lord. She had not been there much above five minutes when Michael Herndon appeared. He still wore his well-tailored riding clothes and boots—clothing that made Anne very conscious of her simple tan frock and inexpensive brown pelisse—but he came forward quickly, a smile upon his handsome face, and she was immediately put at her ease.

"My stepmother begs you will forgive her for not receiving you, Miss Baxter, but she is keeping to her room today."

Anne's disappointment must have shown on her face, for a questioning look appeared on his.

"Is she unwell, sir?"

It was an impertinent question from a stranger, and for a moment Anne thought he meant not to answer. When he finally replied, the tone of his voice was cool. "As one might expect, the eight months since the death of my father have been difficult for her."

"But she is not bedridden? I will get to meet her before I leave?"

Anne bit her bottom lip. Would she never learn to guard her tongue? A flash of anger had shone in Lord Herndon's eyes, and if she was not careful, he would toss her out on her ear before she had been inside the house above ten minutes. "What I mean to say, my lord, is that I hope to have the pleasure of meeting the lady."

The look he gave her was decidedly guarded. "Come," he said, "let us waste no further time in going to the library. It is there we will discover just how long your stay will be."

The book room was situated just behind the hall and was reached by crossing a wide corridor. Unfortunately, the distance was not sufficient for Anne to prepare her mind for the barrage of questions she knew must follow in a matter of moments.

"Please," he said, motioning for her to precede him into the book-lined room.

It was not a large library, though books covered every inch of the wall-to-ceiling shelves. Nor was it opulent, though an ornate walnut desk stood to the right and a handsome oak trestle table to the left. What instantly caught one's eye was the beautiful hand-tooled book that took pride of place in the center of the room. Reposing upon a specially built walnut stand with a glass cover, the large, thick book was immediately identifiable as a Gutenberg Bible.

"Oh, my," Anne said, approaching the treasure, yet not even daring to touch the glass cover. "How magnificent."

Lord Herndon had followed her into the room, and now he stood just behind her, so close she could smell the clean, tangy aroma of his shaving soap. When he reached around her to press a lever just beneath the stand, his shoulder touched her back, and she caught her breath at the sudden contact. Thankfully, her maidenly reaction was mistaken for awe, for the lever worked a mechanism that lifted the glass cover, while at the same time raising the recessed middle of the stand so that the book was level with the two leaves that came up like bird's wings and locked into place.

Without a word, Lord Herndon stepped around her and opened the heavy tome to a place marked with a square of clean vellum. The instant the book lay open, Anne saw the reason for the vellum; it marked the place where a leaf had been torn down the middle. "Oh, no," she said. "Such a regrettable thing to have happened."

"Can it be mended?" he asked.

"I sincerely hope so."

"What I should have said, ma'am, is can *you* repair it? Do you feel yourself qualified to undertake such a task."

Anne swallowed. Mend it? She dare not even touch it!

Stalling for time, she leaned over the book, being careful not to get too close. Not knowing what else to do, she counted the forty-two lines, noticing the intricate scrollwork that ran between the two columns on the left-hand page.

"This copy dates to fourteen sixty," he said.

"I . . . I thought as much," she replied, hoping it made her sound the authority she was obviously supposed to be. "How was it torn?"

"It was an accident. One of my sister's children wished to investigate the mechanism that operates the stand. The lad is but eight years old, and I did not think him strong enough to work the lever." He shook his head. "The blame is entirely mine, of course, for I should have known better. The rascal is forever getting up to some lark or other, and I suppose a hidden lever was just too much of a temptation."

Anne knew a moment's pity for the unknown boy. Having been the recipient of some stiff punishment meted out by a rather unforgiving father—punishment far too harsh for the very minor infractions—she could only imagine what retribution would be considered fitting for one who had committed such a serious misdeed. "I hope your nephew was not too severely chastised."

"Whipped, do you mean? No. Nancy, that is my sister, Lady Phelps, was all for relating the whole to her husband, but I asked her to leave it to me. The lad was beside himself with remorse, and I saw nothing to be gained by inflicting corporal punishment when it was obvious he had already learned his lesson."

Anne turned to look up at Lord Herndon, surprised to hear the forbearance in his tone. Who had been responsible for instilling such fairness in him?

Michael noted the incredulity writ plainly upon her countenance, and as he gazed into those wide, hazel eyes, he amended his initial opinion that they were unremarkable. At the moment, with nothing to show them off but her plain brown pelisse, her eyes were the warm greenish brown of the leaves of the autumn spindle tree, pretty enough in their own way. But if she were adorned in some worthy fabric, like a lustrous silk of emerald or gold, he could imagine those orbs turning the clear, soft yellow-green of the flag iris that blooms in early summer. They would be beautiful, and he . . .

Whoa! The woman was here to do a job of work, and it mattered not at all that he had discovered how comely she was. As master of the house, it behooved him to remember that no female under his roof should be made to suffer the least embarrassment. Recalled to a sense of his responsibility, he took a step back, putting some distance between them.

"You are a very understanding uncle, sir. The lad might have known harsher treatment at other hands."

Michael chuckled. "Not in this house. Mama Lenore would never stand for it."

* * *

Anne could not remember Lord Herndon's words without experiencing a red-hot jolt of anger. As she sat before the looking glass in the pretty guest bedchamber, the room's soft, rose-colored hangings and carpet were wasted upon her. All her concentration was upon his words. *Mama Lenore would never stand for it.*

How noble of her! Especially if she should prove to be Anne's mother, Lenore Carlton.

It was that Lenore who had left her own flesh and blood—her only child—to suffer the vicissitudes of Roger Carlton's changes in mood. It was that Lenore who had left a little girl to be reared by a man whose idea of discipline was learned while a lieutenant in a light infantry company—a company made up of ragtag soldiers.

Anne could not wait to meet the woman he called his stepmother, for if she was Lenore Carlton, then words were not sufficient to excoriate her for shirking her duty to her own child. True, Roger Carlton had been a difficult man—reserved almost to the point of coldness—but that was no reason for a mother to seek her own happiness elsewhere while forsaking her child. The notorious cuckoo was a better parent! At least that unmotherly fowl left her eggs safe and warm in some caring bird's nest.

The sound of the dinner gong interrupted Anne's angry reverie, and though still a bit nervous to be dining with Lord Herndon instead of having her dinner sent to her room on a tray, she quickly finished her toilette. After twisting her long, brown hair into a knot atop her head, she pulled wispy curls loose to lie softly across her forehead and trail against her cheeks. She was rather vain about her hair, considering the thick, natural curls her best feature.

She was less pleased with the plain green dinner dress deemed suitable by the Misses Thwaite. Since it was the best she possessed, however, there was little point in lamenting what could not be helped. Giving the three-quarter sleeves a final tug to

make certain the scar at her left elbow was not visible, Anne
hurried from the bedchamber and down the wide staircase.

Lord Herndon waited for her in the small drawing room at the
rear of the house. He stood beside a pianoforte, idly thumbing
through a collection of songs, but at her entrance he put the music
down and came to her, his approving gaze telling her that he was
not displeased with the appearance of his dinner companion.

Indicating a side table upon which reposed a decanter of sherry
and two glasses, he said, "May I offer you some wine, Miss
Baxter?"

"What? Oh, no, sir, I thank you." Anne had almost failed to
answer to her assumed name, so struck was she by his lordship's
appearance.

She had thought the man handsome in his riding clothes, but
dressed for an informal dinner in his own home, he was breath-
taking. Wearing a mulberry coat that made his dark blue eyes
resemble the sky at midnight, and a creamy white marcella waistcoat that only served to emphasize his almost coal black hair, he
was easily the most attractive man she had ever seen.

Attractive became devastating when he smiled at her. "I see
that I was correct," he said, the corner of his mouth pulling ever
so slightly to the left in a way that made Anne's heart beat unusually fast.

"Correct, sir? I do not—"

"Earlier I made a sort of wager with myself about your eyes."

The pace of her heart accelerated. "What about my eyes?"

"I suspected that if given the opportunity, they would turn that
color. Such a lovely shade. It puts me in mind of the flag iris,
the kind that grows in a little spinney on the far side of the brook
I used to fish as a lad."

Anne could not seem to catch her breath. No man had ever
spoken of her eyes before. Of a certainty, no one had ever likened
their color to a flower's and called it a lovely shade.

"Are you fond of wildflowers?" he asked.

I am now!

When she nodded, he said, "They are my favorites. I find I
much prefer them to the cultivated varieties. It is their freshness,

I think, and a certain uninhibited quality. And for all their seeming fragility, there is that underlying strength one must admire in them, that courage to survive the storms that assail us all."

If she had wanted to, Anne could not have replied, for it was almost as if he described her. Searching for some other topic, she mentioned the collection of songs he was perusing when she entered the room. "Are you musical, sir?"

"Only my ear. It dearly loves to listen."

"Just the one ear?"

He chuckled. "Yes, just the one. The other ear stays alert to saucy replies from impertinent young ladies."

It was Anne's turn to chuckle.

"And what of your ears?" he asked. "Do they like a bit of Mozart or Haydn?"

"Only if played by someone other than myself. Though it was my dearest childhood wish to be proficient at the pianoforte, I fear my desire far exceeded my talents."

"My stepmother was wont to play the pianoforte," he said, a sort of wistful quality in his voice. "Many an evening she played for my father, and I would sit in that chair over there by the fire and listen until I fell asleep."

He was silent for a moment. "Those are some of my most treasured memories. Of course, I never knew who took me up to the nursery and tucked me in. If it was my father, he was good enough never to complain of the task."

The idyllic scene Lord Herndon painted made Anne grit her teeth. A good thing he could not see her eyes now, for they must surely be pea green with envy.

Thankfully, she was not obliged to remark upon his memory of Lenore and her musical talents, for Pilgreen chose that moment to announce that dinner was served.

During the meal, Lord Herndon did all within his power to make Anne feel comfortable, introducing such topics of conversation as were generally acceptable at table. Yet she could not relax, no more than she could rid herself of a growing sense of regret—regret because personable gentlemen did not come in her way very often. Here was a man whose attentions any female would wish to encourage, and as luck would have it, Anne was in no position to do so.

Furthermore, she was in this particular gentleman's home under false pretenses. If he knew who she was and why she was here, he would not be likening her to flowers, but to wolves in sheep's clothing. To deceivers. Apparently he was devoted to his stepmother, and once he discovered Anne's purpose, chances were he would lose no time in expelling her from the premises.

A frisson of fear trailed up her spine, for unless she was much mistaken, here was a man not easily forgiving of deceit. He had told her that until May, when Napoleon was exiled to Elba, he had served at the Home Office, as aide de camp to General Sir Richard McCormick. If all Anne had heard of the general was true, that formidable old warhorse demanded that the gentlemen of his staff possess more than the normal allotment of strength, resolution, and loyalty.

Anne suspected that Lord Herndon was just such a man. And once he learned of her deceit, his gentlemanly manners would probably give way to wrath.

"I have decided to trust you, Miss Baxter."

Anne jumped, very nearly knocking over her water glass. "You have?"

"I have. Furthermore, I wish you to remain here as long as need be. I want your very best efforts where the Gutenberg is concerned, so take as much time as the job requires. No need to hurry."

For Anne there was every need. She had to work for her living, and there were only two weeks before the new school term began. Since she was obliged to be in Dover by the end of the fortnight, or risk losing her position, time was of the essence. She would see Lenore as soon as possible, not only because it would satisfy some unnamed need inside her, but also because she was not certain how long she could keep up this nerve-wracking pretense.

Anything could happen. Mr. Julian Baxter might come hobbling up to the door of the Hall, a crutch under each arm, and expose her as a fraud. Or his Lordship might ask to see the progress of her repairs—repairs she had no idea how to make.

As for the latter threat, Anne had come up with a plan she hoped would solve that problem.

"I do have one requirement, sir. One that must be met if I am to remain."

He raised an eyebrow in question.

"I must have privacy. Complete privacy. I cannot have anyone coming into the library to look over my shoulder, asking what I am doing and why. It would make me nervous when I need a steady hand."

"You are the expert, Miss Baxter. Whatever you need, it is yours."

"When I say privacy, I mean the doors are to be kept locked. No one is to enter the room until I am ready to leave. No maids with their dust cloths." She swallowed. "Not even you, my lord."

"You may have what you need, Miss Baxter, but surely you do not mean to hole up in there. I am persuaded that for such exacting work, long hours would prove detrimental. You will need frequent breaks. Time to go outside. Time to breathe fresh air. Enjoy some exercise."

A slow smile played upon his lips. "And I have just the scheme for all three. Do you ride?"

A shudder ran through Anne at the thought. "I do not, sir. From childhood I have had an unreasoning fear of horses."

"Truly? Why is that? Did something untoward happen?"

"I have no idea."

Without realizing she did so, Anne touched her left elbow, making certain the scar was not exposed. "If something fearful occurred, I was far too young to remember it. In any event, the incident is long forgotten."

They said nothing for a time, then Lord Herndon signaled the butler to assist Anne with her chair. "If I am to surrender my library to you for an extended period, Miss Baxter, I have some papers that must be seen to tonight."

He held the door open while she exited the dining room; then he walked with her to the bottom of the staircase. "And now," he said, taking her hand in his, "I shall bid you good evening."

His fingers were long and slender, and his grip, though gentle, hinted at underlying strength. As he bent forward to brush his lips lightly against the back of her hand, the brightness from the candles in the chandelier was reflected in his thick, black hair, and it was all Anne could do to stop herself from reaching out to feel the lustrous strands for herself.

"Sleep well," he whispered, releasing her hand.

"Good night, sir."

While she climbed the stairs, Anne fancied she could still feel the warmth of his lips upon her skin. She definitely felt the power of his gaze upon her back, and the knowledge that he watched her sent a flush of warmth throughout her entire body.

The man is far too mesmerizing. If I do not keep my distance from him, I risk leaving Herndon Hall with a broken heart.

With that warning still resounding in her thoughts, she had only just reached the corridor when a middle-aged servant in a starched white apron and a cap stepped out of the room next to Anne's. After bobbing a curtsy, she said, "Madam would like to see you, miss."

"Madam?"

"If you please, miss." The maid reentered the room, and after a moment's hesitation, Anne followed.

She had come to the Hall with no other objective than to see the woman called Lenore, yet with the actual meeting at hand, Anne found her knees shaking like a blancmange, and her feet inclined to stick to the floor as though glued. As well, she was having trouble swallowing. How could she give voice to all the things she had planned when her mouth was dry as a desert?

The bedchamber was much larger than the one assigned to Anne, and from what she could see of it, it was decorated in shades of blue and gold. Visibility was limited, for aside from the fire in the grate, the only light in the room came from a small lamp that sat on a tripod table some distance from the heavily carved rosewood bed.

"Come in, my dear," said the person who occupied that bed.

The voice was slightly husky, as though the woman had only just awakened. "I am so glad to have this opportunity to welcome you to Herndon Hall."

Anne strained to see the figure who sat up, her back resting against a bank of pillows. She had been convinced that she need only come face-to-face with her to know for certain if this woman was Lenore Carlton. Unfortunately, a shadow from the bed hangings obscured all but her pointed chin, and it was difficult to discern much else in the dimness, except that the person beneath the covers was slender and possibly of medium height.

"My stepson will have already informed you that I am subject to migraine headaches, so you will understand the necessity for the nearly darkened room. But I am over the worst of this one and should be able to leave my bed within the next few days. I hope to welcome you properly at that time."

"I . . ." Anne sighed. Was this the woman her father had labeled *Madame Whore?* Whatever she was . . . whoever she was, at the moment she was defenseless, and Anne could no more rail at her than she could kick a helpless kitten.

The maid stepped beside Anne and touched her arm. "I'll show you out, miss."

"Good night," said the woman. "Thank you for coming."

"Yes. Good night."

Anne got little sleep that night. Frustration kept her awake. Getting inside Herndon Hall had proved much easier than she had thought possible, but dealing with the inhabitants of the Hall was not going at all the way she had planned. First, she had not considered the possibility that Lenore might be ill, and second, she had never dreamed that the master of the Hall would be so handsome, so exciting. As well, Michael Herndon possessed the kind of character Anne most admired—strong, loyal, fair.

"I hope you slept well," he greeted when she entered the morning room in search of some breakfast. A maid was removing his plate, so Anne knew he had finished with his own meal.

"I slept tolerably well, sir."

Studying her in the bright morning light that streamed through the French windows, Michael took leave to doubt her statement. Faint color smudged the soft skin beneath her eyes, and though it was not unattractive, he could tell she had not enjoyed a restful night. She was not very old, no more than twenty-two or -three, and such a young lady should have fallen asleep easily, even in a strange bed. What could have kept her awake? Certainly not a guilty conscience, for she was too open, too innocent.

She looked particularly guileless in her pale yellow muslin frock, its only adornment a row of little white daisies at the square neck and around the high waist. The style suited her trim figure, and though there was no apparent attempt to do so, it drew his attention to her pretty bosom.

Where, he wondered, had he gotten the idea that Miss Julianne Baxter was average?

Her figure alone must attract any man's attention. Add to that the artless curls that framed her delicate face, and the sweet smile that came slowly, yet genuinely to her lips, and anyone must agree that she was a very pretty girl.

"You should not work a full day today," he said. "I am persuaded that you are not sufficiently rested from your journey."

"But, sir, I—"

"I told you last evening that you needed fresh air and exercise, and I believe I know the very place where both may be achieved. The distance is not great, and it is easily accomplished on foot."

"Truly, I—"

He raised his hand to forestall her arguments. "As your employer, I insist you cease all work today at noon. This edict you must obey. If, however, you have any reservations about being in my company for the afternoon, you have only to say the word. That edict, I will obey."

He paused long enough to give her an opportunity to refuse his invitation.

"I have no such reservations, sir."

Three

I have no such reservations, sir.

The quiet admission had pleased Michael more than he had expected, but for the moment he chose not to examine his response too closely. "Very well, Miss Baxter, I will meet you in the Hall at exactly noon. At that time, I will expect you to have donned your bonnet and your boots, and to be ready for an adventure."

Anne did not let herself dwell on all the reasons she should not spend the afternoon with Michael Herndon, should not share with him an adventure. It was reason enough that she would be returning to Dover soon, returning to her very circumspect existence as an instructress—an existence that was likely to be hers for years to come.

But, the would-be adventurer deep within her insisted, was she not entitled to at least one lovely memory?

If she allowed herself the pleasure of one balmy summer afternoon spent in the company of the most exciting man she had ever met, who but herself would suffer? Whose heart but her own did she risk?

Convinced that the expected joy of the outing was worth the price she might be required to pay, she ate two or three bites of toast, swallowed one big gulp of tea, then took herself to the library where the Gutenberg Bible waited. Of course, she had no intention of touching so much as a finger to the pages of the rare and valuable book, but on the chance that someone might forget her rule of privacy and enter the room, she approached the stand and pushed the lever.

Slowly the glass cover lifted and the recessed middle of the stand rose. As soon as the two side leaves locked into place, Anne moved to the far end of the room, opened one of the narrow casement windows to let in the fresh morning air, and began to scan the shelves for a volume she would not be afraid to touch. She needed something to occupy her time, and Lord Herndon had a wide selection of books, everything from the great literature of Greece and Rome to the works of Lord Byron.

After choosing *Childe Harold's Pilgrimage,* Anne disposed herself in the chair behind the ornate walnut desk and began to read. To her dismay, she soon discovered that when one was obliged to read to kill time, all the pleasure was removed from pleasure reading. Therefore, at half-past eleven, she was quite ready to return Lord Byron's poetry to the shelf.

As soon as she closed the casement window and then activated the lever, restoring the Gutenberg to its usual place, she lost no time in running upstairs to change from her slippers to her half boots. After hastily donning her tan straw bonnet—the only hat she had with her—and her green faille spencer, Anne hurried back downstairs. She was inside the hall, waiting for Michael long before the ormolu clock on the mantel chimed the noon hour.

Seated upon the settle on the dais, she looked around the ancient hall, wondering how it would feel to have grown up in such a house as this, with evidence all around of the generations of relatives who had come before.

Anne scarcely recalled the years she had spent with her father, and as for the dozen or so houses they had inhabited during that time, those had all melded into one blurred memory. Once she was old enough to be sent to school at the Misses Thwaite's Academy for Young Ladies, she had remained there, seeing her father only three or four times in the next fourteen years. She had not even known Roger Carlton was back in the country until she received the letter informing her of his heart attack.

No, Anne could not envision living where one's family had resided for generations. She could not even imagine how it must feel to have a family. She was without roots; without ties to any place or anyone.

"May one ask what you were thinking, Miss Baxter?"

Anne did not answer. She had not heard him come in, but when she looked toward the door that opened from the vestibule, he stood there quietly, his shoulder resting against the doorjamb, just watching her. In addition to having changed into a hunting jacket of tan corduroy, he had slung over his shoulder a well-used leather pouch. He appeared quite relaxed, and dressed in such casual attire, he looked less like a lord and more like a young man bent on adventure. The sight lifted her spirits.

"You appeared lost in thought," he said. "And so very serious I scarcely knew if I should disturb you.

"Serious? Me? You are mistaken, sir, for I am like the lilies. I toil not, neither do I spin."

She did not want to think of the past. Not now. This was to be her happy memory day, and she did not mean to let anything spoil it. She rose and walked toward him, not even trying to hide the joy she felt at the promised outing.

Amusement lit his blue orbs, though his countenance was un-smiling. "So, Miss Baxter, you have the eyes of the iris and the soul of the lily."

"I know little of irises, my lord. However, since my employer has been gracious enough to give me the afternoon off, this lily means to make the most of it."

"I am in perfect agreement with such a sentiment," he said, responding to her smile with one of his own. "No toiling, and most emphatically no spinning."

He looked her over from her bonnet down to her boots. "Since we have already twisted the proverb, so to speak, let me say that I am happy to see that you took thought for your raiment. Otherwise, ma'am, I should appear quite the fool for having given consideration to what we should eat."

At her raised eyebrow, he patted the leather pouch. "I thought you might be hungry after your morning's work, so I asked Cook to prepare us a simple picnic."

Anne had not realized that the grounds of Herndon Hall were so vast until she traveled them on foot. Not that she objected to the expanse of lush green countryside or the many ancient trees, a few so thick it would need three men, their arms stretched wide, to circle each of the massive trunks. Nor did she object when each time they encountered a sheep path to be crossed, Michael took her hands and helped her down one bank and up the next.

Michael. He had asked her to call him by his name.

"And you who spin not, I shall call Lily."

"Please," she said, "call me Anne."

The moment she said it, she realized her error. Fortunately, before she could think how to rectify such a blunder, he did it for her.

"Anne," he said, as if trying it out upon his tongue. "Julianne is a beautiful name, but in this instance I believe I prefer the shorter version. It suits you."

She asked him several times where they were bound, but each time he merely bid her be patient. "I told you this was to be an adventure, and that is all I am prepared to reveal. I want your first impression of the site to be free of any preconceived notion."

"Shall I like it, this mysterious site?"

"That is for you to say."

She tried again. "Do you like it?"

"Oh, no, Miss Trickster, I am not so easily taken in as that. And do not, I warn you, try that thing you do where you look up at me through your eyelashes, for charming though I find it, I will not be beguiled. I said you must wait, and nothing will sway my decision."

Anne caught her breath. Look up through her eyelashes? She had no idea what he was talking about.

As for *charming* and *beguiling,* words she was not used to hearing in reference to herself, those she packed away in her memory, to be taken out and examined at a later time.

"Really, sir, I should like to know where we are going. I promise you I will be delighted, so—"

"Shhh," he said. "It is just beyond that copse of poplars."

Taking her hand, he broke into a gentle run, pulling her along with him. When they reached the beautiful silver green trees, he stopped so she might catch her breath. "Are you ready?"

She nodded and he led her around the natural barrier, pausing to allow her a moment to take in the scene before her. He said not a word, merely waited while she gazed into the quiet, secluded hollow.

"Oh," she said, the single exclamation all she could manage.

Before her was an ancient manor house, or at least the ghost of one, and it was enveloped in silence and completely surrounded by a moat. Almost like a dream it stood there, protected by the still, dark water, while dozens of white swans swam about peacefully, barely disturbing the silver-green reflections of the poplars.

"It is early twelfth century," Michael said.

"It is beautiful," she whispered.

"When I was a lad, this was my special place. I would sit here for hours imagining myself inside the house, the captain of the guards, watching while hordes of enemy soldiers on horseback rode over the downs, their swords drawn and ready for battle. How I and my small band of valiant men would cheer when the foe arrived only to discover the bridge drawn and the moat a barrier not to be denied."

Anne heard every word he said, yet as she searched the latticed windows and scanned the timeless quadrangle of gray, irregular ragstone—so white in the afternoon sunshine it might almost have been new—the feeling it evoked in her was one of stability, continuity. Even in its quiet abandonment, the house gave her a sense of peace.

"I have read of such places, but I never thought to see one. May we go inside?"

He shook his head. "It is far too dangerous. The walls may look substantial, but the least vibration tends to loosen the stones, often sending a shower down upon the unsuspecting."

To Anne's surprise, he put his fingertips beneath her chin, raising it so that she looked directly at him. "I should be very sorry," he said softly, "to see anything happen to this lovely face."

She was drawn into his eyes, almost as if they were the waters of the moat and she one of the swans, and at that moment she asked nothing more of life than to be allowed to swim in those cool, blue depths for eternity.

Fortunately for her sanity, Michael released her chin and went over to set the leather pouch in the shade of a broad horse-chestnut tree. Returning, he took her hand again. "We cannot go inside the house, but there is nothing to prevent us from walking all around it, just as long as we do not cross the moat. If I remember correctly, there are some pretty flowers that grow on the opposite side from here. Perhaps we will find a flag iris."

As it turned out, it was too late in the season for the iris and the forget-me-nots, though remnants of both plants were visible along the banks of the moat, but the heartsease, with its pretty yellow and purple petals grew in abundance down near the water's edge, mingling with the tall, wild grasses. As well, here and there they spotted rust red sorrel and even some water lilies, their waxy white heads floating in the water.

Maul, maul! trumpeted a swan as they circled around to the back side of the manor house.

Anne jumped at the sound, then laughed at her own skittishness when the big male fowl ceased his trumpeting and relaxed his powerful wings. "That fellow is definitely not a muted swan. Did we frighten him?"

"Not at all. The swans have no fear of man."

Shading his eyes with his hands, Michael looked up into the sky. "There," he said, pointing eastward, "there is the cause for the bird's alarm. It is an eagle. It is that mighty predator the swan was warning off."

Anne shaded her eyes as well and was rewarded with an extraordinary view of a golden eagle circling in the sky, the golden-red feathers on its head and neck gleaming like copper in the sun.

"What a magnificent sight!"

Michael chuckled. "Not to the swans."

She was immediately contrite. "Oh, no. Of course not. Will he return, do you think?"

"That is hard to say. We might see if we can discourage him. How far can you throw a stone?"

"On a good day? Possibly twenty feet."

Michael stared at her for a moment, then burst out laughing. "I know you can run. What say you if we see if we can chase the eagle away?"

"Oh, yes."

Having said this, he began to run eastward, whistling loudly and waving his arms over his head. Anne hesitated only a moment before she followed suit, shouting, "Shoo, shoo! Go away, you eagle."

They continued thus for several minutes, and whether or not the bird of prey was frightened, at least he flew some distance away. With his going, Anne collapsed upon the soft, green grass, her skirt billowing out around her.

Michael looked to see if she was all right, and though her breathing was a bit erratic, her face glowed with healthy color from the exercise, and she smiled like a young girl just come in from play.

Enchanted by her uninhibited exuberance, he lowered himself onto the grass beside her, then stretched out on his back, his arms beneath his head. "You were wonderful," he said, looking up at her. "If that horde of soldiers ever does come galloping over the downs, I believe I shall call upon you to help me send them packing."

She gave him a mock salute. "At your service, Captain."

Though Michael lowered his eyelids against the sun's glare, he did not close them altogether, a circumstance that allowed him to observe her at his leisure. As he watched, she loosened the strings of her bonnet, lifted the hat from her head, and began to fan herself. The removal of such an innocuous item as a straw hat was by no means a provocative gesture, yet somehow the action set Michael's pulse to racing—racing out of all proportion.

A light sheen of perspiration dampened her forehead, and the moisture caused the wispy tendrils around her face to curl. Unable to resist the temptation, he raised up on one elbow and reached out to test the springiness of one of those medium brown spirals.

Catching it between his thumb and finger, he tugged gently,

straightening the tress then releasing it, smiling as it slowly crinkled back into its coil. "You have beautiful hair," he whispered.

She had remained perfectly still while he tested the curl, but at his words she drew in a soft, nearly inaudible gasp. As Michael gazed at her parted lips, he knew an almost overwhelming urge to take her in his arms and kiss her.

They sat thus for several breathless moments; then he reached his hand out again and cupped her cheek, letting his thumb move slowly, softly over her mouth.

"Anne," he whispered. "Do you believe in fate?"

Fate?

She believed in the clean, masculine smell of Michael Herndon, a heady aroma that filled her nostrils. She believed in his slightly roughened hand upon her face, and she believed in the magic of his thumb caressing her lips.

"Somehow," he said, "I feel we were destined to meet. Almost from the first moment I saw you, I felt irresistibly drawn to you. As though I already knew you."

He still rested upon one elbow. He had not moved any closer, yet Anne could feel the vitality, the warmth of his body, almost as if it touched hers. Corduroy and faille might not have been there, so strongly did she feel that warmth upon her skin. Mesmerized, Anne could neither breathe nor speak.

His gaze was concentrated upon her lips, and as he looked his fill, his eyes grew dark as midnight. "Anne," he breathed out.

Sitting upright at last, he brought his face close to hers, and while her bones surrendered to a sort of honeyed liquification, Anne closed her eyes, waiting for his kiss.

Maul, maul! Maul, maul!

It was not to be wondered at that they jumped apart at the loud, jarring trumpeting of the swans.

Maul, maul! seemed to come from everywhere at once as at least a dozen birds warned away the eagle that had returned. Even bolder than before, the large predator circled just above the moat. Michael sprang to his feet, waving his arms once again.

Whether the sounds of the swans in the moat or the movement

of the man on the bank frightened the eagle, it immediately took itself off in search of other prey.

As for Anne, she sat as if turned to stone. She was more disturbed by the event than the swans, for those lovely white creatures were already settling back down into their peaceful swim, while her heart thumped so rapidly she thought it might escape her chest.

When peace was restored once again, Michael turned back to gaze down at Anne, and as she looked up at him, he exhaled a loud sigh. "Now do you believe in fate?" he asked, his voice noticeably husky.

He must have seen the disappointment in her face, for he muttered something beneath his breath. "Do not look at me like that," he warned, his breathing no more steady than her own, "or I shall be obliged to finish what the swans interrupted so dramatically."

She reached up her hand toward him. "But I want you to finish it."

"No!" he said, then he smiled to soften the impact of the harsh word. "What happened was for the best, at least for the moment. It would be better if we took things more slowly. Since we have all the time in the world, there is no need to rush that which will be all the sweeter for the wait."

Anne wanted to cry, for she knew what he did not, that there would be no time for them. Once he discovered her deceit, he would very likely despise her.

"Come," he said, holding out his hands to her. "I think we had better return to the Hall."

She placed both her hands in his, and he lifted her to her feet with an ease that sent a shiver of delight from her toes all the way to her heart.

"But what of our picnic? Is it to be forfeited as well?"

He nodded. "I know, even if you do not, my lovely wild flower, that if we remain here for even one more minute, it will be your lips I taste."

"Would that be so bad?"

"Yes," he said, his voice low and tantalizing, "for I am very much afraid that one taste would not be enough."

The walk back to the Hall was accomplished in almost complete silence, and though Michael held her hand the entire way, the warmth of his fingers enveloping hers, Anne knew that the afternoon she had meant to store up as a happy memory had turned into one of heartbreak.

She loved Michael Herndon. It was the height of foolishness. It was insanity. It was asking for a lifetime of heartache. But it was reality. She loved him.

How it had happened, she did not know. How could a rational woman be in love with a man she had known slightly more than twenty-four hours? There was no logic to it. There was only the feeling deep inside her soul that she had found the one man in the world whom she could love. The one man she did love. And no matter if she went away this minute and never saw him again, no other man would ever possess her heart but Michael.

The sound of their boots crunching upon the gravel of the driveway brought Anne back to a sense of where they were. They were nearing the entrance to the Hall, and as they approached the two-story porch, Michael tugged at her hand. "Please," he said, "before we go inside, there is something I would say to you."

She stopped, her back to him, but he took her by the shoulders and turned her around. Then he placed his left hand on the door and his right hand on the stone pilaster, effectively trapping her within his arms.

"Thank you for the picnic," he said, his voice so soft it nearly brought tears to her eyes.

"But we did not eat."

"No, but there will be other days and other picnics."

Anne very much doubted it, but she kept the knowledge to herself.

"I wanted to tell you," he said, "that I shall be away from the Hall for a few days."

At his words, Anne felt bereft. She missed him already.

"Some time within the next hour, my man of business is to meet me here, and we are to travel to Tunbridge Wells to see my sister, Lady Phelps. It is a matter of family business, or I would postpone it."

He bent his elbows so that his face was brought very close to hers. His breath was warm upon her cheek, his voice soft and low. "I shall look forward to seeing you when I return."

He remained thus for several heart-stopping moments; then very slowly he moved that last inch and brushed her lips with his own.

It was the merest whisper of a kiss, but the sweetness, the tenderness of it pierced Anne to her very soul.

Four

Michael stayed in Tunbridge Wells for an entire week, and Anne could not believe how she missed him! Every day she thought to see him riding up the carriageway, and each day when he did not return, she felt as if the empty place that had taken up residence inside her chest grew bigger.

During the morning hours, she kept up the pretense of working by going into the library and closing the door, but each afternoon, after she had partaken of a light nuncheon, she went to the little garden at the side of the house. There she could walk about and get some exercise while watching for Michael.

Unfortunately, even if he had been at Herndon Hall the entire time, it would have made no difference in the impossibility of the situation. And Anne knew it. She was in love with Michael Herndon—loved him with all her heart—but any chance they might have had of sharing a future life together was doomed by the fact that the woman he loved like a mother was the same woman Anne abhorred.

The woman he called his stepmother was, indeed, Anne's mother. Anne was convinced of it now, for the afternoon before she had been invited to take tea in Lenore's suite.

"Come in, Miss Baxter," Lenore had called out in answer to Anne's knock.

It had been six days since she had paid her first visit to the woman, and this time when she entered the bedchamber, it was less a sickroom and more the beautifully appointed suite one might expect. The hangings at the windows had been opened to let in the afternoon light, and fresh air filled the room. The blue and gold of the hangings and counterpane were repeated in the flowers of the Axminster carpet, and the two Louis the Fifteenth chairs that stood near the fireplace were upholstered in gold fleur-de-lis brocade.

As for the woman who had been but a shadowed figure the first time Anne visited, today she sat in one of the gold chairs, the light behind her back. She wore a lovely rose-colored wrapper whose satin cuffs and sash were a darker pink, and upon her silver-streaked brown hair sat a little silk cap that incorporated a lace veil. The veil was only long enough to shade her eyes, leaving the bottom half of her face uncovered, and as Anne studied the face below the veil, there was nothing about the chin, the mouth, or the nose that reminded her of anyone she had ever seen before.

"You will forgive me," Lenore said, touching a finger to the lace. "By tomorrow, when Michael returns, I shall probably be as good as new, but for today I am more comfortable with the light filtered."

Anne did not answer, she could not; instead, she took the chair opposite Lenore's, sitting down before she fell down.

Tomorrow . . . I shall . . . be good as new, said a husky voice inside her head.

When Anne had visited before, the woman's voice had sounded slightly frail, and husky from sleep. Today, however, it was frail no longer, though the huskiness remained.

Tomorrow . . . I shall . . . be good as new.

Anne's breathing grew shallow as the chance remark whirled round and round in her brain. There was something so very familiar about the phrase, though the wording was not quite right.

While the middle-aged maid brought over a little rosewood tea table and set it within easy reach of her mistress, Lenore said, "How glad I am that you accepted my invitation to tea, Miss Baxter, for I—"

That was it! Not *I,* but *you!* Anne remembered now. The woman had said, *Tomorrow you will be good as new.*

Her voice had been husky, and the little girl who was Anne so many years ago was crying. She held her left elbow. Her arm was newly bandaged, and there was blood on her skirt.

For today it will hurt, the voice had said. *But I promise you, little one, that tomorrow you will be good as new.*

Anne could not stop herself from touching her left sleeve; beneath it was the scar she always kept covered—the scar whose source she had forgotten. She remembered it now.

It was her fourth birthday, and her father had come home for her birthday tea. He looked so handsome in his uniform, and he rode a large bay horse he had purchased just that morning. "Come," he said, holding his arms out to her, "Papa will give you a ride on his new horse."

"She is too little," said the husky voice. "There will be time enough for horses when she is older."

Her father had ignored the woman and had scooped the little girl up, setting her in front of him on the bay. The horse had no more than reached the lane when something spooked him and he bucked, tossing both riders through the air.

"One lump or two, Miss Baxter?"

"What?"

She held a cube of sugar between dainty, chased silver tongs.

"No," Anne replied, "no sugar."

Anne reached for the cup and saucer, but when she would have taken a sip of the mahogany-colored brew to help calm her shattered nerves, her hand shook too much to risk lifting the hot liquid to her mouth.

"Is your work going well?" the woman asked.

No. Not the woman—Lenore. Lenore Carlton. That was her real name. Whatever vows she might have exchanged with Michael's father, she was not now, nor had she ever been the man's wife. How could she marry him when she already had a husband? She was Lenore Carlton, recent widow of Captain Roger Carlton, a man who addressed her as *Madame Whore.*

Anne tried to remember the few words that remained of the letter signed Lenore—the letter her father had burned before beginning his own missive. Other than the signature, two charred corners and the direction of the sender had survived the flames.

In one corner were the words, "my daughter," and in another, "so cruel after all these years."

Yes, it was cruel. Nothing could be crueler than a mother who abandoned her child.

"He is such a wonderful man," Lenore said.

What was she saying? Who was wonderful? Anne tried to concentrate.

"He felt it his patriotic duty to serve his country in whatever way possible, but after Lord Herndon's death, Michael resigned from General McCormick's staff and returned to Kent to take his place as the new Baron Herndon."

Lenore set her empty cup on the tea table. "Michael is the kind of man any woman would be proud to call her son."

"But you are not, I think, his mother." Anne was unable to keep the sarcasm from her voice.

"No, I am not, but I love him as though he were my own. Michael and Nancy are the children of my heart."

"I believe his Lordship said you were once their governess."

"That is true. When I became stepmother to him and his sister, it was the second most wonderful event of my life."

For a woman like Lenore, marrying a wealthy baron—even if that marriage was not legal—must surely figure as the most wonderful event in her life. Anne felt sick to her stomach, and she longed to show Roger Carlton's letter to his widow!

"I love children," Lenore continued. "I am persuaded there is no more important calling on earth than rearing a child. Can anything have farther-reaching repercussions than giving a child a solid foundation of love and honesty, and a sense of his responsibility to himself and to the world in which he lives?"

Anne bit her lip to keep from expressing aloud what she thought of this woman's sense of responsibility.

"Caring for children is not unlike learning to play the pianoforte. Do you play, Miss Baxter?"

"A little," Anne replied, though the words were torn from her.

"Then you know it is not enough to perform the music proficiently, for that requires only discipline. Not that discipline is not important, of course. Certainly one must devote time to learning the principals, or there will never be harmony. Once those principals are firmly established, however, the true virtuoso lets the heart rule her fingers, thereby producing beautiful music."

"You said, *her.*"

"Yes, for those entrusted with the care of children are usually female. If such a woman devotes time to nurturing a child, teaching him solid principals while letting her heart tell her when it is time to trust the child's own values, the result is a good, caring human being."

Too angry to remain in the same room with this hypocrite—this woman who deserted her own child—Anne stood. "I cannot remain," she said, "I feel sick to my stomach."

The next day, knowing that Michael would return home at any moment kept Anne on the alert. As usual, she went to the library once she had partaken of breakfast, but after working the lever to open the stand, exposing the Gutenberg Bible, she was unable to sit still for two minutes together. Because of her disordered emotions, reading one of the books from the shelves was out of the question, so she chose instead to pace back and forth, hoping the activity would help her to think. Other than the anticipation of seeing Michael again, she had to decide what to do about Lenore.

She had thought of nothing else since leaving the woman's bedchamber yesterday afternoon save her absolute conviction that Lenore was in reality her mother, Lenore Carlton. When Lenore had knocked at her door later that evening, calling out to inquire if she was all right and asking if she might bring her a soothing potion, Anne had feigned sleep.

She wanted no words of sympathy. She wanted no soothing draughts. Not from Lenore! Not now. The time for such things had come and gone years ago, and at the moment, Anne had not the stomach for dissembling. Any conversation between the two women would have resulted in Anne's giving voice to the anger that gnawed at her insides, like mice gnawing at a loaf of bread left exposed in a larder.

Unfortunately, knowing the truth and acting upon that information were two entirely different things. Her original plan had been to expose Lenore for what she was, to look her mother in the face and tell her what she thought of a female who cared so little for her own child that she could abandon her for the sake of a liaison with a wealthy peer.

But that was before Anne had met Michael Herndon; before she knew that she loved him with all her heart. Loving him as she did, how could she expose Lenore before him? How could she hurt him in this manner?

Those unanswerable questions were interrupted by a tapping at one of the casement windows, and when Anne spun around to see who had chosen such an unorthodox manner of gaining her attention, she saw Michael. At the sight of him, the hollow feeling that had been growing inside her chest all week vanished immediately, like the morning mists before the warmth of the sun.

Feeling as though she trod on air, she ran to the window and pushed open the casement; then, with no other thought than to be as close to Michael as possible, she squeezed her arms and shoulders through the narrow opening until the entire top half of her torso was outside. "You are here at last!"

Michael still held the reins of the chestnut gelding, but when he saw Anne practically climb out to meet him, he let the leather slip from his fingers so he could take her hands in his. "You missed me, then? It was not I alone who wished the days at an end so I could return to the Hall?"

She shook her head. "This was the longest week of my life."

Hearing the sincerity in her slightly husky voice, he raised her hands to his lips. "My sweet wild flower."

She smiled, and Michael wondered what good deed he had done unaware that Heaven should have sent him this wonderful person—this lovely, open, unaffected girl. "Did I tell you," he said, "how beautiful you are?"

"No," she whispered.

It was only the one word, nothing provocative about it, yet Michael felt a pang of desire so intense he thought he might explode if he did not take her in his arms soon. He longed to hold her close and cover her mouth with his own, to smother her with kisses until she was in no doubt as to how much he had missed her.

"I want to hold you," he said. "I want to feel your heart pressed against mine."

"Me, too," she said, then she bit her bottom lip as if to keep her happiness in check.

Michael could not take his gaze from that soft, pink mouth. So mesmerized was he, so aware of the lovely woman who seemed to want him as much as he wanted her, that he found it difficult to resist the temptation to try to fit his frame through that impossibly narrow window and thus climb into the room with her.

His saner self told him he was too large to do so, of course. Furthermore, someone waited for him. Who, he did not know. As luck would have it, when he galloped up the lane several minutes earlier, he had passed the gig hired out by the White Dove in Lamberford.

"Your Lordship has a visitor," the lad from the inn had told him. "Just left him at t'Hall. Seems fair beside himself t'see your Lordship, he does."

Michael had thanked the lad for the information; then, knowing he might be detained by the visitor, he had ridden around to the library window to see if he could find Anne.

"Someone is waiting to see me," he told her, "so I cannot stay long enough to tell you all the things I want to say. Will you meet me in the side garden in half an hour?"

She nodded enthusiastically. "I will meet you anywhere you say. At any time you wish."

He was sorely tempted to kick the damned window right out of the wall, anything to be able to take Anne in his arms, but that saner self took over again, and he was forced to content himself with taking her face between his hands and kissing her.

Heaven help him! She tasted so good. And he had never felt anything so wonderful as her lips. They were so smooth, so innocently eager to please and be pleased that one kiss filled him with an almost overwhelming craving for her.

"Anne. Anne," he muttered, his voice raw with desire. "I cannot even imagine why the fates chose to grant me the gift of your love, but I warn you, I do not mean to let you go."

"You do not?" she asked breathlessly.

"Never!"

Those green eyes stared directly into his, and the joy he saw there filled him with such exhilaration, such wonder, that he wanted to throw back his head and shout at the top of his voice so that all the world would know of his happiness.

He caught her left hand and lifted it to his mouth, placing a kiss upon her third finger. "My mother's betrothal ring has been waiting all these years. Will you do me the honor of wearing it?"

"Oh, Michael," she said, tears of joy spilling down her cheeks. "I do love you so."

Finding nothing to dislike in that answer, he kissed each satiny cheek, tasting warm salty tears before giving his attention to her mouth once again. He kissed her until he thought he would go mad with longing; then, after exerting what seemed superhuman strength, he stepped back, putting several inches between himself and the woman he loved.

"I must go, my sweet."

Unable to stop himself, he reached out and touched one of the curls that rested against her temples, rubbing the silkiness between his fingers. "The side garden," he said. "In half an hour." He gave the curl a gentle tug before letting it go. "Do not keep me waiting."

"I will be there," she said.

Michael backed away from the window, then caught up the gelding's reins and led the horse around to the front of the house. Whoever his visitor might be, he would send the man on his way without delay. Nothing the fellow had to say could possibly be as important as that meeting in the garden. Anne said she loved him, and that was all Michael needed to know.

Eight days ago he had not even known of her existence; yet now, all he could think of was making her his bride. In vain had he told himself that they knew little of one another, that they needed time to learn all those things two people should know before pledging their lives. In this, however, his saner self had not been victorious. Michael Herndon knew all he needed to know about Miss Julianne Baxter, and that was an end to it.

He had only just given the gelding into the hands of a groom who ran up from the stables, when the entrance door swung open and Pilgreen stepped outside. The very proper butler seemed even more formal than usual, and there was about him an air better suited to the day of judgment than to welcoming home the master of the house.

"Good day, my lord."

"And to you, Pilgreen."

As they stepped into the vestibule, the butler said, "Someone is waiting in the Hall, my lord. Shall I announce you?"

Announce me? In my own house? What absurdity is this?

"Thank you, no." Michael handed over his hat and gloves. "I should like you to send a message to Mrs. Herndon, however. Tell her that I have returned, and ask her if she will receive me in an hour's time."

"As you wish, my lord."

While Pilgreen went to do his master's bidding, Michael crossed from the vestibule to the Hall, pausing just inside the doorway for his first look at the visitor. The man was small and thin, with the rather sour expression of the dyspeptic, and he had chosen to seat himself at the mahogany table in the middle of the room. His foot was bound, and for comfort's sake he had propped the injured limb on a small stool. His wooden crutches leaned against the table.

"You wanted to see me?"

"Lord Herndon?"

When the man started to rise, Michael bid him to keep his seat. "I see you have met with an accident, sir. Since it must be quite painful for you to be racketing about with such an injury, may I ask straight away what has brought you to see me?"

The man blinked. "Surely you were expecting me, my lord. I sent word when I would arrive. Of course, I was delayed on account of the accident on the road, but I came as soon as ever I could."

"There must be some mistake. I was expecting no one."

"But you sent for me, my lord. I've come all the way from Dover. To see to the Gutenberg."

"The Gutenberg? But the person I sent for has already—" Michael stopped. Some voice deep inside told him that if he did not say the words, they could not be refuted. Of course, this was some sort of hoax. The visitor was obviously a charlatan. There could be no other explanation.

He looked at the little man with the bound foot and the dyspeptic demeanor. Was ever a person less likely to be a charlatan? Such people were reputed to be comely, with winning ways, possessed of all the traits needed to make others turn a blind eye.

Comely. Winning ways!

A knot formed in the pit of Michael's stomach. "One moment, if you please. There is something I must see."

Without another word, he strode from the Hall directly to the library, the chamber he had not entered since promising Anne that she might have privacy in which to do her work. The room was empty, with the casement window closed and fastened and the Gutenberg tucked snugly in its proper place. Hoping against all the evidence of his senses that there was some logical explanation for the mix-up, Michael went straight to the stand and pushed the lever.

The minute the book was in place, he spied the piece of vellum he had used as a marker. While still searching his mind for some believable excuse, he opened the book and turned to the marked page. It looked just as it had eight days ago. It was still torn, and no attempt had been made to mend it.

Feeling as though he had been cudgeled from behind, Michael grasped the edges of the stand, holding it so tightly his fingers turned white with the pressure he exerted. "No!" he said. "It is not true. Anne is too fine. Too open. Too honest for deception. There has to be some explanation."

When he returned to the Hall several minutes later, he went directly to the visitor. There would be an explanation, of course, but Michael suspected that whatever openness, whatever honesty existed, it resided in the little man with the sour face. "Your pardon for the interruption, but there was a matter I needed to investigate."

"Of course, my lord."

Taking a deep breath, Michael asked the question whose answer he truly did not want to hear. "And your name is?"

"Excuse me, my lord. I meant no disrespect. I just assumed the butler had told you. The name's Baxter. Julian Baxter."

Five

Anne remained quite still, watching Michael as he led the gelding around to the front of the house. Only when he was out of sight did she reach up to wipe away the last of her tears. With his kiss still warm upon her lips, she let herself believe that somehow they had a chance for happiness. He had asked her to marry him, and with all her heart she wanted to say yes.

But could she? Did she dare?

Even if Michael never found out that she had lied to him about who she was and why she had come to Herndon Hall, how was she to conquer the anger she felt for the woman he considered his stepmother? If Anne successfully concealed her enmity for Lenore, what would be the cost to her own pride, to her honor?

Assured of only one thing, that she would meet Michael in the garden as she had promised, she began to back out of the narrow window. The opening seemed even smaller than when she had squirmed through it earlier, and as she strove to ease her shoulders and arms free, her left sleeve caught on the lock piece.

With no room to maneuver, Anne had no choice but to continue her backward movement, and the fragile muslin paid the price by ripping from the top of the sleeve all the way to the band beneath the elbow. Her arm was left completely exposed, but at last she was released.

With more important issues to think about than a torn sleeve, Anne closed the window, pushed the lever to return the Gutenberg to its place of safety, and hurried toward the broad staircase. She had only just reached her bedchamber when there was a knock at the door.

Trying to ignore the sound, she muttered, "No. Not now."

This was no time for interruptions, for Anne had only a matter of minutes in which to come to the most important decision of her life. In those minutes she must decide which was most important to her, her possible future with Michael, or her desire to be revenged upon Lenore. Could she pretend that Lenore was not her mother? Could she, like Lenore, forsake her principals for the man she loved?

As much as she wanted the answer to be yes, she knew better. There were some things a person just could not do.

Yet how could she leave Michael? How could she go, when to do so would surely break her heart?

"Miss Baxter. May I come in?"

Without waiting for permission, Lenore pushed the door open and entered the bedchamber. "My dear, I saw you run up the stairs. Has something happened?"

As Anne turned to stare at the woman whose face was completely uncovered at last, all the anguish she felt must have shown in her eyes, for Lenore stepped forward, her hands outstretched.

"You poor child. Anyone can see that you are distressed. Please, will you not say what has occurred? If you allow me, perhaps I can be of help. Believe me, I know what it is to be alone and heartsore."

Unable to look upon the woman's still lovely face, and not wanting to take the proffered hands, Anne turned away. "I cannot talk now."

"But my dear, you are—"

Anne heard a strangled gasp, followed by complete silence. After a moment of such hushed stillness she might almost have thought the woman gone from the room, Anne felt quivering fingers touch her left arm, pulling aside the torn sleeve.

"That scar. I once knew a little girl with such a scar. How . . . how did you get it?"

Anne had dreamed of this moment. In her mind she had rehearsed every line of dialogue. Yet now that the time for retribution had finally come, she stood paralyzed with fear, unable to speak, unable to move.

"Please," Lenore pleaded, "answer me." When Anne said nothing, Lenore caught her arm and turned her around so they were face-to-face.

After searching Anne's green eyes, Lenore's hand went to her throat. She turned ashen, and for a moment Anne thought she might faint.

"Who are you?" Lenore asked, her voice little more than a whisper.

Because her knees shook so badly she thought she might fall, Anne took a step back, leaning her weight against the dressing table. "Who do you suppose me to be?"

Lenore began to shake as if overcome by an ague. "Are you my Anne? Please tell me," she begged. "Are you my little girl?"

From somewhere deep inside her, Anne's anger erupted, gushing out before she could even consider controlling it. "Your little girl? Madam, you have no little girl, nor any right to claim parenthood. One might expect a stray dog that drops her litter on the side of the road to be a better mother than you."

"Enough!" said a deep, enraged voice from just outside the doorway.

In four broad, angry strides Michael was beside Lenore, slipping an arm around her shoulder to support her trembling form. "Come, my dear," he said, "let me take you back to your room."

"No. I must stay, for somehow my child has come to me." Still dazed, she stared at Anne. "This is my little girl. My Anne. After all these years, my prayers have been answered. Do you not see?"

"I see only that you are upset, and you and I both know that such excitement, following so close on your recent illness, may well bring on another of your sick headaches."

Anne watched the man she loved pull Lenore close so that her head rested upon his shoulder, but when he tried to turn her toward the door, she pushed free of his protective arm. "If you love me, Michael, let me go. I must, I *will* speak with my daughter."

Michael let Lenore have her way, though he insisted that she be seated in a slipper chair near the door and allow him to do the talking. "Who this young woman may be," he said, "I cannot even guess. All I know for certain is that she is a consummate liar."

Anne felt as if she had been struck. "Michael, I—"

"Do not think to deceive me further," he said. "You are very skilled, and I must draw what comfort I may from the knowledge that any man might have been misled by your beauty and your seeming innocence and sincerity. But I am not a complete fool. I know now that everything you said was a lie."

"Not everything," she said. "Not when I said I loved you. I meant that with all my heart. You must believe me."

He turned upon her a look cold enough to freeze the fires of Hades. "Believe you? I think not. Better I should believe the gentleman who has only just arrived. Perhaps you know him. I should be surprised if you did not, for his name is Julian Baxter."

A chilling weight not unlike a block of ice settled in Anne's chest. What she had feared had come to pass, for Michael had discovered her subterfuge and now he hated her.

He laughed, but there was no joy in the sound. "No wonder you worked so fast to catch me in your net. Not able to guess how long poor Baxter would be laid up after his injury, you were obliged to move with all speed. Was money your object?"

"If you will only let me," she said, "I can explain everything."

"Of that I have no doubt. A woman of your talent must have several stories ready to hand."

Lenore chose that moment to intervene. "Enough, Michael. I wish to hear what my daughter has to say."

"Your daughter? Ha! Do not be taken in by her innocent looks, my dear. She has a way of telling people what they want to hear."

"But she *is* my daughter."

He shook his head. "I know you would like her to be, and I am sorry to hurt you, but she is not. She is nothing but a charlatan. No doubt she discovered somehow that you have spent the past seventeen years searching for your daughter, and she thought to use the information for her own purposes."

Even through Anne's pain and shock at Michael's anger, his

words penetrated her brain. "Seventeen years? What do you mean, searching?"

"My stepmother was once most cruelly used by a vindictive husband whose wish to control every aspect of her life spurred him to take their child and disappear. I will not let her be hurt again. Not by him and not by you. I suggest you pack your things immediately. In an hour I will have you conveyed to the village, and if you know what is good for you, you will never stop this way again."

Anne looked across the room at Lenore. Her face was ashen, and her lips quivered, yet her eyes held such unbelievable hope that Anne was forced to look away. "My father is dead," she said.

"What?" It was Lenore who spoke. "Roger is dead?"

"My dear," Michael said, "do not say anything more. I am persuaded she will use what information you give her to raise your hopes."

Though his words tore at her soul like the claws of an angry beast, making her want to flee, Anne stood her ground. "My father received your letter," she said. "Then he burned it. Fortunately, enough of it remained that I was able to read this address, so I came to see you. I used Mr. Baxter's name to insure my entrance into the Hall."

Tears filled Lenore's eyes. "My child," she whispered, "you came to find me?"

"I came," Anne continued, "to tell you what I think of a woman who would desert her child."

"Desert!" Michael swore. "Where did you get that crazy idea? From that swine, Roger Carlton?"

"No," she said, looking at Michael. "My father told me that my mother was dead. And until I found what remained of her letter, I had no reason not to believe him."

Lenore began to sob softly. "My poor baby. You must have been so frightened, and so very lonely."

For just a moment Anne felt a pang of pity, though whether it was for the sobbing woman or for the little girl who had often been lonely and frightened, she could not say. To protect herself from the memories, she said, "Yes, I was both those things. Not that I believe you cared for one minute."

"I cared," Lenore said softly. "I cared every minute of every day for seventeen years. I still care. Oh, Anne. I never stopped loving you."

"No! You are just saying that. You found a rich protector, so you must have had money at your disposal. If you had truly loved me, you would have come for me instead of writing a letter to my father." Her heart was torn in two, pulled in one direction by the anger she had harbored, and in the other direction by her desire to believe her mother's words. Anne turned her back, and as if to clear her thoughts, she leaned her forehead against the cool pane of the window.

For a time, the only sound was an occasional sniff from Lenore; then Michael spoke. "I do not believe for one moment that you are Anne Carlton, but just to set the record straight, I will tell you that you are wrong about Mama Lenore. Just as I was wrong about you. Wrong to care for you. Wrong to think you the most wonderful girl in the world."

As if realizing he had gotten off the track, he stopped and took a deep breath. "Mama Lenore spent thousands of pounds searching for her daughter, but each time she thought she had a lead, it would prove false. The child was never her Anne."

It is true, then. Lenore did look for me.

"When I became aide de camp to General McCormick, I finally had a source of military information. I located Roger Carlton, but in deference to my father, who was ill at the time, I did not tell anyone where the fellow was. Carlton's military record was not one of success. According to the reports, he was universally disliked, which is why he never received promotion to major. According to his senior officers, he would not tolerate an opinion opposed to his own, and that pigheadedness alienated him from officers and men alike."

Anne was not surprised by the report. "He was difficult," she said.

"He was cruel!" Michael amended. "He took you—the child, I should say—from her mother. It was an act of vengeance, pure and simple. He did it not because *he* loved the child—I do not believe he knew the meaning of the word—he took her because he knew how much it would hurt the child's mother. Then, once he had her, he hid her someplace where she could not be found, and he went off to war."

Unable to credit his words, Anne turned to look at Lenore.

Lenore nodded her head. "What Michael said is true. Your father took you away while I was gone to the village to post a letter to Michael's mother, Lady Herndon. She was my dearest friend since our school days, and I had written to tell her I could no longer live with my husband and that I was leaving him for good. She knew of Roger's rages and unfounded jealousies, and she had begged me more than once to come to her if I ever needed a safe haven. In the letter I informed her that you and I would be on the next stage to Lamberford."

Lenore put her face in her hands, and when she spoke again, her voice was muffled. "Roger must have discovered my letter, for when I returned to the cottage, you were gone. Your clothes, the little stocking doll I had made you a week earlier for your fifth birthday, everything gone. It was as if every trace of my little girl had been obliterated."

The stocking doll. Hannah. Anne had not thought of the doll in years. Now she remembered how she had clung to the little cloth baby with its yellow yarn hair and its brown button eyes.

That day her father had taken her away on his horse, riding for so many hours she had finally fallen asleep leaning against him in the saddle, Anne had clung to Hannah. And that night, when they stopped at an inn and Roger Carlton told his daughter that her mother was dead, Anne had held that little rag baby to her heart for comfort, not knowing what else to do, not knowing where else to turn.

Between bouts of silent tears—silent because her father grew more irritated each time she cried—Anne took deep breaths, smelling the doll, fancying she could still detect on the cloth the aroma of lemon verbena from her mother's hands. For weeks she had worn the doll inside her shift, afraid she might lose it—afraid she might lose the only link she had with her mother.

"I remember the doll," Anne said, the words sounding strained, almost tear-choked.

"You named her Hannah," Lenore replied. She lowered her hands from her face, revealing eyes that were dulled by a memory too painful to endure.

"For weeks after Roger took you away, I went from town to town, asking anyone who would stop if they had seen a little dark-haired girl carrying a stocking doll. I must have appeared demented, for people began to shun me, to move away if I came too close. I know I could not have been in my right mind, so desperate as I felt, so anguished for want of my child."

Michael knelt beside Lenore's chair and took her hand. "You were ill for a long time," he said, as if she might not remember. "I recall how frantic my mother became when you did not arrive on the promised stage. After a week had passed and you still had not come to us, she sent Father to find you."

"I do not remember that," Lenore said.

"No," he said, "you were much too ill. For days after he brought you to the Hall, you said almost nothing. Those few times when you spoke at all it was to call for Anne."

He looked up at Anne. "Your father was a cruel, vindictive man, and I hope he has received his just reward. If so, he is even now breathing the sulphured fumes of hell."

Anne wanted to say something in her father's defense, but she could not. "He was very unhappy," she said. "I knew he did not love me, but I always thought it was something lacking in me. I thought it was *me* he did not like."

Lenore shook her head. "It was not you, my sweet. It was himself he did not like. Happiness, love, caring for others, all those qualities come from within a person. If those qualities are missing, then the person cannot love himself. And he who cannot love himself cannot love others."

As if prodded by some unseen hand, Anne felt herself crossing the room to where Lenore sat in the slipper chair. Lenore Carlton, her mother. Lenore, the woman who had been searching for her for seventeen years.

She paused mere inches from the chair, not certain what she

should do next. Because she could not stop herself, however, she reached out and placed a hand on Lenore's shoulder. "I am sorry," she whispered.

Lenore laid her cheek against that hand; then with a sob, she caught Anne's fingers and turned her face so her lips were pressed into her daughter's palm. Again and again she kissed Anne's palm, her fingers, her hand, as though to make up for all the years between the last kiss and that moment. "My sweet Anne," she cried. "My little girl. I knew one day I would see you again."

When Anne could withstand it no longer, she knelt down beside Lenore's chair. Tears all but closed her throat, but somehow she managed to speak. "I am not a little girl any longer," she said. "Is that all right?"

A sob escaped Lenore. "You will always be my little girl," she said, then she took Anne in her arms, holding her as if she meant never to let her go.

Six

The next five days sped by, with Anne and Lenore spending almost every minute together. They had so much to say. So much to hear. And so much to learn about one another. To have a mother again was wonderful, and Anne could not express the joy she felt each morning when she awoke knowing her mother was in the next room, near enough to see, near enough to touch, near enough love.

There was but one sad note in those five days, and it very nearly broke Anne's heart. Michael had taken himself off somewhere so he need not be in the same house with her. He had finally admitted—to Lenore, though not to Anne—that he believed her to be Lenore's child. Unfortunately, he could not forgive Anne for her deception, for the story she told to gain entrance to Herndon Hall. It was her one and only fib, yet because of it, Michael did not believe her when she tried to tell him that she did, truly, love him.

Of course, she had only had one opportunity to speak with him, for he took himself off almost immediately. Now it was time for her to return to Dover, to her position as instructress at the Misses Thwaite's Academy for Young Ladies, and Michael had not returned.

"Please," Lenore begged, "stay here. You need not go. Send a letter to Miss Thwaite, for I am persuaded she will say that your place is with your family."

Anne shook her head. As much as she wanted to stay, she could not. Not as long as Michael hated her. He would return in time, it was his home after all, and loving him as she did, she would be unable to look at him every day, knowing that he no longer loved her.

"I cannot stay," she said. "As much as I should like to, it is impossible."

Her mother had finally agreed that Anne must do what she thought best, so after breakfast Anne packed her portmanteau in preparation to catch the afternoon stagecoach to Dover. Lenore was to accompany her to Lamberford in the gig, but before she left, Anne wanted to see the hollow again where the moated manor house stood, the place where she had discovered that she loved Michael Herndon.

As before, she walked across the expanse of lush green countryside, past the many thick ancient trees, and up and down the sheep paths. Only this time there was no Michael with her to hold her hand and to tease her about the mysterious place they were bound.

And this time, when she spied the copse of poplars, there was no one to run with her, pulling her along until they reached the beautiful silver-green trees, nor anyone to marvel at the scene before them in the quiet, secluded hollow.

As before, the ancient manor house was enveloped in silence, silence made even more complete by the phenomenon of frost hollow. The night before, cold air had flowed down the hillside to accumulate on the valley bottom, and when it warmed after dawn, it rose to meet more cold air, the result being low-lying fog.

Unfortunately, the fog hung just above the water of the moat, all but obscuring it, and if the white swans swam about as before, Anne could not see them. Recalling the joy she had felt the last time she had stood thus, looking down at the moat, with Michael beside her, it was not to be wondered at that tears began to spill down her cheeks.

"Frost hollow," she said, swiping the tears away with the back of her hand.

"Are you certain," said a deep voice from somewhere to her right.

Anne turned to look toward the broad horse-chestnut tree under whose shade Michael had left their picnic when they came here before. He sat on the ground very near the tree, his left knee bent and his elbow resting upon it. The golden chestnut gelding that had frightened Anne the day she arrived stood several feet away, munching peacefully on a patch of dark green grass.

"I did not know you would be here," she said.

"Nor I you," he replied. "I came here to think. To see if my mind would be clearer in my special place."

"And is it? Clearer, I mean."

He shook his head. "Life can be complicated," he said.

She nodded. "I just came to tell the swans good-bye."

At her words, he rose suddenly, the movement quick and purposeful, and came toward her. When he drew near, she looked away.

"What do you mean, *good-bye?*"

"I shall be leaving in an hour. My mother means to accompany me to Lamberford where I will catch the afternoon coach to Dover, but I wanted to stop by here first."

"To say your farewells to the swans," he said for her.

She nodded.

"And what of me?" he asked, the words clipped as if he was angry. "Had you plans to take your leave of me? Or did you mean merely to go as you had come, without warning?"

She still did not look at him, she could not. "I thought you were gone from home; otherwise, I would not have dreamed of leaving without bidding farewell to the master of the house."

"Master of the house be damned!"

At his sharp words, Anne turned at last to look at him. He was even handsomer than she remembered, and the sight of him took her breath away. The wind had blown a lock of black hair across his forehead, and the blue riding coat he wore—the same one he had worn the first time she saw him—turned his dark blue eyes the color of the sea.

"Why are you leaving?" he asked.

"Why? Because I cannot stay. You must see that."

"Must I?"

Anne did not know how to answer him. "You cannot want me here."

"I cannot?"

She wanted to scream. Why must he answer all her comments with a question? Never good at docility, she spoke rather sharply. "You know you do not. Your last words to me were scathing in the extreme, and you left me in no doubt as to your disgust of me. If it had not been for my mother, I believe you would have caught me by the scruff of the neck and tossed me out physically."

"Like this, do you mean?"

He stepped very close, and before she realized what he meant to do, he reached out and slipped his hand around her neck, moving slowly until his long, supple fingers were threaded in the hair at her nape. His touch was mesmerizingly gentle.

"Then what would I have done?" he asked, his breath soft and warm upon her face.

Anne felt the heat of his body from her toes all the way to her scalp, and as she looked up into his eyes, she thought she might swoon from the passion she saw there, passion only just held in check. "Michael," she whispered, "I . . ."

"You?" he repeated; then his thumb began to stroke her earlobe in a way that drove all thought from her mind.

She swallowed with difficulty. "I want to know what you are doing."

"I thought it was obvious," he said quietly. "I am throwing you out." Having said this, he bent down and rubbed his cheek against hers. "Did I ever tell you how much I like your skin? Or that it feels just like silk?"

"No," she replied breathlessly, "you never did."

"What about your nose?" he asked, sliding his lips from the bridge down to the tip, the movement whisper soft. "It is awfully pert. Surely I remarked upon that."

"No," she said, her heart beating so loudly she could hear it in her own ears. "I think I would have remembered if you had."

"And your lips?" he asked, his voice suddenly husky. "Did we ever discuss those?"

Anne's knees seemed to lose their ability to hold her up, and she would have fallen if Michael had not slipped his other arm around her waist and brought her close against his chest. Of its own volition, the tip of her tongue came out to moisten her lips, and as it circled her mouth, she heard him inhale sharply.

"If you do that again," he said, "I shall be forced to kiss you."

"Shall you?"

Never one to back down from a threat, she started to repeat her former action. She had only just touched the tip of her tongue to her top lip when the strong hand behind her neck urged her forward and Michael covered her mouth with his.

For what seemed a lifetime, he kissed her, and when he finally lifted his head, Anne felt tears upon her cheeks once again. Only this time, the tears were an overflow of the joy in her heart.

"There is that frost hollow thing again," he said, gently kissing the tears away. "Perhaps I should take you home where the air is warmer."

Anne did not ever remember being warmer than she was at that particular moment, but she was willing to go any place with him.

"Your mother will be happy to know that you are not leaving today."

She looked up into his dark blue eyes. "I am not?"

He shook his head. "No. Not today."

Anne dared to hope that he was saying he wanted her to stay, but she needed to hear the words. "If not today, when?"

"Oh, I cannot say for sure. In twenty or thirty years perhaps. I could not possibly part with you in less time."

"Oh, Michael, I want to stay with you."

"In that case, my love, perhaps I had better give you this. You did say you would wear it."

He reached inside the small pocket of his waistcoat and withdrew a delicate gold ring bearing a large emerald set in the midst of a circle of diamonds. "It was my mother's," he said, "and if memory serves me, you promised to wear it."

"Yes," she said, "and I try always to keep my promises."

He took her left hand and slipped the ring on her third finger, then after allowing her a moment to admire the effect, he took her in his arms once again, drawing her close. "And now, my sweet wild flower, how do you suggest we seal the bargain?"

"Hmmm," she said, as if giving the matter serious consideration. "Let me think a moment. How should such a bargain be sealed?" Though it was not in the least necessary to assist her brain, she touched the tip of her tongue to her lips.

"Oh, yes," Michael said. "My thoughts exactly." Then without further ado, he claimed her lips for his own.

The Virtues of Patience

Carol Quinto

For my mother with love
on Mother's Day

One

Althea's dark lashes fluttered open. Drowsily, she glanced across the room. Slivers of sunlight seeped between the edges of the pale rose curtains, but Katie had not yet brought in the breakfast tray, nor stirred the dying embers in the huge fireplace. It must still be early, Althea thought, and wished she had not wakened so soon. It made the day unbearably long.

Positioning several pillows behind her, she sat up in the four-poster bed. There was no point in trying to recapture sleep. She never could in the mornings. Sighing, she ran her hand down her thigh, kneading the skin in an effort to relieve the ache that felt as if it came from within her bones. The pain was relentless. She could no longer remember a time when she was without it.

Tempted, Althea eyed the bottle of laudanum sitting on her bedside table. She knew a few drops of the tincture of opium would provide her some relief—but she also knew it would leave her feeling too lethargic to get out of bed. She tried to distract her thoughts from the pain. Of course, she could ring for Katie, but the maid would realize her mistress hadn't slept again, and she would worry. Worse, she would tell Gregory.

Althea's blue eyes widened as she thought of her son. *That* was why she'd unconsciously awoken early. Gregory had promised to return to Norwick today, and he always kept his promises. Particularly those he made to his mother.

Thinking of her son, Althea smiled, and the smile eased the tiny lines of pain had etched about her eyes and around the corners of her mouth. She looked suddenly younger, more like the girl Brummell had once deemed the toast of London. Her deep blue eyes were still heavily lashed, and she possessed the sort of bone structure that only improved with the passing years. Even her hair, a pale delicate blond, had not grayed like that of so many women, but was shot with streaks of pure silver. Her son claimed it made her look like an angel. Althea dismissed such talk as nonsense, but it was true. And when she smiled, her age and her infirmity were nearly forgotten.

When Katie carried in the breakfast tray, she noticed the change in her mistress at once. As she settled the tray across Althea's slender body, she said, "Good morning, Your Grace. No need to ask if you slept well because you look pretty as a picture. Just like a young girl."

"You exaggerate, Katie, but thank you," Althea replied, reaching for the delicate china cup. She cradled it in her hands, savoring its warmth, and said happily, "Gregory is coming home today."

The maid nodded. "You needn't worry, Your Grace. Everything is in readiness. The master won't be finding nothing to complain about."

Althea watched the girl as she drew open the curtains, gathered up a crumpled dressing gown, and retrieved a pair of slippers from beneath the bed. She sipped her tea, then asked idly, "Does he complain often, Katie?"

"I suppose no more than any other man," the maid answered tactfully. She was fond of the duchess, and like the rest of the household, she knew how much her mistress adored her only son. Katie might carp about the duke below stairs, but she'd bite her tongue off before uttering a word of criticism of him to the duchess.

Althea sighed. Gregory was respected by the staff and tenants at Norwick, but he wasn't beloved. Not like his father, or his grandfather, or even herself. And it was unfair. Her son had so many wonderful qualities, but an aura of reserve about him made him seem distant, almost arrogant. Even her sister, Cecilia, often commented on it. Althea remembered the letter she'd received last week, full of amusing gossip about her four nephews.

Cecilia had written she was nearly at wits' end to know what to do about her sons' exploits, and had added, "You are so fortunate, my dear Althea, in having a son like Gregory, whom I am very certain never gives you a moment's worry. To be sure, he is a paragon. But there, I should not complain for I know that whatever mischief my darling boys evoke, 'tis merely due to an excess of high spirits. And they have grown into such charming gentlemen, so well liked and admired, that they are invariably forgiven by all who know them."

The letter had been typical of Cecilia. She often pretended to complain of her sons, but there was no doubting she was proud of them, and that she felt sorry for her sister whose only son was so staid, so respectable, so responsible, he never caused the least trouble. And what vexed Althea most, was that she feared her sister was right. Gregory was *too* reserved, too lacking in any emotion, to be universally liked. Even the matchmaking mothers did not chase after the Duke of Norwick the way they did her nephews—and Gregory was a much better catch. His fortune was considerable, he was darkly handsome, and he certainly outranked his cousins.

"Your Grace?" Katie said hesitantly, afraid the pain the duchess suffered had worsened. She looked tired now, drawn. "Do you wish to dress today?"

The quicksilver smile was back, the eyes full of amusement. "Of course, Katie. I cannot allow Gregory to find me lolling in bed. He treats me as an invalid now, and we must not encourage him. Bring me the blue morning dress—the one with the lace trim."

Katie knew which gown the duchess meant. Although it was perhaps two or three years old, it was still fashionable with its tiny puffed sleeves and low-cut bodice. And, of course, it still fit perfectly. Her Grace had neither gained nor lost more than a pound or two in the five years Katie had been at Norwick. Filbert, the butler who had served the family for as long as anyone could recall, told her the duchess was still just as slender as she was the day the duke first brought her to the abbey as his bride.

Too slender, Katie thought, as she laid out the clothes her

mistress would require. She didn't eat enough to keep a sparrow alive. Of course it was just as well because if she gained weight, she'd have to have new clothes, and there was nothing Her Grace loathed more than the bother of fittings or having a seamstress fuss over her. She, who could well afford to order a new dress for every day of the year, could rarely be persuaded to have a modiste call. There was little need, the duchess said. She never left the abbey, and in the last few years, rarely received visitors.

A pity, Katie thought, as she helped the duchess to dress. It was a long, and tiring process. Her Grace could stand for no more than a minute or two, and even sitting in the specially made wheelchair her son had ordered for her, often aggravated the pain in her back. Katie worked as swiftly as possible. The duchess wore her hair simply, pulled back into a becoming coil at the base of her neck. This morning, perhaps because her son was coming, Althea allowed the maid to lace a blue silk ribbon through the blond strands, but she refused the earbobs and necklaces Katie suggested.

Still, she looked elegant and every inch the aristocrat, the maid thought as she stepped back to admire her work.

The duchess laughed at her. "No need to fuss so, Katie. 'Tis only Gregory who will see me, and I doubt he will notice what I am wearing. You may wheel me into the sitting room."

The maid obeyed, but she privately thought Her Grace was mistaken. The duke noticed everything about his mother, and if he thought she had been neglected in any way, his wrath would fall swiftly on those responsible. Katie had been on the receiving end of one of his scolds when he'd come home unexpectedly and found his mother still in bed, dark circles beneath her eyes from a particularly restless night. The duke had been incensed that the doctor had not been called, or medication given to his mother to ease her pain. It did no good to tell him that the duchess had refused both. Thank heavens she looked well this morning. He would have no cause for complaint. At least, Katie prayed not.

She wheeled the duchess into the sitting room adjoining her bedchamber. It had previously been another bedchamber, but because the duchess had difficulty with the stairs, the duke had converted it into a fashionable salon where the duchess now spent most of her time. She liked to sit by the long windows that lined the south wall. They overlooked the sweeping lawns at the front of the abbey, and from there she could see Gregory's carriage the moment he turned into the tree-lined drive.

Katie brought the duchess her sewing basket, positioning it within easy reach of the chair. Her eyes swept the room, making certain all was in perfect order before the duke's arrival. The polished wood glistened in the morning sunlight, fresh flowers stood on the mahogany center table, and the fire burned cheerfully. Three new novels rested on the inlaid table next to Her Grace's chair, and a Norwick shawl was draped over the footstool in case she felt chilled. Satisfied, Katie asked, "Is there anything I can get for you, Your Grace?"

Althea, with one of her soft smiles, shook her head. "Thank you, but no. I shall do fine until Gregory arrives. I suppose 'tis silly to be so excited. He has only been gone two months, but it seems much longer."

Not to me, Katie thought, but she curtsied and left Her Grace to wait for her son.

The duke arrived at one that afternoon, precisely on schedule. Althea, watching his carriage sweep up the drive, wondered if her son was ever late. Not that she wished him to be. Punctuality must naturally be accounted a virtue . . . but if he just once forgot his schedule, just once gave into an impulse, it would make him more . . . more human. Traitorous thoughts for a mother to have, Althea scolded herself.

It was all Cecilia's fault. She'd written that her son Anthony, who'd recently proposed to Lady Ann Sedgewick, and been accepted, had actually forgotten to attend a supper in honor of his betrothal. Lady Ann had been embarrassed, her parents irate, and Cecilia mortified. Anthony had appeared the following day, all smiles and charm, and apologized profusely. He'd been detained by a friend who had required his services in an affair of honor. Althea had laughed when she'd read the letter. It was just like

Carol Quinto

her nephew, but a nagging thought had prompted her to compare him to her own son. Gregory, of course, would never participate in a duel. Duels were illegal. Nor would he ever forget such an important engagement as a betrothal supper. Of the two young men, her son was the one to be admired, and yet it was Anthony whom everyone adored. Althea couldn't help wishing that occasionally Gregory would behave with some of his cousin's impulsiveness, and forgo some of his dignity.

Such thoughts were immediately forgotten when her son strode into her fitting room. He was taller than most men, and his broad shoulders and trim waist owed nothing to padding or corsets.

"Mother, how are you?" he asked, bending to kiss her cheek. His eyes, a blue several shades darker than her own, studied her with concern.

Althea's heart warmed. How foolish she was to wish to change her son when he was so nearly perfect! She reached up and brushed a lock of dark hair from his brow—the only sign of disarray about his immaculate person. His bottle green coat was without embellishment but was well cut of the finest kerseymere. His tan breeches molded his muscular thighs without the slightest wrinkle, and the highly polished black boots reflected back her own image.

"How handsome you look," she said impulsively.

His dark brows arched as he stepped back. They were not a family given to idle compliments, and he eyed her curiously. "Are you feeling feverish, Mother? I cannot otherwise account for such a statement."

"You are far too modest, Gregory. I know any number of people who consider you an extraordinarily handsome man. Why, even your Aunt Cecilia has often said she wishes your cousins had your height and bearing."

He accepted the cup of tea she poured for him, then took the chair next to her, stretching out his long legs. After tasting the tea, he replied ruefully, "I suppose my aunt also wishes that Anthony or Edward's face be deformed by a scar as mine is."

"Deformed? That is certainly an exaggeration. One hardly

notices the scar," she protested, referring to the jagged cut that ran from beneath his right eye to just below his ear. It had faded with the years, and she was so accustomed to it that she never gave it a second thought.

Gregory fingered the old scar, a memento from his boyhood when he'd fallen from the barn loft and laid his cheek open on a rusted blade. He'd been fortunate not to lose his eye. The disfigurement rarely bothered him. He was not vain, and he seldom thought of it, but he'd too often seen the look of morbid fascination in the eyes of strangers. Most were too polite to say anything, but that didn't stop them from staring.

He glanced at his mother over the rim of his cup, and said dryly, "People do notice."

"If they do, then they probably think it makes you look very dashing," she retorted.

"Dashing? You are very fulsome with the compliments today, Mother. I suppose the scarcity of company at Norwick must make anyone seem appealing to you. However, if we are to talk of appearances, I must say you look exceptionally charming in that gown. Blue always did become you." It was the truth, but he had not missed the pale shadows beneath her eyes, or the way her hand involuntarily rubbed against her leg—a sign that the pain was troubling her. With concern, he asked, "Are you tired? Shall I allow you to rest?"

She stretched out a hand to him. "No, do not go. It has been so long since I've seen you, I am sure that is a better tonic for me than all of Dr. Chamberlain's tonics. And I wish to hear what you have been doing. Who did you see in Town?"

It was always the same when he returned from one of his trips. She questioned him about every acquaintance he met, every affair he attended, and always with the hope that this time he had met a young lady, a lady he might one day ask to be the Duchess of Norwick. In the last few years, his mother had often brought up the question of his marriage. She pointed out that he was getting older and it was past time he set up his nursery.

Gregory knew she was right. He had no inclination to wed, but he was well aware that it was his duty to the family to provide an heir to protect the title and the estates. He smiled now, anticipating the surprise he was about to give his mother.

Althea, watching him, thought that few women would be able to resist her son if he smiled in just that way. It warmed his eyes and softened the sharp planes of his face. Aloud she said, "What is it? You are looking excessively pleased."

"Ah, I have a surprise for you—one which I think you will well like."

"What is it?" Althea demanded again, her eyes lighting with pleasure. She loved surprises, and Gregory frequently brought her back a token of some sort from his trips, a figurine or painting, or some exquisite piece of jewelry. The opal ring she wore, set in gold and encrusted with diamonds, had been one of his gifts. Whatever he'd brought back today, must be equally small for she'd seen no signs of a parcel or box.

He watched her, amused by her excitement. His mother was extraordinarily easy to please, and he suspected his decision would delight her. Aloud, he said, "I have given much thought to what you have said, Mother, regarding my marriage—"

"Gregory! Have you offered for someone? Who is she? Do I know the family?"

He laughed, holding up a hand in mock defense. "You go too fast, Mother. Do you truly think I would offer for a lady without discussing it with you first? After all, whomever I wed will share this house with you, and—"

"No," she interrupted firmly, shaking her head. "When you marry I shall remove to the dower house just as your grandmother did when I came to the Abbey as a bride. A house can have only one mistress, Gregory."

"The cases are very different," he protested. "The dower house would be extremely difficult for you to negotiate in your chair, and the rooms are too small. Think of all the stairs—no, I will not allow it. You will stay here where you belong, and where you can be comfortable. As for my bride, I am certain she will understand. Indeed, Mother, I hope that the lady I ultimately choose for my wife will also become your devoted daughter. That is why I need your help in making my decision."

He paused and withdrew a folded sheet of paper from his pocket. With a rare show of hesitancy, he tapped it against his knee as he sought for words to explain his plan. Finally, he said, "I have narrowed my choice to six ladies whom I think may prove suitable. Naturally, they all possess the necessary breeding and deportment."

Althea accepted the list he handed her, and quickly read the names. She recognized several of the families, but it had been years since she had moved in polite Society, and these girls would have been still in the nursery or schoolroom. She knew nothing of them, and glanced at her son, confusion in her eyes. "I am not certain I understand you, Gregory. 'Tis absurd, of course, but one might almost think you were asking me to choose your bride."

"Not entirely," he said, smiling at her. "But naturally I would not wish to wed anyone with whom you did not feel entirely comfortable. What I propose is that you invite these ladies, one at a time, to Norwick, so that you may become acquainted with them. Such a visit will also give us the opportunity to judge how well they would adapt to our household."

His voice was entirely reasonable, his manner detached. Althea stared at him. Did her son not realize how he sounded? That what he proposed was arrogant?

Gregory saw the astonishment in his mother's eyes, but misjudging the reason, he assured her, "I realize you are not physically capable of entertaining a houseful of guests, but these visits will be quite informal—just the girl and her parents, and I shall make certain they understand your situation. If you think it advisable, we might even ask one of my aunts or cousins to come and act as my official hostess."

Avoiding his gaze, Althea fussed with the teapot. His concern for her was endearing, but his utter lack of regard for his future wife disturbed her greatly. As she freshened her cup, she asked lightly, "Have you spoken to any of these young ladies, Gregory? Are they aware that they are being . . . considered as your possible bride?"

"No, of course not," he replied, a touch annoyed that his

mother did not understand what he hoped to accomplish. "Naturally, I am somewhat acquainted with each of them. They were all at Almack's, and at various other affairs I attended while in Town. One meets the same people everywhere. Surely, you remember what London is like during the Season?"

"Yes, of course. I am not putting this very well, but what I am trying to say is that you seem to be approaching your nuptials in much the same manner you would seek a new hunter. Have you given *any* thought to the young ladies' feelings? I should think it not entirely inconceivable that one or more of them may not wish to wed you."

"Not wish to be the Duchess of Norwick?" he mocked, his dark brows raised. "Not wish to have a position of rank and wealth? I doubt very much that will prove to be a problem, Mother. Indeed, I would own myself astonished if even one of these ladies refused our invitation."

Perhaps he was right. Althea remembered her own parents' elation when the duke had called on her father. For any of these girls, an offer from the present Duke of Norwick would be a feather in her cap. Even if she were not enamored of Gregory, her parents would most likely urge her to accept his offer. Still, her son's cynicism and calm assumption that he had only to make his choice disturbed her.

Glancing at the list again, Althea said softly, "You say you are a little acquainted with these ladies, Gregory. I gather that means you have danced with them, and conversed with them?" When he nodded, she continued, "Then may I ask if you have formed a partiality for one of them?"

"No. To be honest, Mother, there is little to choose between them. However, Lady Anne is at the top of my list. She is considered a diamond of the first water, and even her most severe critic would own she has beauty and grace, but I confess I found her conversation a trifle boring." He considered the matter, then added fairly, "Of course it may have merely been the circumstances under which we met."

"And Lady Barbara?" Althea asked, mentioning the second name on the list.

He smiled and confided, "I almost did not include her. She is not a beauty like Anne, but still there is something about her that draw's one's attention, and I found her to be rather witty. She has a droll sense of humor. I think you might enjoy her company."

Althea merely nodded and struggled to decipher the next name on his list. "Claudia Yarborough?"

"Miss Yarborough is both pretty and uncommonly intelligent. I spent a pleasurable hour talking with her at Lady Jersey's salon. I don't believe I have ever met a lady so conversant with political affairs. I think Sally Jersey considers her a sort of protégée. 'Tis unfortunate that her family is unexceptional, and I doubt she has more than a thousand pounds a year, but still I think she might make an admirable duchess. I shall be interested to hear your opinion of her."

Althea laid the list aside. Nothing Gregory had said indicated his feelings were in any way engaged. This was not the sort of marriage she wished for her son. She sighed and unconsciously rubbed her hand over her thigh.

Gregory noticed the gesture and rose at once. He moved swiftly behind her chair, his hands on the crossbar before she could object. "I have obviously tired you. Allow me take you back to your room."

"You did not tire me," she protested.

But her voice was weak and Gregory had seen the pain in her eyes. He silently cursed himself for being a fool. Aloud, he said, "It is my news that has disturbed you. I should not have sprung it on you in such a manner. I do apologize, Mother, but I thought you would be pleased—"

She reached up to clasp his hand in hers. "You have nothing to apologize for, and I *am* pleased that you have decided to wed, but let us discuss it on the morrow."

"Of course, Mother."

When he had positioned her chair by the window as she requested, and made certain she had everything at hand she desired, he bent to kiss her brow, then took his leave. Althea watched him go with mixed feelings. In some ways, he was very like his father. She'd wager that to those who did not know either man well, there must seem little to choose between them. But to those who had been intimates of the third Duke of Norwick, it was readily apparent that the son lacked his father's generosity of spirit and his warm heart.

Lacked it, Althea wondered, or was he merely untouched as yet?

The following afternoon the duchess was seated at her dressing table, allowing Katie to put the finishing touches to her coiffure. Althea had spent a restless night and it showed in the faint shadows beneath her eyes, but she had insisted on rising and planned to join her son for tea.

When a tap sounded on the door, she half-turned, expecting Gregory. She was surprised when the butler stepped into the room, for he rarely had occasion to come above stairs. "Yes, Filbert, what is it?"

"I beg pardon for disturbing you, Your Grace, but you have visitors."

"Indeed?" Althea asked, surprised. She was no longer "at home" to guests. Her old friends, knowing of her illness, never called, and her family visited Norwick only at her express invitation.

"Lady Cheswick and Miss Cheswick," the butler elaborated. "She says she is your cousin."

Astonished, Althea ordered her guests shown to the drawing room, sending her apologies that she would be delayed in receiving them. She vaguely recalled Hermione. The woman was a cousin, very distant, but Althea had not seen her in over twenty years. Even then, they had not been close. Hermione was a few years younger, and from an impoverished branch of the family. The last Althea had heard, her cousin had married a wealthy baron and moved to the north of England. She had written occasionally to Aunt Agatha, but it had been some years since they had heard from her. What, Althea wondered curiously, had brought Hermione to Norwick?

The duchess dressed with assistance from Katie, and an hour later was wheeled into the drawing room.

Lady Cheswick, seated on the serpentine sofa with her elder daughter beside her, was reminiscing about her girlhood. She heard the door open and turned to greet her cousin. The welcoming words died on her lips as she stared in shock at the sight of the wheelchair. She recovered her poise after a moment, rose, and with outstretched hands, crossed to greet her cousin. "Althea, my dear, what has happened? Have you suffered an accident?"

The duchess, who loathed pity, took the proffered hands and managed a smile as she replied, "I fear 'tis mostly the effects of advancing age, but you are looking very well. Do be seated. Is this your daughter?"

"My oldest," Hermione said with a bit of pride. "Patience, make your bow to your cousin."

The girl obeyed. There was only a slight resemblance between the pair. Hermione was tiny and had grown plump with age. There was a pinched look about her thin lips that spoke of troubles borne, and her once black hair had thinned and was streaked with gray. But her daughter was tall and willowy and moved with a fluid gracefulness her mother had never known. A cloud of burnished dark brown hair framed her delicate heart-shaped face. She had a small, turned-up nose and a wide, generous mouth. Althea decided it was the girl's eyes that resembled her mother's—brown eyes, but hers were larger and more expressive—and at the moment they seemed to hold a trace of embarrassment.

"Do be seated," the duchess said, seeking to put the girl at ease.

But Patience turned to her mother and said softly. "We must not stay, Mama. It is an intrusion that—"

Hermione hushed her and laughingly turned to the duchess. "My daughter has a very poor notion of what it means to be family. As though I could possibly be in Suffolk without stopping to see my favorite cousin. And I am very glad I did. If you are ill, Althea, then 'tis well for you to have family about to help care for you."

Althea did not mention that she had neither seen nor heard from her "favorite cousin" in more than twenty years, but said only, "Of course I am very happy to see you, and you must stay and take a cup of tea. Tell me what brings you to Norwick?"

Hermione smiled smugly and patted her daughter's hand. "It is due to my dear Patience. I wrote to Aunt Agatha, but I gather she did not tell you that I, too, am now a widow? Yes, 'tis sadly true. I lost my dear Henry last year, and suffered such bouts of melancholy that Patience thought a journey might do much to restore my spirits."

Her daughter looked embarrassed at this revelation, and Althea shrewdly deduced that it was Hermione who had insisted on the visit. She poured tea for her guests, then said, "I seem to recall Aunt Agatha writing that you had several children?"

"Yes, my dear, and how sad that we have so lost touch that you are not acquainted with my girls. You would like them very much I am sure. Prudence has just turned sixteen, Silence is fifteen, and my little Temperance is fourteen. I wish I could have brought all my daughters, for they are such a comfort to me, but alas, it could not be."

"All girls," Althea commented softly. She knew well the inheritance laws of England and began to suspect the reason for Hermione's sudden visit.

"A distant cousin of Papa's inherited the estate," Patience said, correctly guessing what the duchess was thinking. Resentment flared in her eyes. "He never saw the place in his life! He knows nothing of the land or the tenants and will likely make a mull of—"

"My dear, you quite forget yourself," Hermione interrupted hastily, and laid a warning hand on her daughter's. To Althea, she said, "Pray forgive her for speaking so. Patience was extremely close to her Papa, and he often consulted her on estate matters." She gave a forced laugh and added, "I daresay my girl here knows more of horses and crops than she does of beaux."

What could one say to such a comment, Althea wondered.

Fortunately, the door swung open and Gregory strode into the room. He had been riding when the Cheswicks arrived, but Filbert had told him of the unexpected guests as soon as he returned to the house. Concerned that his mother not be troubled with visitors, he had come immediately to the drawing room. His expression was not welcoming.

"Gregory," Althea said with one of her quick smiles, "I am glad you are home. Come and meet my guests." She performed the introductions swiftly, but even learning that the visitors were distant relations did little to soften the duke's obvious annoyance.

Hermione, who had not thought twice about addressing the duchess informally, hesitated to take such liberties with the duke. She was not easily intimidated, but there was a formidable air about him. Patience, sitting quietly beside her mother, took measure of his grace and decided she did not care for his manner. When he condescended to address her, her reply was as cool and nearly as incivil as his.

Althea, dismayed by the tension in the room, poured a cup of tea for her son, and said, "Was it not kind of my cousin to call? I have been much entertained."

Gregory saw the appeal in her eyes and made an effort to be polite. He listened courteously as Hermione explained the reason for her journey, and offered his condolences on the loss of her husband. He spoke little to Miss Cheswick, but he was aware of her perusal and sensed her dislike. Unconsciously, his hand fingered the scar beneath his eye.

When an hour had passed and the Cheswicks showed no inclination to leave, he turned to his mother. "I know you have enjoyed seeing your cousin again, but I can see you are tired. Perhaps it is time you rested. I am sure Lady Cheswick will understand."

"I am not that tired, Gregory," Althea replied dryly. "Pray do not fuss."

Hermione, all solicitous care, leaned across and patted her cousin's hand. "You must not stand on ceremony with me, dear Althea. After all, we are family. If there is aught I can do?"

"Thank you, but no," the duchess answered.

Gregory tried another tactic and asked, "Are you staying in the area Lady Cheswick?"

Hermione laughed. Lifting her hands in a helpless manner, she confessed, "Alas, we had hoped to spend a few days at Norwick . . ."

Patience blushed. Her mother's plan had been to spend several weeks with her cousin in the hope that the duchess would help find a suitable husband for her eldest daughter. But that was before they knew about Althea's illness. Patience, knowing full well what the duke would think, twisted her gloved hands in her lap and longed to escape from the room.

Althea, observing the girl's embarrassment, felt sorry for her. Impulsively, she leaned forward and said to her cousin, "Of course you must stay at Norwick. Indeed, I shall be glad of the company, and it will give us a chance to become reacquainted."

"Well, if you insist," Hermione replied before her daughter could foolishly decline the invitation. "We put up at a little inn just north of the village, but I own the accommodations are not what one would like."

"That settles it, then, does it not? We shall be pleased to have you stay."

She spoke for both her and her son—only Gregory did not look in the least pleased.

Two

The duke, his temper growing increasingly short, tolerated the guests for four days. He doubted Hermione's fondness for her "favorite cousin" as she so often referred to the duchess, and he worried that the visit would prove too great a hardship for his mother. Nor was he pacified by the presence of Patience. He agreed with his mother that she was a pretty enough girl, but commented sarcastically that "pretty is as pretty does." In his opinion Miss Cheswick was entirely too opinionated and outspoken.

As a courtesy he had driven her on a tour of the estate. Most guests were impressed by the vastness and abundance that comprised Norwick, but Miss Cheswick had only seen much to criticize. She'd found fault with everything from the layout of the stables to the production of the home farm. And she had not hesitated to put forth suggestions for improvements.

When he'd complained of her interference, his mother said kindly that Patience only meant to be helpful. Gregory retorted that he did not require her help, but Althea suspected that what rankled most was that Patience's ideas contained a certain amount of good sense. Had they come from his steward, or any other gentleman, Gregory might have implemented her suggestions. But he did not take advice from a female. Ladies, in his opinion, were meant to see to the household, not interfere in the tenant farms or stables where they had no business!

But even when his guest busied herself within the house, he was displeased. On Thursday, he learned that Miss Cheswick had visited the stillroom and prepared a tisane for his mother—a

herbal potion that she insisted would do much to ease the pain
the duchess suffered. How dare she, he fumed, as he dressed for
supper that evening. He had the very best physicians in atten-
dance on his mother. He did not need some country girl with her
homemade remedies quacking her, and so he would tell Miss
Cheswick. He went down to supper in a black mood, his brows
drawn ominously together, his eyes glinting with suppressed
fury.

Miss Cheswick appeared not to notice. She chattered through
the first removes, and when she drew little response from the
duke, she directed most of her remarks to her mother. Lady
Cheswick, aware of the duke's mood, had little to say either and
tried by means of frowns and shakes of her head to suppress her
daughter's conversation—to little effect.

Gregory bore most of it in silence, but when the last course
was served, he suggested rather pointedly that Lady Cheswick
must be anxious to resume her journey.

"Oh, not at all, Your Grace," Hermione replied, a wistful little
smile tugging at her lips. "Mayhap others, less sensitive than
myself, could travel on and enjoy themselves, but not I. Why, to
be attending balls and routs in London while knowing my favorite cousin is all but confined to her bed—no, I could not bear it.
'Tis not to be thought of."

"You take too much on yourself, Lady Cheswick," Gregory
persisted. "Naturally, I appreciate your sentiment, but my mother
has managed quite well without your assistance all these years.
And it is not as though you would be deserting her. As you must
have observed, she has a large staff to see to her slightest wish."

"Servants," Hermione sniffed, dismissing them with a wave
of her hand. "However devoted they may be, 'tis not the same
as having family about, do you not agree?"

"No," he replied curtly. "If my mother wishes her relatives'
company, she has only to issue an invitation, but she has often
told me she quite *prefers* solitude."

Patience, listening to the exchange, knew it was best not to
speak. She'd realized from the first that her advice, indeed her
presence, was not wanted. Still, she had grown sincerely fond of

the duchess, and it was for her sake that she said, "I am sure she does, Your Grace, but solitude, however appealing, may not be best for your mother. I believe it encourages one to become more of an invalid than is necessary."

"Do you?" he asked with a ferocious scowl. "And do you also fancy yourself a medical authority, Miss Cheswick?"

"No, of course not, but it is only common sense. Left alone, Her Grace has no reason to make the effort to rise each day, to dress or to entertain. It becomes extraordinarily easy for her merely to remain in bed and—"

"My mother has not the strength to entertain guests—or family," he interrupted, his voice cold enough to freeze the Thames.

Hermione tried to catch her daughter's eye, to warn her not to antagonize the duke further. He'd already made it clear that he did not welcome them, and she'd not put it beyond him to order them from the house. But Patience had the bit in her teeth.

Ignoring her mother, she said calmly, "Naturally Her Grace has not the strength. She has been weakened by idleness. I believe you fence, Your Grace?"

Astonished, he glared at her. "I fail to see what that has to do with my mother."

"I have met Monsieur Dupré. He told me that when you are in residence, he fences with you twice a week. He says he seldom has had a pupil who challenges him as you do."

"I am vastly indebted to Dupré for the compliment, but I still fail to see what that has to do with my mother's health."

She was delighted to tell him, and explained earnestly, "Only think how poorly you would perform if you did not practice so often, Your Grace. Imagine if you had not touched a foil for a year, and then Monsieur Dupré challenged you to a duel. Your muscles would have become weak from lack of use, and your reflexes would not be so sharp as—"

"I see your point, Miss Cheswick," he interrupted. "But the cases are entirely different. My mother is not a malingerer as you seem to think. She does not take to her bed to indulge herself, but because she has not the endurance to do otherwise."

Undaunted, Patience replied, "But that is exactly the problem.

Do you not see? The duchess has not the strength because she has been forced to be idle—"

"Enough!" he thundered, rising to his feet. "You do not know of what you speak, and I will *not* permit you to badger my mother or dose her with your tonics. Is that quite clear?"

"Oh, 'tis perfectly clear, Your Grace," she answered, her own eyes flashing with anger. "Indeed, I doubt that there is anyone in the country who did not hear you."

The barb struck home. She saw the flash of annoyance in his blue eyes, the way the tiny lines about his mouth tightened. She braced herself for a tongue-lashing, but he said quietly, "I am glad we understand each other." With a curt nod to Lady Cheswick, he turned and left the room.

"Gracious," Hermione said, reaching thirstily for a glass of wine. "My dear, I cannot think it wise in you to provoke him so."

"Perhaps not," her daughter replied, feeling unaccountably flushed, "but 'tis time someone spoke for the duchess. Left to his own devices, His Grace would keep her virtually a prisoner."

"I do not like him any better than you, my child, but I believe you do him an injustice. Althea tells me he is devoted to her. You have seen only the rough side of his tongue, but my cousin tells me he frequently sits with her and tells her all the latest gossip and news. He is forever bringing her little gifts and books and whatever else he can think of to cheer her. There are not many sons who would do so much."

Patience pretended not to hear, just as she pretended that the duke's anger had not cut her pride to ribbons and left her feeling as helpless as a newborn babe. Her chin lifted, her mouth firmed in stubborn lines. He had no right! No right to treat her with icy contempt, no right to dismiss her suggestions out of hand when she'd only meant to be helpful.

He was arrogant, opinionated, rude, and full of conceit. He would no doubt prefer to let his mother suffer rather than listen to advice from a mere female. He was just like her cousin, she thought, remembering the way Thomas had brushed aside her offers of help. She, who knew every blade of grass on the estate, every tenant, and the revenue from every farm down to the last shilling. Her father had depended on her and heeded her advice, but not her cousin. With typical male arrogance, Thomas had treated her as though she were only capable of adorning the drawing room or ordering an elegant supper. And the duke was just like him—just as narrow-minded, just as assured of his own supremacy.

Patience sighed and sipped the tea now grown cold. She had not allowed Thomas to disturb her. Although she'd felt sorry for the tenants at Manderly, she'd been happy enough to leave her cousin to suffer from his mistakes. It served him right. And she should do the same with His Grace, should put him out of her mind. Forget that his house, stables, and farms did not operate as efficiently as they could. Just like her cousin, the duke did not want her help—did not even want her as a guest in his house.

Forget him, she told herself. But even as she determined to do so, Patience recalled his dark, compelling eyes, and the strong, dominant lines of his jaw and mouth. The duke had an expressive face, although it was rare that she'd seen him when he wasn't either annoyed or angry. It was regrettable for he had a wonderful smile, and she knew his eyes—those blue eyes that could appear as cold and hard as ice—were capable of great tenderness. Unfortunately those looks were reserved solely for his mother.

Gregory, his fury barely contained, strode through the house. Half-a-dozen footmen snapped to attention as he passed. Not one of them dared to speak. As word spread quickly that His Grace was in one of his black moods, the servants took pains to avoid his notice.

The duke, unaware that his anger had thrown his staff into a state of anxiety, sought only the solitude of his library. It was the one room at Norwick, aside from his bedchamber, where he could be certain he would not encounter Miss Cheswick.

That blasted girl was everywhere, interfering in matters that did not concern her, or offering advice where it was not wanted. He had never encountered such an ill-bred, ill-mannered, outspoken female. She had no concept of the way a lady should conduct herself.

He crossed to the cabinet and poured a generous measure of brandy into a beautifully cut crystal glass. Gregory admired perfection and held a deep appreciation for fine craftsmanship, whether it was contained in art, furniture, cut crystal, or the imported, aged brandy smuggled in from France. But after his contretemps with Miss Cheswick, he didn't notice the way the light reflected off the many facets of the crystal, or savor the smooth, rich taste of the brandy. He tossed the drink down as though it were home-brewed elderberry wine.

Nor did the warmth of the brandy do much to ease his agitation. He settled behind his desk, his brows drawn into a frown, as he contemplated ways of ridding himself of Miss Cheswick's presence. Lighting one of the rare cigars he smoked, he considered ordering the girl from the house. The notion appealed. He envisioned her, cowed, humiliated, trudging with dragging footsteps to her carriage. He almost smiled, but reality intruded.

Gregory knew he could not order Miss Cheswick to leave Norwick. She was his mother's guest, and unaccountably, the duchess seemed to have taken a strong liking to her. His mother would be furious if he ousted the girl, and he'd not put it beyond the duchess to insist that he apologize and ask Miss Cheswick to return—then he would be obliged to do so. He could not, would not, do anything to distress his mother.

Swirling the brandy in his glass, Gregory acknowledged that even if it were possible to evict Miss Cheswick, she would not be humbled. The lady, though it was stretching a point to call her such, had an elevated notion of her own worth. She carried herself with an air of regality that would have done justice to royalty. She spoke that way, too, he thought, remembering the certainty with which she'd dispensed her opinions.

His teeth left deep indentations on his cigar as he recalled the girl's criticism of the way he cared for his mother. Miss Cheswick's remarks had cut deeply. Since he was a child of nine, Gregory had accepted full responsibility for the duchess. He might have his faults, but there wasn't a soul alive who could say he wasn't devoted to his mother. He would sell his own soul to have her well again, and, in fact, he'd spent a small fortune on the best physicians money could procure. Not that it had done much good. The duchess had grown progressively weaker until she now spent most of her day in her wheelchair.

It frustrated him that for all his wealth, he could do nothing more to help the duchess. The knowledge ate at him, destroying whatever pleasure he might have taken in the simple joys of life. He sipped at the brandy, remembering his mother as she was before her illness. She had swept through the house with style, elegance, and a sweetness impossible to define.

Everyone had adored the duchess, but especially the little boy with whom she'd laughed and played. And every night, the last thing the boy remembered was the enticing scent of spring flowers that always seemed to surround his mother. No matter how many guests were staying at Norwick, no matter how busy she was, the duchess always took time to come and kiss her son good-night.

Now it was he who went to her each evening. He glanced at the mantel clock. It was nearly time. He crushed out the cigar, took one more sip of the brandy, and rose. Breathing deeply, he stood still for a moment, trying to set aside his anger with Miss Cheswick.

He succeeded sufficiently well so that when he walked into his mother's bedchamber, he was able to smile as he greeted her.

Althea was settled comfortably in the huge four-poster bed, her back against a number of pillows. She wore a blue silk dressing gown, edged with exquisite lace, and her long blond hair had been brushed and braided for the night. The scent of wild flowers still clung to her, and to Gregory's eyes, she still looked incredibly lovely.

Drawn near the bed was a center table holding an elaborate tea service. It had become their custom to enjoy a cup of tea together in her bedchamber, whenever Gregory was at home. It was a ritual they both took pleasure from.

He bent and placed a light kiss on her brow as he searched her face for signs of fatigue. He was relieved to see that her eyes reflected neither pain nor the confusion that the laudanum sometimes produced.

"You look well, Mother. Were you able to rest this evening?"

"A little, though in truth I did not feel the need." She smiled at him as he sat down in the tall wing chair and poured their tea. "Indeed, I almost joined you for supper. Perhaps I shall tomorrow."

"Well, that *is* good news, but pray do not overtax your strength. Your cousin quite understands that you are not able to entertain as you would like."

Althea nodded as she accepted the cup he handed to her. "Hermione is very good, and Patience, too, of course. I hope you do not find their presence here too annoying? I know you did not like that I invited them to stay, but truly I believe their visit has done much to improve my spirits."

"Then I must hope they remain indefinitely," he said with forced cheerfulness.

Dear Gregory, Althea thought, struggling not to laugh aloud. She knew full well that her son had frequently come to points with Patience. Her own movement through the house might be severely limited, but her servants kept her well informed. She had known of the quarrel at supper moments after it occurred, but apparently Gregory was not going to mention it.

Probing gently, she said, "If Hermione cannot arrange a suitable marriage for her daughter, I thought I might ask Patience to remain here as my companion."

Astonished, Gregory stared at her.

Althea laughed. "You need not look as though I have taken leave of my senses."

"You must forgive my surprise, Mother, but you have never sought feminine company before. If I had known you wished for such, I would have made arrangements to employ someone."

"I know, dear, but 'tis not just merely a question of employing someone, but finding someone agreeable. With Patience, I am at ease. She does not annoy me with constant chattering or idle conversation. Nor does she treat me as an invalid who must be fussed over and carefully watched to see that I do not exert my-self."

"Someone must do so," Gregory replied. "And I am afraid Miss Cheswick does not realize the extent of your illness."

"Perhaps that is why 'tis so pleasant to have her about," Althea said with one of her quiet smiles. "Indulge me in this, Gregory. I enjoy the girl's company, and since I began taking the tonic she prepared, I have felt much stronger."

Rage coursed through him. The blasted girl had gone behind his back and was dosing his mother despite his explicit orders that she was not to do so. His fingers clenched, and he felt a strong desire to enclose them around Miss Cheswick's slender neck. With a supreme effort, he restrained his temper. He could not get rid of the girl, but perhaps he could contrive to show his mother that Miss Cheswick was ill mannered, ill bred, and not at all a suitable companion.

Forcing a smile to his lips, he said, "I am of course delighted that you are feeling much stronger. Perhaps now would be an excellent time to invite Lady Anne Billingsly to Norwick. If you are agreed, I shall write to her parents at once."

The duke retired from her bedchamber triumphant. He'd left his mother little choice. If she'd complained she was not well enough to receive Lady Anne, he would have used her health as an excuse to bring the Cheswicks' visit to a close. But she had agreed, and he would post a letter at once. Within a week, a fortnight at most, he would have Lady Anne at Norwick. She would show that blasted girl how a real lady conducted herself.

He was so pleased with his scheme that when he encountered Miss Cheswick in the hall, he smiled sweetly and wished her a pleasant evening.

Patience stared after him, her heart beating erratically.

Three

Two tall wing chairs were drawn close to the fireplace in the small sitting room that adjoined Althea's bedchamber. Between the chairs, on an exquisitely carved mahogany table, rested an elaborate tea tray. Boots, the fat spaniel belonging to the duchess, slept contentedly at her feet, his snores occasionally punctuating the conversation of the two ladies.

It had been quiet for several moments, the peaceful kind of silence that sometimes occurs between friends when talking is not necessary. The duchess was engrossed with her needlepoint, and content with the companionship of her cousin.

Hermione, too, was content, and loath to disturb Althea's serenity, but she felt it was necessary. Aloud she said, "I have been thinking 'tis time I took my leave."

"If you wish to retire early, you must not allow me to detain you," Althea replied. She smiled warmly, for it was still a novelty that she was not the first to take to her bed in the evening. Only in the last few days had she felt sufficiently strong to not only join the others for supper, but to sit in her room afterward, sewing and chatting with her cousin.

Hermione smiled too, but it did not reach her eyes, and when she spoke her voice was troubled. "I was not speaking of bed, my dear duchess. It is time I continued my journey . . . time I took Patience to London."

Disappointment darkened Althea's eyes. She had grown very fond of her cousin in the month she had stayed at Norwick. And Patience. Althea knew it was foolish of her, but she'd secretly hoped that one day Patience and Gregory might make a match of it. She knew the two of them quarreled constantly, and would argue any point—even whether the sun was shining or not.

It was hardly the behavior one associated with marriage. But at least Patience had aroused some emotion in Gregory, even if it was only animosity. That was more than any other female had ever managed. Distressed by the news, the duchess unconsciously ran her hand up and down her leg.

Hermione noticed the gesture and was instantly contrite. "The pain has returned, has it not? You must retire at once, Cousin, and I shall have Patience make a sleeping draught for you."

Althea shook her head. "It is not the pain that troubles me, but the thought of your leaving. *Must* you go?"

Hermione hesitated. In truth she had no desire to leave. She was comfortably situated. The duchess treated her with a degree of intimacy that was flattering to one in her position. She had come to Norwick intending to take advantage of her distant relationship to Althea, and to use that connection to find a suitable husband for Patience. But in the past month, Hermione had developed a true affection for her cousin. If it were not for Patience . . . But she had to consider the future.

Regretfully, Hermione said, "You know how Manderly was left, Cousin. I have no choice but to see to it that Patience marries well, and unfortunately she will not meet any suitable gentlemen here."

Althea did not wish to raise her cousin's hopes unjustly, so she said nothing of her own dreams that one day their children might wed . . . but Hermione had given her an idea. "Suppose I could arrange it so that Patience does have the chance to meet some eligible young men?"

"At Norwick?" Hermione questioned with a laugh. "Why, we have not met anyone but servants, not unless you count Monsieur Dupré. And I assure you, a fencing master is *not* the sort of match I have in mind for my daughter."

"No, of course not, but Lady Anne Billingsly will arrive any day, and I am certain Gregory will wish a few of our neighbors to call—gentlemen as well as ladies. I can think of several who might appeal to Patience."

Hermione freshened her cup of tea while she considered the notion. It held several advantages, not the least of which was that she would be put to very little expense. The remove to London would be costly. Clothing, accommodations, carriages and all the accoutrements necessary to present her daughter in the proper style would seriously deplete her small savings.

Althea saw her indecision and urged, "Do consider staying on, at least for another month. It would give me the greatest pleasure. I have grown extremely fond of you and Patience."

"I will think on it," Hermione promised. "But . . . well, 'tis only I know His Grace will not be pleased. You saw how he behaved at supper. I do not know why it should be so, but putting your son and my daughter together is like trying to mix oil and water. And his opinion of me is little better. He has made it quite clear that he feels I have outstayed my welcome."

"Leave my son to me," Althea replied with the look of a lady quite accustomed to having her own way. Then, because she did not wish her cousin to think too harshly of the duke, she tried to explain, "Gregory is really very sweet, but I fear he has spent far too much time at Norwick with only me for company. It is not good for a young man to be so isolated from his friends—and from young ladies."

Hermione smiled her understanding. "I suppose one could say the same of Patience. Instead of taking an interest in balls, fashions, and such as girls usually do, she spent the past few years immersed in the affairs of Manderly. It has set her apart from other young ladies. I have no doubt His Grace thinks her ill bred."

"I think she is charming, and I suspect some of the young gentlemen in the neighborhood will agree with me when they meet her. Now, let us plan. Lady Anne is expected any day. If you will help me, I will send invitations for an informal supper on Friday to welcome her."

"I will help you, of course, but . . . oh, Cousin, I cannot help wondering how Patience will fare when seen next to someone like Lady Anne. If His Grace is considering offering for her, she must be a diamond of the first water. How can Patience hope to compete with such perfection?"

"Perfection has its drawbacks," Althea said. "I have often observed that gentlemen may admire a great beauty, but yet be afraid to approach her. I think Patience will do very well. Still, it will not hurt to make certain."

Seeing the gleam of mischief in Althea's eyes, Hermione demanded, "What have you in mind?"

"Gregory has a friend, Charles Villars. He has not visited here in some years, but he used to come often, and I grew most fond of him. I am certain that if I asked him, he would oblige me by conducting a discreet flirtation with our Patience."

Hermione looked doubtful that such a measure would serve, or that it would even be wise to involve her daughter in so dubious a scheme.

The duchess patted her hand. "You must trust me, Cousin. When I was a girl, I observed that young men are much like a flock of sheep. Where one leads, the rest follow. It is true," she insisted, laughing, and sounding much like a young girl herself.

So it was that when Gregory came to bid her good evening, he found his mother with color in her cheeks, her eyes sparkling, and a smile on her lips. However much he'd feared that supper had taxed her strength, he could not deny she was looking very well.

Hermione took his entrance as her cue to withdraw, and after an exchange of brief remarks, she slipped from the room.

Gregory took her seat and smiled at the duchess. "I am very pleased to see you enjoying yourself, but should you not be abed? 'Tis after nine."

"Once I danced until three."

"Once you were seventeen," he replied teasingly, then added, "Not that you look much older now. When I came along the hall, it sounded like two young girls in here, chatting and giggling."

"Thank you, Gregory. I confess it feels quite wonderful to be able to sit down after supper with our guests, and to *plan* things again . . . almost as if I were normal."

"And just what are you planning?" he asked, amused.

"I thought, perhaps, a small supper to welcome Lady Anne and her mother. I shall invite some of the neighbors and—"

"I assure you, Mother, that is not necessary. I do not want you tiring yourself."

"Hush," she commanded, holding up her hand to stem the flow of his words. "It may not be necessary, but it is what I wish to do—and what I intend to do. And if you are truly concerned that I do not tire myself, then you will not exhaust me by arguing about it."

Gregory eyed her in astonishment. He could not recall her ever speaking so harshly to him. Rising stiffly, he said, "I am sorry if my concern for your health annoys you."

She caught his hand in hers. "I know you mean well, darling, and I am deeply thankful to have so considerate, so thoughtful a son . . . but allow me a little freedom to pretend I am capable of doing more than sitting in bed."

Not proof against her entreaty, he shrugged. "If it means so much to you, I cannot gainsay you."

"It does," she answered softly, and brought his hand to her lips to lightly kiss his fingers. "Hermione will help me, and I promise that if I grow the least tired, I will rest."

He had to be content with that, and a few moments later, he took his leave. Lady Anne was due to arrive on the morrow. He could only hope that her serenity of manner and unusual good sense would help to convince the duchess to have a care for herself.

Patience blamed her sleeplessness on the moonlight streaming in the casement windows. She rose, slipped on a wrapper, and crossed the room to look up at the star-studded sky. A full moon bathed Norwick in its gold light. A harbinger for good or bad, she wondered. Ancient myths credited the moon with both. At the moment, she could easily believe it possessed some magical power that worked on her mind.

Her thoughts were not her own this night. No matter how she had tried to compose her mind for sleep, his grace, the Duke of Norwick, insisted on intruding. She'd tried to banish him, but with his usual arrogance, he persisted in dominating her thoughts. Each time she closed her eyes, she could see his cool blue ones—glaring at her, or appraising her contemptuously. Even in her dreams, it seemed she could do nothing to please his grace.

Not that she cared! She would not grant him the smallest civility were it not for the kindness of his mother. It was only because it so obviously distressed the duchess to see them at odds that Patience had made an effort to placate him—an effort he had returned with his usual rudeness.

Tonight at supper, all he spoke of was the arrival of Lady Anne, as though she were some sort of goddess descended from the heavens. Patience was surprised that any female could win approval from His Grace, but apparently this one embodied all the attributes he considered essential in a true lady. She could still hear him, remarking to the duchess that he was certain she would enjoy the company of a lady so refined, so elegant, so well mannered as Lady Anne. And with maddening condescension, he had even hinted that Patience might profit from association with such a lady.

It had taken all her willpower not to toss the oxtail soup in his lap. But she'd clenched her hands beneath the table, determined not to give him the satisfaction of goading her to behave in an ill manner before the duchess. Still, her palms had itched, and she'd had to bite her tongue to keep from retorting to his barbs.

Lady Anne Billingsly. Even the name annoyed Patience, and she wished she could persuade her mother to depart for London at once, before the paragon's arrival. She had tried, but Mama had said the duchess implored her to remain for a few more weeks, and she had not the heart to refuse her cousin. Patience did not blame her mother. She doubted anyone could refuse the duchess anything. She was as sweet, as kind, as warm and generous as the duke was cold and haughty. Indeed, it amazed Patience that the two were related, so different were their natures.

She turned from the window, glanced at the rumpled bed, and knew she would not be able to sleep yet awhile. Idly, she picked up the book on her bedside table. It was a Minerva Press novel— an improbable love story with a swashbuckling hero. Unfortunately, his arrogance reminded her too strongly of the duke, and the fainthearted heroine behaved so meekly, Patience tossed the book down in disgust. She needed something far more absorbing to settle her mind. Of course there were hundreds of books in the library . . . the mantel clock showed it was a quarter past two. The household would be asleep. Surely, it would disturb no one if she crept quietly below stairs and borrowed a book or two.

Making up her mind, Patience lit a tall taper and then opened her door. The hall was dark and eerily silent, but her candle cast a sufficient glow to see the way to the top of the long stairs.

Odd, how different the hall looked by candlelight, she thought, her heart pumping faster than usual. A suit of armor gave her a momentary fright, and she scolded herself for behaving as hen-heartedly as the silly heroine in that book. There was nothing to be frightened of at Norwick. Repeating those words as though they were a charm to ward off evil, she approached the library and pushed open the heavy oak door. The scent of stale tobacco and the musty smell of old books assaulted her senses. She found that strangely comforting and entered the enormous cavern of a room with more assurance.

She had not had the opportunity to explore the library. More often than not, the duke was closeted within. The room suited him, she thought, glancing at the austere furnishings. The huge mahogany desk was swept bare, its polished surface gleaming in the candlelight. No clutter here, no cozy comfort. None of the small warm touches that turned empty rooms into a home. Throughout the rest of the house, large vases of flowers graced table tops. Tiny porcelain and china figurines drew the eye, as did numerous oil paintings. Embroidered cushions added splashes of color and beckoned invitingly. But not in the library. Even had the fire been lit, she would have thought the room as cold and unwelcoming as its master.

Patience shivered in her thin wrapper, and quickly crossed to the nearest tier of shelving. Lifting the candle, she studied the titles. This section appeared to be composed of historical texts— dry, dusty reading to judge from the titles. But mixed among the heavy tomes, her eyes picked out a slender volume of verse. She was about to reach for it when she heard footfalls behind her. Startled, she whirled around.

"Miss Cheswick, may I inquire what you are doing?"

The duke stood close enough that she could see the small swirls of blue and gold in the pattern of his brocade dressing gown. He'd spoken quietly, but she felt as though she'd been caught stealing the silver. He eyed her with such derision, she stammered, "I was just looking for something to read."

One brow arched as he glanced at the shelves behind her. "I would not have supposed a historical account of the rise of the House of Norwick to be to your taste. Or perhaps it was the *Treatise on Man and Architecture* by Colbert that drew your attention?"

She blushed but held her ground, her chin lifting in defiance. Her voice barely quivered as she replied, "No, Your Grace. I was merely seeking to . . . to familiarize myself with the arrangement—assuming, of course, that the books *are* arranged in some order?"

He nearly grinned. She was the one caught in his library at two in the morning, clad only in a thin wrapper, yet she had the audacity to criticize the placement of his books. He might have laughed even then, but the truth was the library was not in any kind of order. It irked him to admit such, but it also gave him an idea.

Torn between annoyance and amusement, he said, "No doubt the knowledge will be abhorrent to someone of your efficiency and organizational skills, but no, the books are not yet catalogued. I have meant for some time to engage someone to set them straight, but it is difficult to find anyone to undertake the task in so remote a house. However, it occurs to me, Miss Cheswick, to wonder if you might be willing?"

Surprised, she looked up at him. Was he mocking her? With only the light from their candles it was difficult to tell what he was thinking. As her gaze met his, she was suddenly conscious of his nearness. She caught the intriguing scent of deep woods that always surrounded him, and imagined she could feel the warmth of his breath on her brow. Her own breath seemed trapped in her throat. Nervously, she took a step backward.

Gregory forgot what he was saying. He was uncomfortably aware of the way her thin wrapper draped her slender figure. Uncomfortably aware of the impropriety of their being alone together at this hour. Uncomfortably aware of the tug of desire that made him wonder how it would feel to hold her in his arms.

The spell was broken when she stepped backward. Appalled at his thoughts, and determined to keep her from guessing the effect she had on his senses, Gregory spoke scornfully. "I beg your pardon, Miss Cheswick. For a moment, I quite forgot that your talent lies only in criticizing the work of others. No doubt such a task would be beyond your capability."

Stung, she retorted, "You mistake the matter, Your Grace. Even a child could improve on the disarray in this library. If I had sufficient time—"

"Take as much time as you desire," he interrupted. "Or was that intended only as an excuse?"

Her dark lashes swept down to cover the confusion in her eyes, and she turned slightly away from him. She found it difficult to think clearly when he stood so close. She murmured, "I was thinking only of the inconvenience to you, Your Grace. I am aware of how much time you spend in here, and would hesitate to disturb you."

"Disturb me?" he echoed with a harsh laugh. She had done little but disturb him for several weeks. She had disrupted his household; defied his orders, and somehow wormed her way into his mother's affections. He encountered her every time he turned around. The absurdity of her sudden burst of consideration was sufficient that he nearly lashed out at her.

He meant to ring a peal over her head—as she deserved—but at that instant she glanced up at him. He thought he saw fear in her eyes. That, too, was absurd. He knew well enough that she wasn't afraid of him. He dismissed the notion as nonsensical, but instead of the lecture he'd intended, he heard himself saying, "If we are agreed then, you may begin cataloguing the books on the morrow. I assure you, you will not disturb me."

"Very well," she replied. She would've agreed to almost anything to escape his presence at that moment, but the task of cataloguing the duke's books appealed to her. He no longer seemed quite the ogre she'd imagined, and she envisioned them both quietly working in the library during the long afternoon hours. Perhaps even sharing a cup of tea and discussing the various books she listed. She offered him a tentative smile.

Her eyes were the color of garnets, Gregory thought, and when she smiled they warmed to a degree that made one forget all else. Only the chiming of the mantel clock recalled him to his senses. He blinked, dispelling the sense of intimacy, and said abruptly, "As I was saying, you need not fear disturbing me. Lady Anne arrives on the morrow, and no doubt I will be much occupied in showing her Norwick, and the surrounding countryside."

The light dimmed in her eyes. "Naturally, Your Grace," Patience said, and with all the dignity she could command, added, "and now, if you grant me leave, I shall retire." It was not until she reached her bedchamber, and set down her candle, that she realized she'd come away from the library without a book. She picked up the novel she'd left on her table. She'd thought the heroine silly, but the girl could not possibly behave more foolishly than Patience herself had done. Resigned to a sleepless night, she opened the book.

Lady Anne Billingsly arrived the following morning with sufficient pomp and ceremony that one might already believe her to be the new Duchess of Norwick. She and her mother, Lady Yardly, traveled in a luxurious, well-sprung chaise, with the family crest emblazoned on the door, and were accompanied by two coachmen, two footmen, and two outriders. A second carriage, not quite so lavish, followed, carrying Lady Yardly's dresser, Lady Anne's maid, and sufficient baggage for a visit of substantial duration.

The duchess, watching from the windows of her bedchamber, remarked to Katie, "Heavens, our guests seemed prepared to stay for several months, although I am certain Gregory suggested a fortnight's visit."

Katie glanced at the tall young lady busy issuing orders to her servants, then smiled at the duchess. "You've forgotten what it's like, Your Grace. A proper lady like that, why she'll be having dresses for every hour of the day most like—morning dresses, walking dresses, riding dresses, supper dresses, and probably some I ain't never thought of!"

"Are you implying that *I* am not a proper lady, Katie?"

Flustered, the maid flushed crimson. "Oh, no, Your Grace. You're the finest lady I ever saw."

"And yet I change my gown no more than once a day."

Forgetting herself for a moment, Katie said, "But you ain't needing to impress nobody. That one there, she's looking to catch herself a duke."

Althea nodded. In another time, or even now had circumstances been different, she, too, might have traveled with such a retinue. Still, as she observed the continuing commotion in the courtyard, the duchess felt a surge of annoyance. Lady Yardly and her daughter had been told that this visit would be quite informal. There would be no theater, no balls to attend, no rout parties, no lavish entertaining. And Althea was also certain that Gregory had told his guests his mother was partially confined to a wheelchair and frequently did not come down to supper. So why such elaborate preparations? *To catch a duke.* The maid's comment seemed to hang in the air.

Perhaps she was being unfair, Althea thought. Perhaps Lady Anne merely wished to appear at her best. She was, after all, young, and had received a most flattering invitation. To be a guest of the Duke of Norwick would be, to her, no small matter.

Beside her, Katie chuckled. "She'll sure put Miss Cheswick in the shade."

Unknowingly, the duke thought much the same as he came out to welcome his guests. Lady Anne was as coolly elegant as he'd remembered. His gaze swept over her with approval. Although she had been traveling, her deep blue carriage dress was as neat and as fashionable as if she'd just stepped out of a London salon. It complemented the stylish hat with its wide brim and becoming sweep of dyed ostrich plumes. Beneath her bonnet, not so much as a stray curl dared to slip out of her meticulously styled coiffure.

She descended from the carriage with grace and dignity as she saw the duke approaching. She curtsied prettily. Gregory drew her up, and after kissing her gloved fingers, told her she honored the House of Norwick with her visit.

"Thank you, Your Grace, but 'tis I who am honored. I can think of no place I would rather be . . . and of no one whose company could give me greater pleasure."

The duke was largely unaccustomed to feminine flattery, but although he was uncomfortable, he also felt gratified. After enduring weeks of Miss Cheswick's criticism, Lady Anne's admiring glances and generous praise were balm to his soul. Happily, he escorted his guests into the house, expressing the hope that their journey had not been too fatiguing.

Lady Yardly sighed with the air of one much put upon. "I fear the accommodations available for anyone traveling in these parts leave much to be desired. And the servants! Well, I can only say 'tis most fortunate we brought our own attendants."

"Oh, Mama, it was not so terrible," Anne declaimed, smiling at the duke. "Only a trifle inconvenient."

Lady Yardly, who enjoyed nothing so much as complaining, wished to make certain the duke understood the hardships she and her daughter had endured in order to accept his invitation. It never hurt to have a gentleman of rank and fortune obliged to one. Sounding utterly exhausted, she replied, "You may say so, my dear, but I fear I have not your stamina. Indeed, I am feeling a little faint. I only hope I will not swoon."

Alarmed, the duke led her to the sofa in the blue drawing room and quickly urged her to be seated. "Is there aught I can get for you? A cup of tea, perhaps or . . . or a brandy?"

Annoyed with her mother, Anne glared at her from behind the duke's shoulder. But when she spoke, her voice was honey sweet, "Pray, do not worry, Your Grace. Mother often feels faint, but I am sure she will be better directly. All she needs is Simpson and her smelling salts."

Gregory looked uncertain. He was too used to the duchess, who would *have* fainted before confessing she felt unwell, to take Lady Yardly's complaints lightly. He gestured to a footman near the door, and ordered him to have someone bring Lady Yardly's smelling salts in at once. "And then, let the duchess know our guests have arrived."

The footman hurried out of the salon and nearly collided with Patience as she was crossing the hall. As she regained her balance, she laughed. "Gracious, Danvers, what is the rush?"

"I beg your pardon, Miss Cheswick! Lady Yardly and her daughter have arrived, and she—Lady Yardly—almost swooned. I got to find her maid and her smelling salts."

"Well, do not let me detain you," Patience urged. "I shall see if I can do anything to help." She smoothed the skirt of her day dress, brushed an errant curl behind her ear, and then quietly opened the door of the salon.

She saw Lady Yardly at once. The elderly woman lolled on the sofa, her massive bosom rising and falling heavily. One of her pudgy hands clutched the duke's, imploring him not to leave her, and her other hand rested across her pale brow. Patience noted the tightly crimped curls, dyed an improbable shade of red, the near panic of the duke as he hovered over her, and the decided expression of annoyance on Lady Anne's patrician features.

Before Patience could comment, Danvers flung open the door, and Simpson, Lady Yardly's dresser, rushed in, waving a vial of smelling salts. The duke disentangled his hand and stepped back with relief.

Lady Anne Billingsly turned at that instant. Her green eyes narrowed as her gaze raked over Patience. The look was readily returned. Sparks of animosity flew between the two females, sparks hot enough to ignite the fire laid ready in the hearth.

Having been told that there would be no other guests at Norwick, Lady Anne was at first inclined to dismiss the girl as some sort of maid. But her manner was not at all subservient, and her dress, however unstylish, was cut too well and made of fine muslin. Anne moved closer to the duke, laying a hand upon his sleeve to draw attention to the interloper.

Gregory glanced around and nearly smiled when he saw Patience. She was not his favorite person, but at least she could be depended on not to swoon—or do anything else foolish. He adjusted his collar and then performed the introductions, explaining, "Miss Cheswick is a cousin . . . of sorts."

"A very close cousin," Althea amended as Hermione wheeled her into the drawing room. The duchess spoke softly, her voice was pleasant and she smiled impartially at the various persons in the room. But Lady Anne felt compelled to immediately remove her hand from the duke's arm. Lady Yardly waved away the smelling salts and sat upright, gazing in astonishment at her hostess.

Gregory crossed the room and with very real pleasure said, "Mother, I am so pleased you are able to join us. May I present our guests?"

The duchess, with her usual charm, soon had everyone at ease, and gathered about a lavish tea service. She complimented Lady Yardly, saying, "My son told me your daughter was quite beautiful. I see he did not exaggerate."

"How kind of you to say so, Your Grace," Lady Yardly gushed. Seated next to her mother, Lady Anne smiled as she modestly lowered her eyes.

Gregory could not resist a glance in Miss Cheswick's direction. This, his look seemed to say, is a real lady. He added his own compliments, then remarked, "I thought that tomorrow, if you are agreeable, I could show you something of Norwick."

"Oh, yes, please do," Anne agreed. "I said to Mother that I have seldom seen lovelier country, and everything so neat and tidy. Mother says 'tis so picture-perfect, it could be in a story-book." She sighed and glanced out the window at the neat sweep of lawn. "It is so beautiful. Do you not agree, Miss . . . uh?"

"Cheswick," Patience supplied. "And, yes, as far as *appearances* go, Norwick does seem perfect, but one cannot always rely on appearances, can one?"

"I beg your pardon," Anne said. "I am afraid I do not quite understand."

"Miss Cheswick often speaks in riddles," the duke said with a trace of annoyance. "You must not pay her any heed."

Ignoring him, Patience continued, "I only meant to say that one must be careful. Looks can be deceiving. Take the gentleman who falls in love with a beautiful lady at a ball. He courts her, is accepted, and the banns are read. Then on their bridal trip he discovers the silky blond hair he wrote sonnets to is only a wig, the lady's own hair thin and gray beneath it. The alluring beauty marks, ah, mere patches. And the figure he admired, alas, due only to the efforts of a tightly laced corset and perhaps straw padding."

Lady Yardly shifted uncomfortably in her own tight corset, but Anne merely laughed. "One hears of such artifices, of course, but a man of discernment and intelligence would surely not be deceived."

"Men have been deceived by clever females since time began."

"My dear," Hermione scolded. "You must not say such things or you will give Lady Yardly a very wrong impression."

The duchess laughed. "You will, indeed, Patience. You must make it equally clear that just as many ladies have been deceived by gentlemen."

There was a great deal of laughter at the duchess's words, but Patience knew she'd behaved badly, and she rose to beg leave. Althea, too, decided it was time she returned to her room. Gregory rose at once, and as Hermione wheeled his mother from the room, he held open the door.

Patience followed, but her steps were slower. She heard Lady Anne angrily whisper, "I thought you said his mother was confined to her room? If you expect me to snare the duke, you'd better keep the old lady out of my hair!"

Four

Patience spent the following morning working in the south corner of the cavernous library. Away from the windows, this area received the least light, and consequently the least attention. She stifled a sneeze as the dust flew. Her dark hair was concealed beneath a white sarsenet cap more suitable for a dowager than a young girl. Her dress, too—a plain muslin with a deep square neck—did little to flatter her, and she had covered most of it with a voluminous apron borrowed from Mrs. Hodgkins. It was one of her oldest gowns, but she had chosen it for practicality rather than appearance. She knew the cataloguing would be a dusty business.

Time proved her right. She had not worked above an hour or two before streaks of dust marred her cheeks and cobwebs trailed from the hem of her dress. She suspected this section of the library had not been touched in years, but she remained determined to set it straight.

The duke's challenge to her to catalogue his books may have been only a taunt, but she looked forward to the task, or at least beginning it. Her hands ran reverently over the leather bindings, and her fingertips gently traced the gold engravings. Her father had instilled in her a deep love for books. She read Shakespeare, poetry, philosophical tomes, and cheap Minerva Press novels. Nothing that contained the printed word was beyond her curiosity or interest. If she did not finish the cataloguing, it would likely be because she'd allowed herself to be distracted with the individual books.

Only this morning it was not the books that diverted her. None seemed to hold her interest for more than a few moments. She couldn't stop thinking about the duke, who, she knew, was driving Lady Anne on a tour of his estate.

Patience had said nothing about the remarks she'd overheard Lady Anne make. It was not her concern if the duke was deceived by a female whose only interest was in his rank and fortune. Indeed, it was undoubtedly no more than what he deserved . . . only there was the duchess to consider.

Her Grace had been kindness itself, and every time Patience remembered the unkind remarks she'd heard, anger simmered in her anew. But at least Lady Anne would not have it all her own way. The duchess had improved tremendously, and this evening she planned to entertain her guests at an informal supper. Far from being "out of her hair" as Lady Anne had so inelegantly phrased it, the duchess would be on hand to observe for herself the young lady her son was considering as his intended. And the duchess was no fool, Patience reminded herself.

Engrossed in her thoughts, she didn't hear the door open or the soft fall of footsteps on the faded Aubusson carpet as someone crossed the room. Not until the duke spoke, did she turn. Startled, she dropped the book she was holding.

They both knelt to retrieve it, and her hands brushed against his. Patience drew back immediately, embarrassed at the blush she felt heating her cheeks.

The duke picked up the book and rose effortlessly to his feet. He offered a hand to Patience, but she scrambled up without assistance.

"I did not mean to frighten you," he apologized. She reminded him of a skittish filly. He fought an urge to run a hand down her back to gentle her, in much the same way he would the nervous chestnut mare in his stables. Nearly the same, he silently amended. His horses had never evoked this odd feeling in his chest.

Patience managed a laugh, and with a composure belied only by her shaking hands, said, "I was not frightened . . . merely surprised. I had not expected to see you this morning. I thought you were giving Lady Anne a tour of Norwick."

"I was, but we had to return. There was a . . . a slight accident."

"An accident? Oh, I do hope no one was hurt?"

"No, not hurt," he answered, a strange look in his eyes as he recalled the sight of Lady Anne sprawled indelicately in a mud puddle outside Henry Mulligan's cottage. She had not appreciated Mrs. Mulligan's dandelion wine or the sampling of fresh cheeses. In her rush to leave the tiny cottage, she had collided with young Andrew Mulligan who had brought his prize sow around to show His Grace.

Lady Anne, apparently under the delusion the pig meant to attack her, had dashed off the footpath and tumbled into a deep, muddy puddle. Nothing the duke said had eased her anger, and all he could do was drive her as quickly as possible back to the house. She was in her bedchamber now, changing her gown.

Patience watched the duke curiously. Was it only her imagination or was there a glint of humor in his blue eyes? For a moment, he looked almost approachable. Unwilling to spoil the mood, she curved her lips into a tentative smile and then said, "I am sure Lady Anne was impressed with what she saw of Norwick. 'Tis a beautiful estate."

His eyebrow lifted in that odd manner he had due to the scar beneath his eye. The touch of humor she'd seen was more pronounced now, and his lips stretched into a grin as he said, "I am flattered, Miss Cheswick. 'Tis high praise coming from one with your impeccable standards. Somehow, I thought you found little to admire here."

"How can you say so, Your Grace?" she asked, truly astonished. "One would have to be difficult to please, indeed, not to find Norwick an exceptional estate."

"Inasmuch as all your comments have been criticisms—"

"Suggestions," she corrected, stung that he could be so unjust. Her chin tilted upward. "Merely because I see room for improvement does not mean that I cannot appreciate the whole."

Their discussion might have evolved into their usual argument, but he was fascinated by the streak of dust across her cheekbones, the tendrils of soft curls that had escaped from her cap. With her turned-up nose high in the air, she still maintained her aura of grandeur. Only now he found it absurd—absurd and strangely appealing.

"Why . . . why are you looking at me that way?" she demanded uneasily.

Without conscious thought, his hand came up and he used his thumb to gently brush the dirt from the curve of her cheek. "It looks as though you encountered a cobweb or two."

"It is frightfully dusty in here," she muttered, color rising in waves of heat to flood her face. She stepped back, needing the distance between them, needing the air to catch her breath. Her heart beating erratically, she tried to regain her composure by taunting him. "Does no one ever dust in here?"

"Not often," he owned. "I prefer to be disturbed as little as possible. However, if you are going to work in here, I shall see that Mrs. Hodgkins directs some of the maids to set it to rights. There is no reason for you to undertake such drudgery."

"I am not above a bit of hard work, Your Grace," Patience retorted. She was uncomfortably aware now of the cobwebs trailing from her gown and the streaks of dust on her apron. Embarrassed she wished only that the duke would leave.

Before he could reply, the door swung open and Lady Anne strolled into the library. She had changed her gown, combed her hair, and after a brief lecture from her mother, mended her temper. Glancing around the room, she quickly spotted the duke and hurried toward him. She dropped a curtsy, then twirled around. With a mischievous smile, she teased, "I hope you find my appearance much improved."

"You look lovely," he replied honestly as he admired her figure in the fashionably cut pale blue riding dress.

"Was anything ever so foolish," she began, then paused as she realized the female she'd mistaken for a maid was Miss Cheswick. Anne's eyes, full of contempt, raked over the stained dress and the serviceable cap perched precariously on the girl's dark curls. "It appears you, too, have had an accident, Miss Cheswick."

Aware of how dowdy she must appear next to Lady Anne's elegance, Patience barely heard her.

Anne, however, had little time to waste on a woman whose status was little better than that of a penniless relative. Once she wed the duke, she intended to put a stop to such visits. For now, she turned her back on the girl and fastened her attention on Gregory. Looking provocatively up at him from beneath her lashes, she said, "Shall we resume our tour, Your Grace? I can hardly wait to see the rest of Norwich."

He bowed slightly in acquiescence, then offered her his arm. He glanced back at Miss Cheswick, but she said nothing as she stood motionless next to the steps. No doubt it was only his imagination that fancied he saw disappointment in her dark eyes.

Five

Excitement permeated the air of the house on Friday as servants bustled about in preparation for the duchess' supper party. In all, twelve persons would grace the table, a small party by most standards. At one time the duchess had seated thirty or forty guests and thought nothing of it. But Hermione and Patience were the first to dine at Norwick in more than three years, and the staff was as pleased to have guests coming as the duchess herself.

It seemed the only person not gratified was the duke. He continued to worry over his mother's health, but no one agreed with him except for Lady Anne. She had expressed her surprise that the duchess should so exert herself.

"I am sure 'tis most kind of her," she murmured as they strolled together one afternoon in the rose garden. She gave him one of her charming smiles and continued, "But I understood that she was not sufficiently well to act as your hostess. Indeed, I am certain I recall your saying that she seldom even dined below stairs."

Gregory, taking her remarks as concern for his mother, nodded his head gravely. "Until recently that was true, and I will tell you I have doubts that it may prove too onerous for her—but she is quite determined."

"I hope it is not on my account," Anne replied, her voice masking the annoyance she felt. At first she'd been pleased to learn of the small supper party, for she was bored with the monotony of meals at Norwick. But when the duke told her about each of the guests, she lost all interest. Of the gentlemen invited, only three were titled and two of those, Lord Philpot and Sir Alex Bonaby, were elderly. They would serve as escorts for the duchess and her own mother, Lady Yardly. The only other gentleman with a title was Sir Edgar Marshall, and he a mere baron. It sounded to Anne like the most tedious of affairs, and worse, she would have to cope with the duchess, whom she sensed did not quite approve of her.

Anne idly picked a rose and turned to the duke. Looking up at him from beneath her lashes, she said persuasively, "Perhaps you should insist that your dear mother remain in bed. I realize she invited these people for my pleasure, but I would feel simply dreadful if she suffered because of it. And truly, Your Grace, I am most content to dine quietly . . . alone with you."

He smiled tenderly down at her. "Your sentiments do you justice, my dear. You are as sweet as the rose you hold."

"Then you will speak to your mother?"

He laughed then. "It would do no good. She may look fragile, but I assure you Mother has a will of iron, and she is insistent that she entertain her guests. In truth, she is in better spirits than I have seen her in some time. We simply must hope she does not overdo and suffer a relapse."

"Yes, of course," Anne replied, turning away to hide the frustration in her eyes. A relapse would please her fine, but barring that she comforted herself with the thought that the first thing she would do when she was the Duchess of Norwick would be to see her mother-in-law removed to the Dower House. Although it would hardly matter. Anne had little intention of spending long, dreary months at so isolated an estate as Norwick. Once she wed the duke, they would buy a house in London. Then she could take her rightful place in Society.

The duke, walking beside her, glanced down and caught the satisfied smile on her perfectly shaped lips. He teased, "What are you thinking of, my dear? You look vastly contented."

"How could I be otherwise in such a charming garden, and with such a charming companion?" she asked, her lashes fluttering. She daringly lifted the rose to brush it softly against his cheek.

Above them, a white lace curtain fell back into place as Patience stepped quickly away from the window. She had not meant to spy on the duke, but she had heard voices and obeyed an impulse to glance out the bedchamber window. When she'd spied his grace strolling innocently with Lady Anne, a heavy weight had seemed to settle about her shoulders and in the region of her heart. They'd made a handsome couple. Unable to turn away, she had watched the duke, noting the way laughter softened the harshness of his countenance and observing the tenderness of his gaze as he spoke to Lady Anne.

Yearning, strong and achingly sharp, stabbed at Patience. No gentleman had ever looked at her in such a manner, and doubtless none ever would. She had not Lady Anne's beauty or practiced art of flirtation. Patience watched for a moment longer, until she saw the coy way Lady Anne plied her rose. Embarrassed, Patience stepped swiftly back.

She felt a stab of jealousy which was quite ridiculous. Until yesterday in the library, she had exchanged very few civil words with the duke. She reminded herself he was arrogant, opinionated, stubborn, and every bit as conceited as her cousin. Too proud to listen to advice from a mere female. But her thoughts carried little conviction, and she dreaded attending the supper planned for the evening. If she could only think of a plausible reason to remain in her room, she would do so. Unfortunately, she was disgustingly healthy. Lady Anne might enact a swoon or plead fatigue, but no one would credit Patience with so much sensibility.

A tap on the door startled her. She flushed guiltily—almost as if she'd been caught spying on the duke. But it was only Katie with a message that Her Grace wished to see her. Patience nodded and promised to come directly.

She took a deep breath to compose herself, and managed a shaky smile before walking down the long hall that led to Her Grace's suite of rooms. She was bidden to enter at once, and found her mother sitting next to the duchess on the small love seat. Both looked well pleased and greeted her warmly.

Hermione's eyes glinted with pleasure. "Her Grace has a splendid surprise for you, my dear."

"I would not call it splendid," Althea said, laughing. "But I do hope you will like it. Katie, bring in the gown, please."

Confused, Patience stared at them. "Gown?"

"You see, my dear, I know from Hermione that you planned to have new dresses made up in Town and might not have anything suitable for our little supper party this evening. Since we are much of a size, except that you are taller, I had Katie unpack one of my old gowns. If it fits you, which I am nearly certain it will, Katie can let down the hem."

"I . . . I cannot take one of your dresses, Your Grace, though 'tis most generous of you to offer."

"Nonsense. In truth, it never suited me, but I think it will do you admirably."

Katie returned then with a satin gown of pale burnished gold draped over her arm. Patience drew in a sharp breath as she saw it. She had never laid eyes on anything so exquisite. Her protests died on her lips.

"Let Katie help you on with it, my dear," Hermione ordered.

Numbly, Patience stepped behind the screen and allowed the maid to undo the long line of buttons on her muslin day dress. Nervously, she stepped into the gold. The satin rustled. Unable to resist, she fingered the lush material and prayed it would fit just to see how she might look.

"Perfect, 'tis perfect," Katie crowed, hooking up the back. "Too short of course, but that's easily mended. Her Grace was right. The color favors you."

Patience needed neither the maid's words nor the looking glass to know the gown flattered her. The low-cut neck fit snugly across her bosom, and the puffed sleeves narrowed into long sheaths of gold that caressed her arms. Russet ribbons, laced beneath the bodice, marked the high waist and allowed the material to fall in elegant, shimmering folds. She had never worn a gown so grand and she felt almost . . . almost pretty.

"What's taking so long, Patience? Let us see how it fits," Hermione called impatiently. But words failed her as her daughter stepped from behind the screen. With a mother's natural prejudice, she had always thought her daughter a pretty girl, but now she looked quite lovely.

The burnished gold of the gown gave Patience's complexion a warm glow, and the russet ribbons deepened the color of her eyes and heightened the highlights in her hair.

"It might have been made for you," the duchess said happily. "Step up on the stool and allow Katie to let down the hem. She is brilliant with a needle and will have it done in a trice."

Reluctantly, her fingers fondling the satin, Patience protested, "I cannot accept such a gift, Your Grace. If Katie alters it, you will not be able to wear it again, and 'tis such a beautiful gown."

"On you, my dear." Althea rose and gave the younger woman a warm hug. "I assure you it never flattered me in the least. The color made me appear dreadfully pale, and it has lain uselessly in the bottom of a trunk for more than a year. I am pleased to have you make use of it."

"But it must have cost a great deal . . ."

The duchess waved her hand as if to dismiss the notion. "The gown is not half so dear to me as the tonic you make which has given me back a small measure of my health. Surely, you will not deny me the pleasure of giving you something in return?"

Patience had not the heart to argue further. She *wanted* to wear the gown that evening. Wanted to see the look in the duke's eyes when he saw her. Wanted, just once, to feel as though she were pretty. Perhaps it was wrong of her to accept such an extravagant gift, but all the same her heart lifted as she climbed up on the stool.

The supper guests proved not to be as boring as Lady Anne had imagined. Half the gentlemen may have been older than her father, but they *were* titled, and they gathered around her in the drawing room with flattering attention. And there was Charles Villars. He may have been untitled, but he was exceedingly handsome and had a degree of charm she found most agreeable. It would not hurt to let the duke see how admired she was, Anne thought, smiling impartially at Lord Philpot, Sir Edgar, and Mr. Villars. She only hoped the duke noticed, trapped as he was in conversation with a little nobody from the neighboring estate.

Gregory did notice. Like most of the gentlemen, he had difficulty keeping his eyes from raking over the elegant figure of Lady Anne. She looked particularly stunning this evening, clad in a shimmering blue silk that clung tantalizingly to her slender form. Even his friend, Charles, had not been impervious and had immediately engaged her in conversation.

Hermione observed that young gentleman with a disapproving eye. Muttering low enough so that Lady Yardly could not hear, she said, "Disgusting the way they all gather around that chit. She's vulgar in the extreme, and I don't doubt she dampened her petticoats."

Althea hid a smile. Patience had not come down yet, but Charles Villars had promised to play the besotted suitor and she trusted him to remember that, even in the face of Lady Anne's more obvious charms. But Althea had another reason to be pleased. Gregory, far from joining the circle of admirers about Lady Anne, had settled beside Miss Diana Villars, and gave every appearance of being content in her company. Whatever faults her son might have, none could say he was not a true gentleman.

The duchess was about to reassure Hermione when Patience entered the room. In her gown of gold cloth, she immediately drew every eye. Althea had the satisfaction of seeing Lady Anne's gaze narrow as she observed the effect of Miss Cheswick's entrance. One could almost see her appraising the cost of the satin gown.

Patience apologized prettily for her tardiness, but she was instantly forgiven and it was the duchess who introduced her to the other guests. Lord Philpot and Sir Alex Bonaby beamed at her, declaring themselves charmed. Sir Edgar, without any prompting from Althea, was plainly delighted to make her acquaintance, and even Gregory seemed to look at Miss Cheswick with new interest.

Charles Villars set her to blushing as he wondered aloud what gods he had to thank for granting him the privilege of leading her in to supper.

Lady Anne was not so well pleased, nor was Lady Yardly. Standing next to her daughter, she gave her a small nudge in the duke's direction.

Anne, regaining some of her poise, laid her hand on his sleeve. Gazing adoringly up at him, she said, "I must hope you are as contented with your supper partner, Your Grace?"

It was brazen, rather bold, but she smiled to make a jest of it, and he answered, "I am undoubtedly the envy of every gentleman in the room."

The duchess led the way into the dining parlor on the arm of Lord Philpot. The rest of the guests followed, being seated in the order of rank—which left Patience at the lower end of the table. She did not regret it. She had Mr. Villars' company, and his sister, who seemed most agreeable, was seated across from her. Had not she been uncomfortably aware of the duke seated at the head of the table with Lady Anne on his left, she would have been quite happy.

"You are looking exceptionally pensive, Mr. Villars," Patience said after supper, becoming a trifle uncomfortable beneath his steady regard. Had she suddenly spouted horns or an unsightly spot on her nose?

They were seated in a corner of the drawing room, a little withdrawn from the others as they had listened to Lady Anne's accomplished performance on the pianoforte. Patience had declined to play, and had half expected Mr. Villars to desert her. But he had remained firmly ensconced beside her, his attention flattering if a little unnerving.

"I was merely regretting the circumstances that make you a guest in the house," he replied with an air of practiced gallantry that made him a favorite among young ladies.

Confused, she turned her clear gaze in his direction. "Regret? I fear I do not understand . . ."

"If you were not a guest, my dear Miss Cheswick, I could

offer to see you home. 'Tis a lovely night for a carriage drive beneath the moon."

The color rose in her cheeks as her lashes swept down to hide the embarrassment in her eyes. Unused to such flirtation, she knew not how to answer him.

She was saved from replying as the duke approached with Lady Anne. Gregory made a joke of it, laughing indulgently at his friend. "Come, Charles, are you being deliberately unsociable this evening, or do you seek to monopolize Miss Cheswick?"

Villars rose in deference to his friend's rank, but there was nothing deferential in his manner as he grinned. "Why, monopolize your cousin. I never guessed you possessed such charming relatives." To Lady Anne, he added, "Be warned, my lady, His Grace has any number of tricks up his sleeve. His air of innocence can be most deceiving."

"Perhaps that runs in the family," she replied, with a tart look in Patience's direction. But when the duke glanced down at her, Anne smiled sweetly and asked, "Are you certain we cannot tempt you to perform for us, Miss Cheswick? Your mother says you play beautifully."

"My mother listens with a mother's ear," Patience said with a fond look across the room to where Hermione was seated by the duchess. "I fear no one else would be so complimentary. Certainly, I cannot hope to compete with your talent, my lady. It was a pleasure to hear you play."

"We all possess different accomplishments," Charles told her loyally. "For myself, I am content to sit and observe you. Your eyes, my dear, are most expressive."

Unaccountably annoyed, Gregory snapped, "We know you are a connoisseur, Charles, but if you can tear yourself away from my cousin's charms sufficiently long enough, Mother would like a word with you."

Villars hid his amusement at his friend's small show of temper with a courteous bow, then begged leave from the ladies to be excused. He was nearly sure he knew what the duchess was up to, and if he was right, her plan was succeeding well. He'd seldom seen the duke so rattled, certainly never over a mere female.

As Patience watched Charles Villars walk away, she frowned slightly, and her dark eyes mirrored her concern.

Gregory, noting her expression, said with uncharacteristic rudeness, "You need not worry, Miss Cheswick. I am sure Mother will not detain your cavalier for long."

She flushed but met his gaze squarely. With her chin lifted defiantly, she retorted, "If I appeared concerned, Your Grace, it was for the sake of the duchess. I believe she is tired and should be persuaded to retire as soon as possible."

"I thought the same," Lady Anne said quickly. Perhaps some of the evening could yet be salvaged if Her Grace would go to her rooms. Supper had been vastly uncomfortable beneath the duchess' critical eyes.

With a measure of remorse, Gregory observed his mother. She had seemed so much like her old self at supper that he had momentarily forgotten how ill she truly was. He was accustomed to making the duchess his first concern, and it came as something of a shock to realize that during the interval since supper, he had not given her a thought. It had taken Miss Cheswick to point out that the duchess was rapidly tiring. He could see it now—in the tiny lines etched about her mouth, and the way her hand unconsciously rubbed against her knee as she conversed with Charles Villars.

"I'll speak to her," he said aloud, but to Lady Anne's dismay, added, "And I'll suggest to our guests 'tis time they took their leave. I am sure they will understand."

Patience agreed, although she, too, had no wish for the evening to end. It had been quite the nicest she could recall. Mr. Villars had made her feel as though she were being courted. He had flirted with her and flattered her. She knew of course that it meant nothing. It was merely his manner, and aside from Lady Anne and his sister, she was the only other young lady present. He was only amusing himself, she thought. His attention sometimes embarrassed her, sometimes made her nervous, but it also made her feel attractive. It was a delicious feeling, and she was sorry that the evening would end so soon.

Charles Villars, as though reading her thoughts, returned to her side with a promptness that was most complimentary. A devilish grin on his lips, he teased, "Did you miss me, my dear?"

"Give way, Charles," Gregory muttered. "What did my mother say? Did she seem overtired to you?"

"A little perhaps. She inquired about my parents' health. I must say 'tis grand to see her entertaining again. I can't think how long 'tis been since I have dined here."

"Too long," Gregory said, conscious that he'd been unnecessarily rude to his old friend. "If Mother's health continues to improve, we shall have to invite you to return."

"Too late," Charles said impudently. "The duchess gave me leave to call tomorrow. Miss Cheswick, I was hoping I might persuade you to ride out with me. There is an old abbey nearby, and many people find the ruins interesting. The duchess thought you might enjoy seeing it, if you will allow me the honor of escorting you?"

Patience felt a shiver of pleasure. "I . . . I should like to, sir, if Her Grace does not have need of me."

Gregory disliked the notion, though he could not say why or think of any reason to gainsay it. Instead he said, "A splendid idea. Lady Anne, what say we make a party of it? I am sure you will find the ruins intriguing."

"Why, that sounds charming," she agreed. She might have to cope with Miss Cheswick's presence, but at least she wouldn't have the duchess scrutinizing her every move.

"That's settled then," Gregory announced. But he sounded more like an executioner than someone planning a pleasant excursion.

Six

Patience awoke slowly the following morning, with a feeling of euphoria that for a moment puzzled her. Something good, something pleasant was afoot, she thought dreamily. Then she remembered the supper party and Mr. Villars' determined flirtation. He had promised to take her to see the ruins of the old abbey today. She smiled as she sat in bed and sipped the hot chocolate Katie had brought her.

She, Patience Cheswick, would be driving out with a handsome gentleman—just like any other young lady. Her feelings warmed her as much as the chocolate, and she wrapped herself in them. For a short while at least, she could luxuriate in the knowledge that she was being courted, that a gentleman found her pretty and her company desirable.

"The duchess says you are going to visit the old abbey," Katie commented as she drew open the curtains. "It looks to be a fine day for an outing."

Naturally it would be, Patience thought. Nothing could possibly go wrong today. The sun would shine, and the ruins would prove to be enchanting. Wanting to talk about her plans, she glanced at the maid and asked, "Katie, have you ever visited the abbey?"

"Once," the maid admitted. "It was years ago when Her Grace didn't need her chair. A large party from the house went. There's not a lot to see, miss, just crumbling walls and old moss-covered stones. Except . . ."

"Except what, Katie?"

"Well, now mind you, it may be only my mind playing tricks, but it seemed a sort of magic place."

"Magic? Do you mean like with elves and fairies?"

"You laugh, miss, but when I was there, I could almost see them old monks walking about beneath the trees. You could feel their presence . . . like 'twas a place that oughtn't to be disturbed."

Patience shivered. She did not believe in ghosts, but there was something in Katie's voice that unsettled her. Whether the abbey was haunted or not, the maid obviously believed what she'd said.

Katie, however, harbored no specters. She prosaically removed a dark green riding habit from the wardrobe, and laid it across the bed. Her charge would have no cause to blush for her dress today. The habit was as well made and stylish as any that Lady Anne owned. Lady Cheswick had confided that when her other daughters had new dresses made, all Patience desired was a riding habit. She spent most of her time riding around the estate with her Papa, so Hermione had not argued. Instead, she had spent more than she customarily would on the one riding dress. Still in excellent condition, it had been adorned with elegant black braiding that made it look almost new. Patience had not had a chance to wear the habit since coming to Norwick, but today would be the perfect opportunity.

The riding dress, with all its promise, lay on the bed, and when Patience looked at it, she happily anticipated the afternoon. Oddly enough, it was not Charles Villars who came to mind, but the duke. He, too, would be of the party—and, of course, Lady Anne.

"Now, what's brought that frown to your pretty face?" Katie demanded. "If it's your hat you're worrying over, you needn't. Your mama and Her Grace between them put new feathers on your bonnet, and it looks a treat. The duchess has a way with such things."

"How is she this morning?" Patience asked contritely. She belatedly realized she had not even inquired, and the evening before must have been taxing to Her Grace.

"Right as rain, miss. She slept through the night for once, and if you was to ask me, that supper did her more good than all her medicines. Like a young girl she is, with her head stuck to your mama's, planning something. She'll be wanting to see you before you leave."

Patience wanted to see the duchess, too. To see for herself that Her Grace had not suffered any ill effects, and to thank her again for the gold satin gown and all her thoughtfulness. The duchess had given her an evening she would long remember.

Patience waited until she was dressed and Katie had done her hair, then hurried down the hall to tap on the door of Her Grace's bedchamber. Bidden to enter, she found the duchess alone.

"Come in, my dear," Althea encouraged when Patience opened the door. "How very pretty you look. Your mama will be most pleased."

"Thank you," Patience replied, and smiled shyly. She was unused to compliments and quickly sought to turn the conversation. "Are you feeling well, your grace? I hope the supper was not too tiring?"

"Not at all. I quite enjoyed the evening. I hope you did as well. One couldn't help noticing that Mr. Villars was most attentive to you."

"He is very kind."

"Kindness had little to do with it, my dear, but I shall not tease you. However, I understand that gentleman is taking you to view the old abbey today, and that my son is joining you as well?"

"Yes, Your Grace," Patience answered, and as she thought of the duke, a slight blush colored her cheeks. She added quickly, "And Lady Anne, of course."

"Yes, so I heard. Well, one cannot have everything."

"I beg your pardon?"

The duchess laughed. " 'Tis nothing, my child. Pay me no mind. As one gets older, one tends to ramble. What I meant to say, is that I am most appreciative that you have enticed my son into an outing. He does not spend enough time with people his own age. Indeed, with the exception of the Villarses, I fear he has lost touch with most of his friends."

"He is very devoted to you, Your Grace, and one cannot blame him for that."

"You are sweet to say so, Patience, but there is a time and a place for all things. Today, I should like my son to simply enjoy himself without worrying over me. I hope that you will see to it that he does."

"Me?" The word came out as a high squeak, and she could only stare in astonishment at the duchess. When she finally regained her voice, she protested, "The duke is most unlikely to take my advice, Your Grace. He—"

" 'Tis not your advice I meant," Althea interrupted with a laugh. "But never mind that. Come tell me what you think of your new hat. Your mama and I found some feathers to refurbish it. Is it not pretty?"

Patience stared at the confection the duchess held up. The single, limp feather that had not quite matched the dark green of her habit, had been replaced with three lush ostrich feathers. Two were dyed dark green and the last a rich, silky black. They swept from the wide crown and curled beguilingly over the side.

"Oh, 'tis lovely!"

"I do think it worthy of a London modiste," the duchess agreed, observing the hat critically. She rose gracefully to her feet, and carefully positioned the confection on Patience's dark curls, then stepped back to admire the effect. "You do look very pretty, my dear."

"Thank you, your grace" Patience replied, dropping a swift curtsy. She knew the duchess was merely being kind, but strangely enough, she *felt* pretty.

Althea smiled. "Run along, now. My son—and Mr. Villars—will not like to be kept waiting."

Patience leaned forward and caressed the silky neck of the bay mare she rode.

"She's a sweet goer," Charles Villars said as he brought his own horse alongside her.

"She's wonderful," Patience agreed. But then she thought all of the horses in the duke's stables were wonderful. It was Lady Anne who had complained because she wasn't given one of his stallions to ride. The duke had insisted such horses were too high-strung and too powerful for a lady to handle. He had mounted Lady Anne on a well-mannered chestnut mare. She had barely spoken a word since.

Patience, too, had been given a gentle ride, but she did not blame the duke. He had never seen either lady ride, so why should he entrust what her Papa would have called "prime goers" to their care? And, of course, he was overly protective of females. She supposed it came from all those years of shielding his mother from the slightest care. The duke seemed to think ladies incapable of handling any problem. For herself, she didn't mind. It was rather sweet of him to be so concerned, and if she stayed at Norwick long enough, she would prove him wrong. Lady Anne, however, was plainly miffed.

Patience stole a look at her. Anne appeared incredibly lovely with her long, blond hair falling in enticing ringlets beneath her stylish blue riding hat. Her chin was raised imperiously, but it only emphasized her exquisite profile.

Charles Villars followed her glance and said softly, "The frown rather spoils her beauty, does it not? I find 'tis not half so charming as your pretty smile."

Color seeped into Patience's cheeks at his remark. It was Mr. Villars who was charming, but she wished he would not be so effusive with his compliments. They embarrassed her, and the words came so easily to his lips, she wondered at his sincerity. She knew it was foolish to feel that way. No doubt ladies in London were accustomed to, even expected, such compliments. And Mr. Villars was adept at paying them.

She chided herself for behaving like a green girl, but her gaze involuntarily flew to the duke, who was riding beside Lady Anne. *He* did not pay empty compliments. He did not pay compliments at all—at least not to her. Not that she wanted him to, she assured herself.

"The abbey is just ahead," Charles said, breaking into her thoughts. "There is a bridle path, of sorts, that leads up to it.

Once it was a decent carriage drive, but 'tis heavily overgrown now and can only be reached by horseback. We turn here." He gestured toward the right where a narrow path opened beneath an awning of trees.

The shaded path looked inviting in the afternoon sunlight. Patience glanced up, admiring the way the tree limbs formed an arch above their heads, random shafts of sunlight piercing their darkness. Beauty was everywhere. Wild flowers grew in profusion at their feet, and beyond the path she could pick out the pinks and reds of rambling roses. Katie had been right. There was a special ambiance here. Not magic, perhaps, but a feeling of peace and serenity that was timeless.

The path was so narrow, only two could ride abreast. Patience went ahead with Charles Villars at her side. At first, she sat stiffly, uncomfortably aware of the duke riding behind her. But slowly the sheer beauty of their surroundings made her forget everything else. One could imagine long-robed monks as they trod on the same hallowed ground.

The trail wound gradually upward until they reached a clearing at the crest of the hill. With mutual accord, the four riders reined in and sat silently staring at the remains of the ancient ruins. Although most of the walls had fallen, enough remained that one could envision the way the abbey must have looked when the monks were still in possession.

" 'Tis said to have been built in 1210," Charles said, breaking the stillness. "It changed hands several times, then was finally abandoned around 1630."

"Gracious, no wonder there is so little left," Anne said. "But I wonder no one ever built here. 'Tis such a beautiful site for a house. Can you not imagine it? Think of the view it would command."

"There has been talk of that from time to time," the duke explained. "The Allersfords own it and should much like to sell it, but there are also a great many rumors and superstitions surrounding the land which has frightened away any prospective buyers."

"Oh, fiddlesticks," Anne declared. "Who believes in a bunch

of old superstitions? Not I!" And to show she was not the least intimidated, she turned to the duke with a smile. "May we not dismount and explore a little?"

"We can, but you must be careful. Some of these stones will crumble at a touch," Gregory warned as he dismounted and came around to assist Lady Anne. Charles was as quick to help Patience, and the four of them strolled across the clearing. Some of the stones were carved by hand, and Patience lingered to study the century-old etchings, but Anne wasn't interested. She wanted to see the best view from the hilltop.

On the north side of the abbey the walls were barely three feet high, but in their center a flight of wide stone steps remained almost intact—steps leading only to the open sky. On the west side, the wall rose to perhaps five feet in spots, but they could see where the old stones had fallen, and in some places given way entirely. There were partial inside walls still standing that allowed them to discern the different rooms.

"It wasn't very large," Lady Anne commented, observing a series of small rooms that could not have held much more than a bed and chest of drawers.

"These were probably the sleeping quarters," the duke said, amused at her expression. "It's my understanding monks did not require much in the way of furnishings."

"My maid has a bigger room," Anne said with a sniff.

The duke took her arm as she stepped over a low portion of an interior wall. "Careful."

Patience and Charles joined them as Anne lifted her chin. "You worry too much, Your Grace. There are ruins near my home, and I grew up playing among them with my brothers. We must have climbed walls like these hundreds of times." She glanced around disdainfully, then added, "Much higher walls as I recall—and I was never harmed."

"You were most fortunate then."

"I believe His Grace is right," Patience said, her voice a gentle rebuke. "The walls here are not safe. One can see how easily they might fall."

"Then *you* be careful," Anne snapped. She twisted away from the duke's hold on her arm. "For myself, I intend to see the view from the top of those stairs."

"Anne, don't!" the duke ordered, but she ran swiftly across the remains of the abbey floor and started up the flight of stone steps. There was no banister, no handhold of any sort. The walls on both sides had fallen away so the stairs rose in the air without support. But they were wide, the stones looked substantial, and Anne danced upward with as little concern as though she were at home. Patience and Charles stared at her in horror, but the duke hurried after her.

He halted at the bottom of the steps. Anne was slightly built and the stairs had taken her weight—so far. But he feared the steps would crumble if he dared to add his own bulk. Standing helplessly at the bottom, he pleaded with her to come down.

"You come up, Your Grace," she taunted. "The view is splendid."

" 'Tis not worth breaking your neck over," he replied, his voice low with barely contained fury.

Ignoring him, Anne called down, "Miss Cheswick, will you not join me? Let us show these gentlemen that not all females are fainthearted. Come up. 'Tis perfectly safe, and you will much admire the vista."

"I would rather you came down," Patience said as she crossed the abbey with Charles.

"I should have known you would agree with His Grace," Anne retorted scornfully. She held out her hands to Charles. "What of you, Mr. Villars? Pray tell me you are not afraid to climb a small flight of stairs."

"You are behaving foolishly, Lady Anne. 'Tis not a matter of bravery, but of common sense. You have had your fun—come down now."

Anne looked at the three disapproving faces below her. Her lips curved into a pout, and she complained, "If I had known how utterly dreary this ride would be, I would have remained at Norwick." Reluctantly, she started down the steps.

The duke breathed a sigh of relief, but as Anne took the second step, the stone beneath her foot crumbled. Her ankle twisted, and she pitched forward with a cry of terror.

With reflexes that came of parrying dueling thrusts, the duke moved swiftly. He caught Anne in his arms, breaking her fall. But the impact of her sudden weight caused his right leg to twist beneath him. Still holding Anne, he crashed to the floor.

"Help me up," Lady Anne cried the instant she realized she was not truly hurt, but was sprawled in a rather unladylike position across the duke's broad chest.

Charles held out his hand and assisted her to her feet. Patience looked down at the duke and, with an odd feeling in the pit of her stomach, observed the grim lines of his mouth. Heedless of the dirt, heedless of the others' presence, she knelt beside him and reached for his hand. "Are you badly hurt, Your Grace? Is there anything I can do?"

"I fear your tonics will not heal a broken leg," he muttered. But at the look of concern in her grave eyes, he managed a wry smile.

"Broken? But . . . but that cannot be," Anne protested. Her gloved hands twisted together helplessly. "If your leg is broken, you cannot ride."

"He will have to be carried down to the road, then taken by carriage to the house," Patience told her, keeping her own voice calm. She glanced up at Charles. "I shall need you to ride back to Norwick for help. As quickly as you can."

"I'm on my way," Charles said. He grinned down at the duke and gave him the small salute that had been common between them as boys. "I leave you in good hands, Your Grace." When he got an answering salute, he turned and strode toward the horses.

Lady Anne watched him leave in silence until he started to mount, then cried out, "But what about me? What am I to do?"

It was Patience who answered her. "I suggest you find somewhere to sit down and wait quietly. If the duke is correct, I shall have to put a splint on his leg. Right now I must remove his boot before his leg becomes too swollen."

Anne stared at her and took two steps backward. Aghast, she said, "You cannot do that. 'Tis so . . . improper."

Patience ignored her. She squeezed the duke's hand and smiled at him. "I do have to remove your boot. I warn you, it may hurt."

"Lady Anne is right," Gregory murmured, though the effort to talk was substantial. He groaned slightly, then, and, his voice barely above a whisper, ordered, "This is no job for a lady. Wait . . . wait until Charles returns."

"It would be much worse by then," Patience said and moved to kneel at his feet. The boot was, naturally, custom made, and it fit as tightly to his calf as his gloves fit his hands. She wished she had a knife. But wishing paid no tolls. Patience braced herself and grasped the shiny black Hessian boot.

"She was wonderful," Charles Villars told the duchess later that evening. They were gathered in the old blue drawing room. It was seldom used for guests, but it contained a rather long sofa, and as the duke refused to be confined to his bed, they had placed him there.

"By the time we returned to help," Charles was saying, "Miss Cheswick had his leg in a splint and had made him as comfortable as possible. Dr. Chamberlain was well pleased and said he could not have done better."

Patience wished Mr. Villars would hush. She had done only what was necessary. And the doctor may have been pleased, but he'd replaced her makeshift splint the moment the duke had returned home. She stole a glance at His Grace as he lay on the sofa. His eyes were closed, and there was still a pinched look about his mouth. It was due, in part, to his refusal to take any laudanum. And in part to his annoyance with her.

Far from being grateful, the duke had been furious with her for setting his leg—furious and deeply embarrassed. She knew he would have given all he owned to have been able to walk out of the abbey. He had barely spoken to her since, and she was certain that was not due to the pain he suffered. Nor did it help matters to have Mr. Villars extolling her praises, reminding the duke over and over again of what had occurred.

In an effort to divert him, she said, "Truly, you exaggerate, Mr. Villars. Anyone would have done the same."

"Not Lady Anne." Charles chuckled. "Egad, I never saw a female with her feathers so ruffled."

"I am sorry if she was disturbed," the duchess said. "But I am sure her decision to return home is for the best. Norwick did not seem to agree with her."

"She could not stand not being the center of attention," Hermione opined, but low enough so the duke did not hear her.

And that was another thing the duke would blame her for, Patience thought. She had been abrupt with Lady Anne in the abbey and had spoken to her curtly when the woman had complained of being bored while waiting for help to arrive. The duke, of course, had heard their altercation. He had said nothing, but Patience knew he was not pleased. Lady Anne was above stairs, packing, and the duke's hopes of making her his duchess were destroyed.

"Would anyone care for more tea?" Althea asked. She sat in a high-back Queen Anne chair with the tea table drawn up in front of her. From her chair, she could keep an eye on her son. At the thought, she smiled and said, "How very odd that I should be watching over Gregory when 'tis usually the other way round. Now, my dearest son, you shall learn how frustrating it is to be an invalid."

The duke opened his eyes. "I sympathize with you, Mother, as I always have, but our positions are not quite the same. I do not require anyone to nurse me. Time will heal my leg."

"Of course, darling, but while you wait you will need some assistance. Do be reasonable about this, Gregory. You can walk no better than I."

"Albert will do all that is necessary."

"Your valet is very competent, but I do not think you should refuse Patience's help. She is very skilled in these matters. You must admit her tonic has done wonders for me."

"For which I am deeply grateful, but as I said, our positions are different. Tonics do not heal broken legs."

"I was thinking more that she might help to entertain you," the duchess rebuked him softly. "Trust me, you will become exceedingly bored confined to the sofa or a chair."

Patience blushed. She knew, even if the duchess did not, that the duke did not want her help—or her company—not under any circumstances. Aloud she said, "Perhaps it is too soon to make any decisions. I suspect what His Grace needs most is peace and quiet."

"Thank you, Miss Cheswick," Gregory said sarcastically. "As usual, you are quite right."

"Feeling a trifle testy, Your Grace?" Charles teased.

" 'Tis not an experience I would recommend."

"Then I shall leave you to bask in your misery, but if you like, I'll call tomorrow and bear you company."

"No! I don't need company."

Charles lifted his brows, but said nothing more. He rose to his feet and bowed to the duchess. "I believe 'tis time I took my leave. Your Grace, if you will permit?"

"Certainly Charles, and even if my son is too incivil to thank you for all your help, I hope you know you have my deepest gratitude."

He said his goodbyes to Lady Cheswick and her daughter and had taken a step toward the door when Gregory called to him.

"Charles, wait. I hope you will accept my apology, and if you are still agreeable, I should like very much to see you tomorrow. Perhaps we can have a game of chess?"

"You *are* a glutton for punishment," Villars said with a grin. "It will be my pleasure to teach you the game." With one of his jaunty salutes, he waved at them, then was gone.

The room was quiet for a moment. The duchess set down her teacup, saying, "Well since you desire peace and quiet, Gregory, I believe I shall retire myself. I pray you will sleep well."

Hermione rose to assist the duchess, and Patience followed suit. She held open the door for her mother to push the wheelchair through, then paused to glance back at the duke.

Senseless to worry over him when he had a large staff at his disposal. She knew his difficult mood was due to his embarrassment and his dislike of being dependent on anyone, particularly her. But she hated to see him suffer needlessly, and was about to suggest again that he try the laudanum when he forestalled her.

"Miss Cheswick . . . if I might have a word with you before you retire?"

"Certainly, Your Grace," she said, coming back into the room.

He was uncomfortable looking up at her, and waved to the chair near the sofa. "Please, do be seated." He waited until she was settled, then cleared his throat. It was difficult to find the words he wanted. He was seldom in the position of apologizing, and he'd already made amends with Charles. However, he knew his behavior had been intolerable. Swallowing his pride, he admitted, "I . . . I wanted to thank you."

"Please, Your Grace, 'tis not necessary."

"No, Mother was right. I have been incivil. I owe you a debt of gratitude that I cannot hope to repay. I hope you will be generous enough to forgive me."

She would forgive him the world, she thought, as she gazed into his deep blue eyes. There was pain reflected there, but sincerity, too, and her heart ached for him.

"Miss Cheswick?" he queried when she did not respond. "I realize 'tis asking a lot of you, but I—"

"Oh, no, Your Grace," she said hurriedly as she realized she had been sitting in stunned silence. "There is nothing to forgive. Indeed, I would have been astonished had you minded your manners when you were in so much pain. Not that I mean to say you *were* incivil—just naturally feeling the effects of your fall. I nursed Papa when he broke his leg, and although one should not speak ill of one's father, I must say he was most . . . most difficult." She knew she was rambling. The duke would think her run mad.

If he did, his return of good manners prohibited him from showing it. He smiled at her instead, in such a way she wished once more that there was something she could do to ease his pain.

"All the same I should like to make amends," he told her. "If you will only tell me what I can say or do to convince you that I sincerely regret my behavior, I am at your command."

"Well, there is one thing . . ." she murmured, deciding to take advantage of his offer.

Gregory had not meant it literally. He'd thought she would refuse and simply forgive him. He shifted his leg and stifled a groan. He could not go back on his word. With an effort, he managed a smile. "You have only to tell me what you wish."

"Then promise me you will take something to ease your pain."

"One of your tonics?" he asked, reluctant to hear the answer. But he was surprised when she shook her head. "Not laudanum," he pleaded. He loathed the drug.

She smiled, mischief in her eyes. "I was thinking more of a shot of brandy. It is said to have excellent medicinal qualities."

His sudden smile was her reward.

Seven

Charles Villars kept his word. Not only did he call on the duke the day after his accident, but every day for the next three weeks—although it was questionable whom he came to see. He spent every afternoon playing chess with His Grace, but Charles always tried to persuade Patience to ride out with him in the morning, or take a stroll in the rose garden before he left.

Gregory knew his old friend was spending time with Patience, but there was little he could do about it. Not that he *wanted* to do anything—not really. He merely felt frustrated every time Charles stepped out of the house with Patience on his arm. He told himself his aggravation was due to his injury and being confined to the sofa, but he only believed that when he'd had sufficient brandy to dull his senses. Cold sober, he admitted it was Patience who roused his frustration, Patience who had somehow got under his skin and crept into the corners of his mind so that he thought of her at the oddest times. He couldn't even escape her in sleep. She haunted his dreams.

As though he had conjured her up, Patience entered the drawing room. She was modestly but neatly dressed and moved with her usual composure. There was none of the animosity that had once marked all their encounters. They had cried friends after his accident. The duke had apologized for his behavior and even owned that the tonic she prepared had helped his mother a great deal. Patience had waved aside his apologies and never mentioned the matter again. She treated him as a good friend, and now smiled warmly at him.

"Good evening, Your Grace. How are you feeling?"

"Tired of this sofa," he complained, wondering how he had ever thought her not attractive. Her smile lit up her face and made her dark eyes sparkle. She did not possess Lady Anne's classical features, but she had a radiance all her own. It was little wonder Charles was courting her.

"Dr. Chamberlain says only another week and then you may try walking with a cane," she said to console him.

Another week seemed an eternity to the duke, but he responded to her smile and gestured for her to be seated near him. "Come tell me what you have been doing today."

"This morning I visited the Pidgeons," she said and nearly laughed aloud at his expression.

Despite the fact that he could think of no conceivable reason for Patience to visit one of his tenants, Gregory restrained his temper admirably. If nothing else, he'd learned that she was exceptionally sensible and generally had an excellent reason for what she chose to do. His brows lifted slightly, but he said only, "Indeed? What took you to the Pidgeons?"

"Your mother," she confided. "Her Grace learned that Mrs. Pidgeon has been in bed for a week with the gout, and thought I might be of some help."

"And were you?" he asked, already knowing that Patience would have given his tenant one of her tonics and a great deal of comfort. She was better at handling such matters than he was. Patience was like his mother when it came to making the tenants feel they were important. He could give them advice on plant rotation or what crops they should sow. Problems with livestock or horses he could easily handle, and he oversaw the maintenance of all the buildings on his estate. But he'd always had difficulties when it came to the tenants' personal problems. It wasn't that he didn't care. He did. He just didn't know how to express his concern. His mother had the knack and so did Patience. He watched her now, admiring the way her eyes constantly changed.

"She should be fine in a day or two," Patience was saying. "I know you do not believe in tonics, but—"

"Not as a rule," he interrupted, "but I believe in yours. Be fair now. I owned that it is due to you that Mother has improved so much. Speaking of which, how is she?"

"Fine," Patience replied and laughed. "I do not know what they are up to, but she and Mama are planning something. They have been closeted together all day."

"Mother is probably scheming to redecorate the drawing room. She has been complaining for years that it has grown shabby, but until now she never had the energy to refurbish it. And with *your* mother to help her, there is no limit to what she may do. I only hope she will wait until I've recovered enough to escape the house. You have no idea what 'tis like when my mother decides to redecorate. No corner of the house will be left undisturbed."

He expected Patience to laugh with him, but her lashes swept down hiding her eyes, and she stared silently down at her hands.

"Patience? What is it?"

She looked at him then, her gaze troubled. The corners of her mouth quivered as she tried to smile. "Nothing, Your Grace. I am behaving foolishly. 'Tis just that I should like to see the duchess redo the drawing room, but Mama has said we must remove to London soon."

"London! You mean . . . leave Norwick?"

She smiled in earnest at his open astonishment. "There was a time when you wished me gone."

He reached out a hand to her. "I never—" he began but broke off when she laughed. "Well, perhaps just at first, but that was before I came to know you. Now it seems that you have always been a part of Norwick."

"That is kind of you, and you have made it easy for me to forget that this is not my home."

His thoughts were jumbled. The idea of her leaving, of never seeing her again, was unbearable. He sought for a reason for her to stay and said impulsively, "What of Charles? He has been most marked in his attention to you. I half expected to hear an announcement."

The color flooded her cheeks and she withdrew her hand. "Charles Villars is a good friend, nothing more."

Relief flooded through him, although he didn't recognize it as such. He only felt his heart lighten and was struck by a sudden surge of joy. Then he silently cursed the fact that he was incapable of standing because now he knew, knew with absolute certainty that he could not let Patience walk out of his life. It was not an auspicious time to be incapacitated. But perhaps it was just as well. He didn't want to frighten her.

He said gently, "Patience, my dear, if you are disappointed in Charles, I am sorry."

"I am content with his friendship, Your Grace," she answered, her eyes cast down. Softly, she added, "I never wanted more than that from him."

Blast that broken leg! If he were capable of it, he would stand and sweep her into his arms. He was not good at expressing his emotions, but he could have shown her how he felt. Now, he had only words. Hesitantly, he said, "Dare I hope that your reluctance to leave Norwick means you will miss me?"

"Of course I shall," she said, blushing furiously. And as she didn't want to wear her heart on her sleeve or place him in an awkward position, she said, "And the duchess. She has been wonderful to me. Indeed, I shall miss everything about Norwick."

"Even the inefficiency of my home farm and the stables?"

"Even that," she agreed.

"If I . . . if I consented to make the changes you suggest, would you stay to make certain your designs are carried out as you intended?"

Her heart sank. For a brief moment, she'd thought he cared for her and that he meant to declare himself. They had been so much at ease together of late, so much in agreement. They had shared laughter and long discussions before the fire in the evenings, and she had cherished absurd hopes. She tried to hide her disappointment, saying lightly, "I fear such improvements would take too long, Your Grace. Mama spoke of leaving within the week. I doubt I could persuade her to change her plans."

Her eyes gave her away. Gregory saw the flash of yearning

followed by her disappointment, and he, too, dared to hope. Her feelings gave him the courage to say, "Once I vainly thought that any lady would be honored if I asked for her hand. I know now that is not true, and I almost fear to put my luck to the test, but Patience, my dearest Patience, I cannot just allow you to leave Norwick, to leave me."

Her lashes flew up and she gazed deep into his blue eyes. Her own mirrored the love she saw in his.

"Will you do me the honor of becoming my wife, Patience? Will you give me your hand? I know I have not always behaved as you would like, but I swear to you, I will do everything in my power to see you happy."

He held his breath for what seemed an eternity, but was only a matter of seconds. Then she shyly reached out and placed her hand in his. "Yes, Your Grace. I would be honored to wed you. Nothing would give me greater joy."

Happiness exploded within him. He forgot the pain in his leg, forgot that a servant might enter the room at any moment, forgot everything but the beautiful woman who had just agreed to wed him. He tugged gently on her hand. "I believe 'tis customary to seal a betrothal with a kiss. Since I cannot get up, would you come to me?"

"Yes, Your Grace." Sudden shyness kept her eyes from meeting his, but she rose gracefully and repositioned herself next to him on the sofa. She could feel the heat of his body and luxuriated in his closeness. Giving in to an urge, she reached out and smoothed his dark hair from his brow.

"You must learn to call me Gregory," he teased, kissing her fingertips.

"Gregory." She said his name softly, testing the sound and the feel of it on her lips. For weeks she'd whispered his name when she was alone, heard it in her dreams, but now she could speak it aloud. "Gregory," she said again as he reached up and gently traced her lips with his fingers.

How blind he had been, the duke thought. He'd had heaven close at hand and nearly lost it. His hand caressed her cheek, then brushed through the silkiness of her hair. With slight pressure, he urged her closer. His lips savored the taste of hers, and it was several moments before he released her.

Grinning foolishly, he told her, "I believe I fell in love with you the first day we met, only I was too pigheaded to realize it."

Her gaze was all tenderness, her voice teasing. "I thought you arrogant, opinionated, rude . . . and incredibly handsome."

He laughed at that and drew her head down again to capture her mouth. Neither noticed as the door swung open and Hermione wheeled the duchess into the room. The two older ladies exchanged satisfied glances.

Hermione waited a moment, then announced, "Well, at last. I must say, Your Grace, 'tis about time."

The pair on the sofa broke apart, but the duchess noticed how her son retained Patience's hand in his while his other hand rested firmly about her waist.

"She has agreed to wed me."

"I should hope so," Hermione sniffed, but her eyes were suspiciously damp. She added gruffly, "Took you long enough."

Too long, the duke thought. He had almost not said a word, almost let her walk out of his life. He didn't like even thinking about it, and said, "Well, 'tis done now, and no reason for you to remove to London. You may stay here and help Mother redecorate the drawing room."

"The drawing room?" the duchess asked, looking puzzled. "I shall leave such matters to my new daughter."

"But isn't that what you were planning? Patience told me the pair of you were closeted together all day."

Both the duchess and Hermione laughed. It was Her Grace who explained, "We were trying to figure out a way to bring you up to scratch, my dear. It was my idea to tell Patience she would be removing to London. I rather thought that might turn the trick."

The duke shook his head in exasperation. "If you were so determined I marry Patience, why did you not just tell me it was what you wished?"

"Because I wanted you to marry to please yourself, not me."

The duke's grin was back in place as he squeezed his bride-to-be's hand. "Oh, I shall, Mother. You may be certain of it."

LOOK FOR THESE REGENCY ROMANCES

FROM ROSANNE BITTNER:
ZEBRA SAVAGE DESTINY ROMANCE!

#1: SWEET PRAIRIE PASSION   (0-8217-5342-8, $5.99)

#2: RIDE THE FREE WIND   (0-8217-5343-6, $5.99)

#3: RIVER OF LOVE   (0-8217-5344-4, $5.99)

#4: EMBRACE THE
    WILD WIND   (0-8217-5413-0, $5.99)

#7: EAGLE'S SONG   (0-8217-5326-6, $5.99)